A LETHAL BETRAYAL

COAST GUARD HAWAI'I

LORI MATTHEWS

ABOUT A LETHAL BETRAYAL

Chief Petty Officer Dane Landry is injured and burning through his last chance with the US Coast Guard. His new team is tasked with finding stolen military-grade technology, but he finds himself in the crosshairs of an investigation as the prime suspect in the murder of a former teammate. With his career and freedom on the line, his top priority should be clearing his name while navigating the complex web of suspicion and betrayal that surrounds him. Being thrown together with the beautiful investigator is a distraction he doesn't need.

Coast Guard Investigative Service Special Agent McKenna Rankin is determined to find out who killed the Senior Chief, but it soon becomes obvious there's so much more at stake. Her attraction to the prime suspect is an obstacle she hadn't anticipated, but one she isn't sure she wants to overcome. As her investigation heats up and tensions run high, Dane and Mac must find a way to reconcile personal feelings with professional obligations while racing against the clock to uncover the true culprit before it's too late.

Filled with pulse-pounding action and heart-wrenching drama, "A Lethal Betrayal" is a thrilling ride through the high-stakes world of the US Coast Guard, where loyalty and duty are put to the ultimate test.

A Lethal Betrayal

For my kids.
You make my life so much more interesting.
Now, knock it off.

ACKNOWLEDGMENTS

Thank you doesn't cover it when it comes to my rock star editors, Corinne DeMaagd and Heidi Senesac. They are truly the most patient people. Thanks also goes out to my amazing assistant, Sara Mallion and my FaceBook guru, Amanda Robinson as well as my beta reader, Jenn Herman. My personal cheer squad which I could not survive without: Janna MacGregor, Suzanne Burke, Stacey Wilk, Kimberley Ash, and Tiara Inserto. My husband and my children who make me laugh everyday. And to you, the reader. Your emails and posts mean the world to me. The fact that you read my stories is the greatest gift ever. Thank you.

CHAPTER ONE

"They're late," a voice said in his earbud.

Chief Petty Officer Dane Landry had been thinking the same thing. It was zero-zero-forty-five hours. Cain Maddox, his team leader, wasn't impatient. He was just stating a fact, one that made Dane's gut tighten.

"You sure your guy had the right spot?" Cain asked.

"Yes, Senior Chief," Koa Kilani responded.

Cain swore. The entire team knew how much the senior chief hated being called by his title.

Dane smiled in the darkness. Koa didn't like to be questioned. Using Cain's rank was his little revenge. *Hilarious.*

Hidden in the bluff of the beach, Dane was lying in some grass and keeping his eyes on the shoreline. He shifted his position to reduce the pressure on his back. It was starting to ache ever so slightly, and he wanted to stop it before it got unbearable.

The night was quiet. The smell of the ocean and spring flowers drifted to him on a light wind. The breeze also kept the bugs at bay. Plenty of those on Oahu. The sound of their chirping and clicking came from the nearby bushes.

Their new team was coming together. The fact that they were already needling each other was a good sign. When he'd hurt his back, he'd thought his career was over. He'd never see action again. Being number two on a team like this was a dream he didn't think was in his grasp. He was so damn glad he'd been wrong about that.

"Anybody got anything?" Jace asked. "My ass is going numb."

"You were the one that wanted to sit on the rocks," Chief Petty Officer Tacitus—Tac—Holden reminded him.

Jace growled, "Sand. I hate the way it gets into every nook and cranny."

Chief Petty Officer Cassidy St. James snorted. "This could be interesting. Exactly how many nooks and crannies have you got?"

A few muffled guffaws came through the earbud before the night got quiet again. Yeah, it was shaping up to be a good team and Cassidy, being the only woman, added a whole new dimension to things. As a crack shot, she was the team sniper and even he had to admit as much as they were all good, she was the best by a wide margin. It didn't hurt that she had a great sense of humor and was tough as nails. A killer combination. She could also be cold and scary as hell. Dane ranked her as the second scariest member of the team. The first place was a tie between Cain and Koa. Those two took badass to another level. He was so glad they were on his side.

Dane scanned the horizon once more. Nothing. Then movement. Way out on the waves. He couldn't be sure yet, but he thought there was a boat. "On my two o'clock."

Silence and then, "I see it," Tac said.

"Got it," Jace agreed.

Cassidy chimed in, "Pickup truck coming down the road."

"Look lively." Cain wasn't big on commands unless absolutely necessary. That was about as command-like as he got.

"Roger that," they all responded in turn.

The pickup pulled into the lot and turned off its lights. Then instead of parking, it drove onto the sand past the bluff.

That was unexpected.

"Shit," Tac mumbled, who was forced to scramble to get out of the way.

Dane held his breath. Tac had been damn lucky that the pickup didn't have its lights on. The driver didn't slow, so it was a safe bet he didn't see Tac crabwalk out of his way. He turned and focused on the approaching speedboat. It was slowing as it approached the shoreline. "Incoming at the beach."

"Roger." Cain's voice was soft. "Four, you good?"

"Yeah. I'm awake now," Tac grumbled.

The night was a bright one. The moon was three-quarters full, which made it easier to see; good for them on the one hand but bad on the other. Sure, they could see better, but they could also be seen. Not ideal.

The team had spread out across the bluff and on some rocks that marched out into the water. Cass had been on the far side of the car park but was moving quickly to a new position by the beach. She ducked behind some palm trees and then flattened on her belly in the sand.

"Who's got sand in their nooks and crannies now?" Jace mumbled.

Dane cracked a grin. *Love this team.*

The pickup did a wide circle and then backed up to the waterline. The powerboat shut down its engines and coasted in with the tide. The pickup driver hopped out and waved a high-powered flashlight. The guy in the powerboat signaled back.

Dane squinted into the darkness. His gut tensed. *No fucking way.* He brought his binoculars up and flicked on the night vision. He zoomed in and made the images as clear as possible. *Sonofabitch.* He closed his eyes for a brief second. This could not be happening. His stomach lurched.

Dane's biggest nightmare just pulled his boat up onto the beach.

"Got visual," Cass said. "Boat man has bags. Multiple backpacks. It looks like three in total."

"Pickup driver getting something out of the back of his truck," Tac reported.

Cain confirmed. "An exchange, like your guy said, Three."

"Roger that," Koa responded.

Cass stated, "Driver handing duffel over and taking backpacks. Wait… They seem to be arguing. The pickup driver is shaking his head. He's taking back the duffel."

Dane's throat closed over. He was struggling to hear what his teammates were saying over the sound of his pounding heart.

"Is he opening it?" Jace asked and then answered his own question, "He is. He's taking something out. Too fast. I didn't get the shot. He stuffed it in his jacket. Now he's handing over the duffel. The boat driver doesn't look happy. Exchange complete. Got the pictures."

Dane finally managed to make his vocal cords work. "We have a problem."

"Repeat, Two," Cain demanded.

"We have a problem," Dane said again.

The guy in the pickup put the backpacks in the cab of his truck behind the driver's seat.

The boat's engine revved and eased away from the shore.

Cain demanded, "What problem?"

"The guy in the boat is one of us." Dane finally managed to get the words out.

"Coast Guard?" Tac asked.

"Yes, MSRT. My former team leader, Craig Owens."

"You sure?" The sudden tension in Cain's tone crackled through the comms.

"Positive."

"Well, shit."

"Yeah." And that didn't cover the half of it. Dane let out a breath as he watched the boat pull away. "We don't need to follow the boat, not that we were planning on it. I know where to find it. But we've got to abort the rest of the plan."

Tac swore. "You think he has guys watching."

"Affirmative. We've just been damn lucky they haven't spotted us." They were at a secluded beach off a nature preserve on Oahu's north shore. They'd come early to get into position and then stayed in place. That had worked in their favor. If they'd moved around, then Owens's scouts would have seen them. The fact that the handoff had happened meant that no one had seen Tac or Cass move. But it also meant Dane's team hadn't seen Owens's men arrive. How had they come? Where were they?

Dane swore. "They're behind us on the left. They have to be. That's the only place they could be where they wouldn't have seen Four and Six move."

On the other side of the road was just a rocky cliff front. If they were on top of it, they would have a great view of the beach, but the palm trees would block Owens's team's view of the road and give them only keyhole views of the beach parking lot, including most of the bluff.

Dane resisted the urge to turn and scan the surroundings in that direction. "Five—"

"On it," Jace whispered.

He had the best view because he was out on the rock

jetty that curved slightly on the right side of the beach, facing the rest of the team. Owens's team was in front of him, off to his right. Dane held his breath.

Jace's voice vibrated in his ear. "Shit. Got one at my two o'clock. Another on my four."

Fuck. They were stuck until those guys moved. The pickup drove up the beach and over the bluff. He went back through the parking lot and made a left back onto the road. A few seconds later, his taillights disappeared. Nobody moved.

Damn. He hated that the guy got away with the drugs. Tension vibrated along his body like tight guitar strings. Pins and needles stung his back, but he didn't move. He brought the binoculars up slowly. Owens stayed just off the beach in the speedboat. He hadn't left yet. *Why?*

"Two, got any insight into why he's hanging around?" Cain asked.

"None." What the fuck was Owens waiting for? A sound reached his ears. A buzzing. "Shit. Drone." Dane froze. Moving even slightly now would give them away.

The drone swooped in over the boat and hovered. It was carrying something, some sort of basket. *What the fuck?* It wasn't looking for them. It seemed to be looking for Owens. Maybe confirming he was there? The drone did a swooping circle and then came to a stop chest-height, hovering above the beach.

Owens brought the boat in and dropped the anchor on the sand. He hopped out and then reached over the side of the basket. He pulled out a small, black square box, the size of carry-on luggage, only square.

"Five, are you getting this?" Dane whispered through his comms.

"Yes. Lots of shots."

Owens put the square bag back into the basket and

stepped back. The drone dipped, almost like a bow, and then took off, first over the water, and then back over the trees. It was gone from view in seconds.

"Some sort of handoff," Tac mused.

Owens got back in his boat and turned out to sea.

Dane stayed still. The churn in his gut matched the burn in his back. This was not how this night was supposed to turn out. They were supposed to follow the pickup and arrest the guy for drug smuggling, but he was long gone. Jace probably had pictures of the truck's license plate, but the likelihood of it being legit was small.

Jace's voice broke into his thoughts. "Watchers are bugging out."

Dane heard the distant sound of a motor. Thirty seconds later, an SUV went down the road to the left. They all stayed where they were for another couple of minutes. Satisfied they were alone, Cain called it.

Dane got up and swore. His back had stiffened up so much that he moved like a one-hundred-year-old man. He was also crunching sand in his teeth. Jace hadn't been wrong about the nooks and crannies part.

They rallied in a parking lot three-quarters of a mile away. Dane was the last to arrive. His back was too stiff to move quickly if it wasn't necessary. He walked up to Cain's vehicle, a black pickup ironically enough, where the rest of the team was waiting.

"So, what the fuck?" Jace asked. "Your old boss?"

Dane blew a breath through his clenched teeth. "Senior Chief Craig Owens. I knew that guy was up to no good. I even spoke to base command about it, but I was told to talk to CGIS. I did, but they screwed me. Owens found out, and then I…had my…incident." He couldn't bring himself to call it an accident because he was sure it wasn't. He knew in the pit of his stomach that Owens had been behind the shit that happened the night Dane suffered his back injury…the reason for his persistent pain, but there was no proof.

"Cass, you're Tactical Law Enforcement. What do we do?" Cain asked.

Cass leaned her slender frame against the truck. "We don't have enough to charge him with anything at this moment. We have to see what the pictures captured. For all we know, he could have had rocks in that box and the duffel bag could've been full of laundry." She held up her hands to stave off any kind of argument. "I'm not saying it's likely. I'm saying what we know and what we can prove are worlds apart. We need more."

"What do we know?" Koa asked. "Cass is right. We were told there would be a drug deal. That's what we saw, but we don't know for sure that drugs changed hands. Zero proof on that. We know Owens is involved, but in what? And we know he gave three backpacks in exchange for a duffel bag and then he put a black case in a basket of a drone. We can fill in the blanks, but it's supposition, not fact."

Tac leaned on the side of the truck. "So, again, what do we do?"

Cass sighed. "Realistically, we're supposed to hand something like this off to the Coast Guard Investigative Services unit."

"No fucking way," Dane said bluntly. "I tried them last time. I just told you what happened. I put Owens on their radar, and they shut me down and then offered me up on a platter." He clamped his jaw shut. It was a long story, and he didn't want to get into it, but he could tell by the looks he was getting he was going to have to at some point. It just wasn't going to be on this beach in the middle of the night.

Cain unstrapped his body armor. "We start poking around."

"You mean we're going to stay on this?" Dane asked. He

didn't want to get his hopes up. Nailing Owens was something he'd been dreaming about.

"We're the Coast Guard. Our job is drug interdiction. We just watched a man presumably bring drugs onshore. That falls under our purview. I will confirm with Admiral Bertrand since he's our direct boss, but I think he'll go along with it. One of our own is the man in question. I don't know about you all, but I hate the thought that someone, who took an oath to protect and defend, is bringing drugs onto our shores. It pisses me off."

That was probably one of the longer speeches Cain had ever given, and Dane found himself agreeing. However, his doubts rose when they started to talk about the next steps.

Cain tucked one of his weapons into the gun locker on the back of his pickup. "Jace, get those pictures uploaded and let's see what we have. Cass, run the plate and see what pops. Cross-reference the names that come up with names of Guardsmen just in case. I don't think the guy in the pickup was one of us, but you never know. Koa, see if you can find out anything else from your friend who gave you the details of this meet." He ran a hand through his hair. "Tac, see if you can come up with a best guess of what could be in that square case. I got a bad feeling about that one."

Dane waited. Cain looked at him. "Go home and take care of your back."

Fuck.

"I need you in the best shape possible. Figure out what you have to do to get yourself there and do it. That's an order." Cain tapped into his phone and studied something on the screen. A clear dismissal of the topic.

Dane's heart thumped like a damn rabbit, and heat crawled up his neck. Cain hadn't assigned him a task other than "get stronger," which seemed like an insult. Hell, he was trying. It just wasn't working out.

"Now, go home. I just got word that the container ship will be available tomorrow for training. See you at oh-five hundred. This opportunity doesn't come up very often, and I want to take advantage. You'll be tired and pissed, the perfect way to board suspected drug ships. Dane, it's your turn to bring the coffee and food." With that, Cain climbed into his truck.

Dane walked over to his SUV and let out a string of curses as he hoisted himself in. Koa pulled alongside on his Ducati motorcycle. He flipped up his visor.

Dane put down his window.

Koa, true to form, didn't mince words. "He didn't give you a job because he can't have you too closely involved. You have history with Owens and the CGIS. You're pissed about it. That could affect things."

Dane paused and stared at Koa. He hadn't thought of that. *Shit.*

Did this mean he was going to be detrimental to the unit? He started to say something, but Koa drove off. Typical Koa. A man of few words, but what he did say was usually spot-on. He'd understood what Cain was doing while Dane still had his head up his ass. Ego was blinding him to the realities of life.

Koa was right. He did have history with Owens, and none of it good.

CHAPTER TWO

"Don't sit down. We have to go," Tom Rutledge said as he breezed past her desk.

McKenna Rankin had just touched her ass to her seat, coffee in one hand and cranberry orange muffin in the other. Hitting snooze one too many times had cost her the time she'd budgeted for breakfast. Instead, she'd hustled through her shower and then driven into the Coast Guard Investigative Service where she worked, only stopping at the cafeteria downstairs to get the muffin and second cup of coffee.

"Seriously? Can it wait, like, five minutes so I can eat?" she asked as she looked down longingly at her muffin. It smelled divine, and it would taste even better because she was starving.

"Cross called a meeting. All agents," he said over his shoulder as he walked away.

"Damn," she mumbled as she got up from her seat and followed in his wake.

Since moving to Oahu six months ago, life had finally settled down a bit. She loved her new job with CGIS far more than she'd enjoyed her seven years with the

Minneapolis Police Department. Thanks to the NCIS TV show, people understood what she did, and she didn't have to explain all the time like she thought she might have to. She was a civilian as most of the other CGIS agents were. A background in law enforcement and investigation were the job requirements but it helped to know more about the Coast Guard. She'd been learning lots since she moved here and last night she'd stayed up late reading some old cases, which was her excuse for oversleeping this morning.

It was odd that Cross would call an all-agent meeting. It had only happened once before, and it was at Christmas to tell everyone how well they were doing and to wish them happy holidays. Today wasn't a holiday as far as she was aware. They'd missed April Fools by a couple of weeks.

At the elevator, several other agents walked up, including her direct boss, Senior Special Agent Quinten Lawrence, AKA Casper, because of the long white hair he always wore pulled back in a ponytail.

"Casper," she said.

"Mac, how are you doing today?"

She just nodded. Casper wasn't her favorite person. There was something off about him, something she couldn't pin down. He was too cagey for her. Rutledge, on the other hand, she had liked immediately even though she was sure he was keeping secrets as well. He was just a nicer person. Casper was…slimy. It was the only word that suited him.

She nodded to two other agents, Barnes and King, and they all got onto the elevator together. The ride was short, only one floor up. The doors opened, and they walked into the main hub of the CGIS.

Two agents stood just outside the elevators with boxes filled with cell phones. Dumbarton said, "Put them in here." His partner, Cutler, held out another box for King and Barnes.

Mac cocked an eyebrow. Dumbarton met her gaze but didn't say anything. *The plot thickens.* She tossed her cell in the box.

She walked into the space and found a place to stand where she could lean on the wall. There were desks in cubicles, but the barriers were short so people could see each other while sitting. The conference room on the far wall was all glass. It had a great view of Honolulu Harbor and the dockyard next door. To the left of the conference room were the offices of the CGIS head honchos.

John Bishop Cross was standing outside his office. He was the Deputy Director for CGIS for Base Hawai'i. He was from back East, but she couldn't remember exactly where. Connecticut maybe? She knew he'd gone to Princeton and had been the quarterback on their football team. He had pictures of his university days in his office. She'd gone in to meet him right after she started. He was not her cup of tea, but she could see why others flocked to him. He was good-looking and charismatic. Headed for the top, there was no doubt.

In case anybody didn't realize his ambitions, he also had pictures of himself with various members of Congress, including senators. Even one Supreme Court Justice. Mac wouldn't have hung that picture if her life depended on it. The Justice in question was a complete asshole as far as she was concerned.

Cross was a tall man, lean, and well-groomed. She guessed he was in his mid-thirties. With his athletic good looks and easy smile, he must have been popular in high school and college. He wore pinstripe navy suit pants with a snowy-white shirt, sleeves rolled up halfway. That was his concession to being casual. He was like herself, a civilian, but unlike her, he was a total politician. He was warm with the Guardsman but made it seem like he was in awe of them. He projected the attitude of *we're all in this together* with the civilian staff, like herself, and most of the other Special Agents.

Hovering behind him was Neil Ainsley. She couldn't remember Ainsley's exact title, but everyone knew he was Cross's right-hand man. Cross didn't move without Ainsley in tow. In contrast to Cross, Ainsley was on the short side of average, with thinning medium-brown hair and a growing paunch. She guessed his age in the mid-forties, and always looked rumpled, like his clothes just didn't quite fit.

He and Cross were polar opposites in presentation and almost everything else. Ainsley did not do well speaking in public, nor did he inspire the kind of confidence Cross did, but he was aces at organization, or so she was told. The perfect working relationship. Except for tech. Neither one of them knew anything about technology. She'd heard that Cross kept deleting things accidentally, and Ainsley had no clue how to get them back, so he had IT on speed dial. The techs were in her shared office space and one of them was always going upstairs to fix whatever Cross and Ainsley had screwed up. She'd never spoken directly to either one of them other than to say good morning, and she wanted to keep it that way.

Cross stepped forward. "Thanks everyone for coming. Sorry to drag you up here," he said toward her and the other agents that had come up from downstairs. There were only about seven agents downstairs, and the rest of the staff on that floor were in the IT department. She'd discovered having the computer techs so nearby had its advantages when her laptop had decided to stop working the other day.

The group settled down. She and the others from downstairs stood against the side wall and waited.

Cross began, "I know this is a little bit odd. We normally do everything through email and the like, but there's something I need to communicate to you, and I need to be clear about it. No gray area. No wiggle room." He stood straight and made eye contact with as many agents as possible.

She glanced at Rutledge who was next to her. "Sounds pretty serious," she murmured.

He nodded but didn't take his eyes off Cross. Rutledge actually looked like Cross. Same tall, athletic build and classic good looks, but his eyes were green and showed a hell of a lot more depth. He was a bit too serious in nature for Mac but otherwise a good partner.

She focused on what Cross was saying.

"What I'm about to tell you must be kept in the strictest confidence. And again, it seems odd I am telling all of you together in a large space, but believe it or not, this is safer than email. I had the room swept this morning, and your cell phones are on a lower floor. I could have spoken to small groups of you, but that would take more time than was necessary."

Mac crossed her arms over her chest. She knew from her time chatting with Manu, the tech who'd fixed her laptop, that they had very tight security on their email system, and everything was encrypted. If Cross wanted to, he could have sent an email, which meant this was all about grandstanding.

"I don't want you discussing this outside these walls. As a matter of fact, I don't want you to discuss it at all. Do not send any emails about it. Don't put anything in writing unless I tell you." He paused again for dramatic effect.

Despite herself, she was intrigued. He was a great showman. This was just a stepping stone for him. Someday, she'd be watching him cross the Senate floor, or perhaps even in the White House. Nothing would surprise her.

"The Navy has informed me that some weapons and... other military equipment have been stolen from Naval Base San Diego. They have reason to believe it might be heading in our direction. Needless to say, the Navy wants its weapons back, but it also wants the perpetrators caught. And, of course, they want it done quickly and quietly. They do not want word to get out about this." He cracked a quick grin. "They're a tad embarrassed, as you can imagine."

The assembled agents all chuckled.

But then he spoke again in a somber tone. "I need all of you to see what you can find out about this, but I need you to do it leaving as small a footprint as possible. Don't ask your sources about weapons, ask about any contraband coming in. Don't reference the Navy. Ask if there's anything big coming down the pike. I won't tell you how to do your jobs."

He just did.

"I will ask, however, that if you get the slightest whiff of anything, you come directly to me. Don't write a report. Don't send an email. Don't talk on the phone. Come see me in person. My door will be open. I will put everything aside for this.

"I know we have a slightly fractious relationship with the Navy at times. They treat us like their annoying little sibling, but in this case, they need our help. They're going to be searching themselves. Stay out of their way, but"—he held up a finger—"also come see me first if you find out anything. Do not go to them. This is on a need-to-know basis, and I'm unsure who needs to know."

"In other words," Rutledge said in a quiet voice, "this is a competition. Find the missing weapons, make me look good."

It was her turn to nod. That was exactly what Cross had said. Now Oahu was going to turn into the wild west, a free-for-all to see who could come up with a lead first. *No, thank you.* She had no interest in being caught up in that mess. Inevitably, something bad would happen and someone would have to take the blame. A lowly new Special Agent like herself would be a prime candidate. She understood political games, and she was having none of it. Let the glory-seekers go for it. She'd just plunk her ass at her desk and eat her muffin.

After the meeting broke up, it took ten minutes to get her cell phone back. She was heading for the stairs when she heard her name being called. Turning, she was surprised to see Ainsley approaching. She hadn't done more than nod in passing at him before this.

"Sorry to hold you up." He offered her a smile.

A wave of cologne hit her, and she started to cough. Did he bathe in the stuff? "No problem. What's up?" She tried to appear relaxed and friendly even though she was freaking out. She'd been through way too much back in Minneapolis to find dealing with the bosses anything but stressful.

Ainsley touched her on the arm in sort of a weird, jerky motion and then pulled his hand back.

Her first instinct was to move back, but she held her ground and kept a smile pasted on her face. *What the hell did he want?*

"No cause for alarm. I just wanted to let you know that you're through your probationary period. I'm sure Casper would've told you eventually, but he's tied up now with this Navy mess." He gestured over his shoulder.

Casper was in with Cross, which wasn't remotely surprising. Casper knew everyone, but he was very cognizant of which side his bread was buttered on. It was just one of the many things she didn't like about her boss.

"Well, thanks for telling me. It was nice of you."

Ainsley smiled again. "I just thought I would share the good news. HR will be in touch next week to finalize the paperwork, but we're happy to have you with us permanently. Keep up the great work."

"Thanks," she said again.

There was a sudden commotion behind her. She turned to see a man standing just off the elevator, shaking hands with one of the other Special Agents. He was average height but heavyset. His hair was white but full, and he wore a light gray suit with a white shirt and red silk tie. "He looks familiar," she muttered.

"He should," Ainsley said. "That's Senator James Weston. He's here for an informal visit before he's off to Asia on official business. He'll be with us for a few days, checking things out. He's on several committees that can help with what we do."

Great. Another politician. No wonder Cross is all hyped up about finding the Navy's weapons. It would be a big score for him. "Well, I won't hold you up then." She started to walk away as the senator came in their direction.

"Senator," Ainsley said as he extended his hand. The man barely acknowledged him and kept going toward Cross.

Ouch. She quickly headed for the stairs and made her escape. She entered her floor and headed toward her desk when she saw Rutledge. He was speaking quietly into his cell, but he stopped altogether when she got closer and hung up abruptly. That was the third time he'd done that in as many days. She let out a sigh.

"What did Ainsley want?" Rutledge asked as she walked by his cubicle.

"To tell me I passed my probation, and I'm now permanent."

"Congratulations. Casper told me the same thing a couple of days ago."

"Congrats." She paused by his cubicle. "I don't know why Ainsley told me, though. Why not Casper? Ainsley said he was busy with the Navy issue, but he could have sent me an email or something. It was weird."

Rutledge chuckled. "Seriously? Ainsley rushed up to tell you some good news and you wonder why? He's known for dating some of the women that work here. Does that make it clearer for you?"

"Oh. Yuck."

Rutledge grinned. "Yup. Lucky you."

Shit. Well, that sucks. She rounded the corner to her desk and stopped abruptly. Her coffee was cold and her muffin was gone. It was going to be one of those days.

CHAPTER THREE

Dane hit the deck of the cargo ship and swore. His back was a mess, but he couldn't stop. He quickly moved away from the rope and scanned the deck with his machine gun raised, fighting the glare of the sun off the water. Reaching the first row of containers, he did a quick peek. Empty. He moved quickly across the opening to the second row. He was leader on this incursion, so he was One.

His earbud crackled. "One, coming up on your six."

"Roger that, Four," he responded. A second later, Tac Holden joined him next to the container.

"Two, Three, are you in position?" He peeked around the corner of the container, looking to the far side of the ship's deck. The rest of his teammates should be at the other end of the row of containers. From here, they would fan out across the deck and then proceed to clear the areas they'd been assigned on the small container ship.

"Roger," came the response from both Koa and Jace.

"Five?" he asked.

"Roger that," Cass responded.

Dane glanced up. He couldn't see her but knew she was

perched on top of the first container, gun up, sweeping the deck, ready to lay down cover fire if necessary.

He nodded to Tac. "On my mark." He waited a beat. "Now."

He stepped out from behind the container, kept his gun up, and cleared the deck. He moved rapidly over to the forecastle and then turned, keeping his eyes sharp until the other three were next to him. He turned and swept his weapon in an arc, ready to lay down cover fire for Five as she jumped down and crossed the open expanse.

When Five made it to the corner, he turned, and ducked inside the forecastle. Suddenly a whistle blew, and he straightened, pointing his gun at the floor. He stepped back onto the deck and waited for his team leader.

"Did we do something wrong?" asked Jace.

Koa, Jace's partner for the drill, answered, "No."

Cass shook her head. "I agree with Koa."

Tac looked at Dane, but he just shrugged.

Dane didn't think they'd done anything wrong either. As a matter of fact, he thought it was their best one yet, but what did he know? Not much, or at least, that's how he felt these days. He was still cranky from last night. Seeing Owens had brought back some heinous memories and, for the three short hours he'd been in bed, he'd had nightmares about falling. The oh-five hundred start time had crushed him, but he'd dragged his ass to their hangar and had food to boot.

Leaning against the forecastle, he looked out over the water. The sun was shining, and he was sweating in his body armor. Hawai'i was hot in April. Not that he truly minded. He was from New Jersey. April could be warmish or snowing in his home state.

He squinted to cut the glare of sunlight bouncing off the water. Way out, maybe half a mile away, a small speedboat was bobbing on the waves. The diving flag was still in the water. He glanced at his watch.

"Team," Cain said as he approached, "it's time to go. The captain of the cargo ship informed me they need to head into port."

"So, we didn't screw up?" Jace asked.

Cain gave him an assessing look. "Do you think you screwed up?"

"No," Koa answered for him.

"By far our best run," added Dane.

Cain nodded his head. "Agreed. I'll review everything with you when we get back to the hangar, but you guys did great today. You're really coming together as a team. I know you're all tired after last night, but we couldn't miss the opportunity. Thanks for bringing your A game." He started to turn but stopped. "Make sure you load your weapons when we get back to the RHIB. I don't want anyone empty. You never know what trouble we might run into."

Dane didn't blame his team leader for making them run drills. Since they were all somewhere on the injured roster, Cain needed to be sure his team of misfit toys was ready. That's how Dane thought of them. He with his back, Koa with his stomach, Jace with his knee, Tac with his hand, and Cass…well, no one knew what Cass's issue was. Dane had a sneaking suspicion her injury was not physically obvious. She was a beautiful woman, and it wasn't hard to imagine some asshole trying to force himself on her. Dane hoped that was not the case. Physical issues were tough enough to deal with but, that was a nightmare. Yes, they were damaged. Not quite good as new. More like a group of Frankenstein monsters, all stitched and patched up, just trying to make it through.

They were going back to base via a thirty-three-foot rigid-hull inflatable boat. In the front, it had a gun mount and then a windscreen with seats behind it. There was also a fiberglass wing overhead with communications equipment so they could stay in touch while they were on the water. Dane always had liked riding in the inflatables before the incident, but now crashing through the waves wreaked havoc on his back. With little sleep and rappelling out of helicopters all morning, he was already in hard shape.

He started across the deck and his gaze snagged on the speedboat again. He had a bad feeling in the pit of his gut. *Keep your mouth shut.* He'd opened his mouth before, and it had gone south. It was better not to get involved, better if he wasn't the one to see it. Cain wanted him to distance himself from the Owens thing. This would put him front and center. *Just let it go.*

But of course, he couldn't. "Cain," he said as they stood at the top of the stairs waiting for the RHIB to come alongside. "I think we should check out that speedboat."

"Why?" his senior chief asked as he looked over at the boat. Dane waited while Cain studied the boat and then looked at him. "You think so?"

He nodded. He could say he recognized the lines of the boat or the paint job, but really it was his gut telling him it was Craig Owens's boat. "We got here at oh-five-thirty. It's just oh-ten-thirty now. I haven't seen anyone on the boat or come out of the water since we've been here. I know we've been back and forth in the helo, but that's about a twenty-minute trip. Even if they were shallow diving, there's no way they could have come up and gone back under again in only twenty minutes. Their tanks would have run out of air, and they'd have to switch them more than once. There's no way we would have missed every switch. At least not if they were being safe. No one could be under that long."

Cain tipped his head. "You think Owens's abandoned his boat?"

He shrugged. Owens loved his powerboat. It was just one

of the things he liked to show off. Dane didn't think he'd just leave it out here, but who knew?

"Okay, we'll swing by it."

They descended the stairs and boarded the RHIB. Cain told the Boatswain's Mate to head to the speedboat.

"What gives?" Cassidy asked immediately.

Cain pointed to Dane. "He wants to check it out."

"Why?"

Dane explained to Cass and the rest of the team what he'd observed, or hadn't observed, since they'd been running drills. "But honestly, I think it's Owens. I'm pretty sure it's his boat."

Cass looked at him with disbelief. "How do you know?"

He shrugged. "I just know. The way it sits in the water. The paint job. It's his boat."

Cass looked at the speedboat they were rapidly approaching then looked back at Dane. "I hadn't even noticed it." She had to yell over the sound of the powerful engines along with the wind and spray.

He shrugged. "It's always been part of my job to notice things." What he didn't say was he made an extra effort to be aware of his surroundings at all times since his injury had occurred.

The Boatswain's Mate, a kid named Peter Slake, slowed the boat down as they approached the Yamaha with two large engines off the back. It had four seats and an awning covering the seating area. There was some sort of lower cabin, too. The boat was white with a blue stripe. Just like Owens's.

They pulled up alongside, and Dane jumped on board. He yelled out, "Coast Guard," but there was no response. He looked down the stairs. There were built-in bench seats in the shape of the hull. If two people sat there, they would be knee-to-knee, and toward the bow where it was narrower, there wasn't even room for seating like that.

He straightened. "Nothing." He went and peered over the side. The water in Hawai'i was a beautiful blue and somewhat clear. He squinted but couldn't make anything out. "Anybody see anything?"

The team peered over the side of the RHIB, but it was too deep for them to get a clear view.

"You're going to have to get in the water if you want to see anything," Koa pointed out.

Damn. He was right. Dane let out a long breath. Was it worth it? Did he really want to get wet?

Cain seemed to be reading his mind. "You'll regret it if you don't. It will haunt you."

"Fuck."

Cass's grin lit up her face. She didn't smile often, but when she did, it cheered the whole team. Most of the time, Cass looked fierce. It was probably because she had one bright green eye and one deep brown. It made it hard to read her mood. "Goin' for a swim," she chortled.

"Yeah." Dane went back over to the RHIB and stripped off his gear. The coolness of the water was going to hurt his back. Never mind wearing wet clothes after. Still, Cain was right. He'd be haunted if he didn't check for people in trouble. He stripped off his tactical gear and uniform down to just his pants then dove in.

The water was a big shock compared to the heat of the sun. He'd been sweating under his body armor. Under the water, he clenched his teeth and looked around. His vision was blurry, and his eyes stung from the salt. It took a minute for his eyes to adjust, but finally he could see a bit.

Was that a shadow? He came up, filled up his lungs again, and dove down using powerful strokes. His back hurt, but his certainty there was something down there kept him swimming downward. *Shit, was there something attached to the anchor chain?*

He swam upward, broke the surface, and sucked in air. "I can't get deep enough to see, but I think there's something down there. I need a mask or something so I can see better." He looked to Slake.

"Sorry, they cleared all the spare dive gear last week and haven't returned it yet. Standard maintenance," Slake said with a frown.

Jace hopped over to the speedboat. "Let's see if Owens keeps a spare mask." He started picking up the cushions and checking the storage boxes at the rear of the boat. With no luck above deck, he disappeared below.

Dane treaded water, trying to keep his back from tightening up. It was going to hurt like a bitch later. He was having second thoughts about this whole thing when he heard a yell.

Cain and Tac jumped over to the speedboat. Cass and Koa swung their weapons up, aimed at the boat.

"What is it?" Dane demanded.

Cass shook her head.

A minute later, Jace emerged and spoke with Cain and Tac. Cain pulled out the sat phone and made a call. Jace turned toward Dane. "Dude, you were right. The boat is registered to Craig Owens. I found a kilo of off-white powder, likely drugs. Cocaine or meth or even heroin. And there was a small pool of blood. It looks like someone cut themselves or was cut on the edge of the storage bin that was under the seat. The blood looks like it soaked into the drugs so that's why he must have left it behind. Could be from the shipment last night."

"Shit." The shadow on the anchor suddenly clicked into focus in his mind. "A body."

"What?" Tac asked.

"There's… I think there is a body attached to the anchor chain. I couldn't figure out what it was at first. Just a shadowy lump, but as soon as Jace said blood, it clicked. It's a body." He didn't bother saying what they were all thinking. *Owens.* His stomach knotted. This wasn't good.

Tac nudged Cain. He turned while still on the phone. Tac pointed at Dane.

"There's a body attached to the anchor chain. At least, I'm pretty sure it's a body," Dane called. Then he said a small prayer he was right. If it wasn't, he'd look like a big freaking idiot, but his gut was telling him he was right. It was a body.

Cain nodded. He'd gotten the message and relayed it to whoever was on the other end of the phone and then hung up. Dane swam to the RHIB. Tac and Cain got back on board, and they pulled Dane out of the water.

"One of our cutters is on the way. They'll have dive gear." Cain handed Dane a towel.

Koa asked, "Which one?"

"*Spencer Wallace.*"

"Thank God," Cass murmured.

They liked the skipper and the XO of the *Wally*, as it was called. Frank Valentine, the CO, was always good to them when they were training with his guys. They'd gone on a few rescues with him, too, and he always treated them with respect. His second in command, XO Nathan Calder, was also a good guy.

"Calder say when they'd get here?" Dane asked. It was a good bet that Cain spoke with the XO.

"About an hour. Might as well take a seat and dry off."

Dane nodded and sat down on the deck. He leaned against the gunwale, closed his eyes, and tried to relax. The sun was warm, and he hoped it would help keep his back from totally locking up. The sound of the gulls overhead, along with the waves bumping the boat, were soothing, but the saltwater drying on his skin created an itch that could only be showered off.

"Hey, sleeping beauty, wake up. No falling asleep on the job," Jace joked.

Dane cracked open one eye. Jace offered him a bottle of water. He was about to say "no" when Jace shook it at him. Dane took it, and then Jace opened his other hand that held two Advil. Dane nodded his thanks and took the ibuprofen. He opened the water and downed the pills. He gave Jace a nod of thanks. Jace always had pain relievers on hand. He'd blown out his knee somehow. Dane never asked for details from Jace or any of the others. The details would come when they wanted to share.

He'd been pissed off when he'd been assigned to this team. Just another dead-end post, one step closer to forcing him out of the Coast Guard, or so he'd thought. But gradually he came to realize Cain was offering him and the others a chance at being on a real team again. A chance of doing good work. And it *was* a good team.

Over the last three months, they'd been attached at the hip. They'd trained together, ate together, hung out together. They were close and getting closer every day. He hadn't realized how much he needed that comradery until it started happening. He hadn't felt that bond with his last MSRT. There had always been an undercurrent, as if he didn't belong there. He'd only been a fill-in. One of the regular guys had gotten hurt and mustered out.

"Drugs," Cass stated out of the blue.

Dane glanced up at her. "You seem surprised."

"Nah. Just...depressed. The war on drugs just never ends, does it?"

"No, I guess not." She was not wrong about it being depressing. Dane was about to close his eyes again, but Jace came over and squatted down.

"You know what kind this is?" Jace pulled a picture up on his phone. It was a block of off-white powder wrapped in plastic. There was a skull and crossbones inside a circle that had wavy lines off it.

"Is that supposed to be a skull in the sun?" Dane asked.

"That's what it looks like," Cass agreed.

Jace frowned. "That's not exactly good marketing, using a skull."

"Addicts don't care. How much marketing do you think drug dealers need to do?" Cass demanded. She snorted and went over to sit in one of the jump-seats.

Jace turned back to Dane. "So, did you recognize the boat because you'd been out in it?"

He shook his head. "It wasn't that kind of team, at least not for me. Maybe I was looking for it subconsciously, or maybe just because I was staring at it last night. Dunno, I just recognized it." He didn't want to go into detail about Owens and his old team in front of the yeoman, but it hit him that he was going to have to explain because, if it was Owens down there on the anchor chain, then all kinds of questions would be asked. Most of which he did not want to answer.

CHAPTER FOUR

"Forget the bagel," Rutledge said as he leaned over the half-wall of her cubicle.

"Oh, for shit's sake," Mac snarled. "I just got it. I need five minutes to eat it. When I left this morning, my muffin disappeared. Casper has had me chasing my tail for the last two hours, talking to supposed CIs who might know something. A load of bullshit if you ask me." She frowned. "I haven't had breakfast yet, and it's almost lunchtime. I need to eat something."

"Trust me, you don't want to eat. They pulled a dead Guardsman out of the water. One Senior Chief Petty Officer Craig Owens. He was probably in there for twelve hours, at least. He ain't going to be pretty to look at. But hey, it's up to you." Rutledge smirked before he turned and strode to the elevator.

Mac's gut rolled just thinking about it. She stood, grabbed her bag, put it over her head so it hung across her body, grabbed her coffee, and started toward the IT department, but then stopped and went back for the bagel. She needed something in her belly, or she'd be hungry and grumpy for the rest of the day.

She hurried down the aisle of cubicles and made a right at the end. Coming to the next row, she stuck her head over the top of the first one. "Manu, you gonna be around later? I have some email questions I want to ask you."

The kid looked up from his computer and grinned. "You bet. I have to fix a couple of laptops, but I should be here."

Manu was the resident computer genius at CGIS at the ripe old age of twenty-five. The kid knew everything as far as Mac was concerned. He was also a huge geek. Tall, reed-thin, with brown hair and big brown eyes. Everyone treated him like their kid brother. He was just a nice guy. She hoped life wouldn't kick that out of him.

She walked over to join Rutledge at the elevator. He glanced at her. "You checking up on what Cross said?"

"Maybe. Manu would know. The kid's brilliant," she said in a quiet voice.

"Then what's he doing here?" Rutledge's voice barely rose above a whisper.

She shrugged. "Apparently, he had a failed tech startup. Something to do with AI. It didn't go so well, so he came home." The elevator doors opened. "Where are we going?"

"About two miles out."

So much for the bagel. Her stomach knotted up. The move to Hawai'i had been a huge change and a godsend in her life, but she still hadn't gotten used to being on the water. She'd never been one for boats, and growing up in Minneapolis, she didn't have to worry about being seasick. Might be the land of ten thousand lakes, but she avoided water easily enough.

"Don't worry," Rutledge said with another smirk. "It's a calm day. There shouldn't be too much roll."

Easy for him to say.

The elevator doors opened, and they exited through the lobby where they met Casper, on the way in. "What's up?" he asked as he stopped in front of them.

Rutledge grimaced. "You need to check your phone."

"It's dead. I forgot to charge it last night, and you know I can't charge it in my car. It's a classic. No way to plug in."

Mac was sure she heard Rutledge grind his teeth. She knew it drove him crazy that Casper was so cavalier about things. She also knew it was an act. Rutledge hadn't seemed to cop on it yet, which surprised her, but the team had only been together six months, so maybe Rutledge was still settling in.

Casper ran a hand over his white hair, which he had pulled back into a ponytail and his forehead crinkled. "So, what'd I miss?"

Mac knew as sure as she was standing there that Casper was lying. His raised eyebrows when he was lying was his tell. He was telling the truth about not being able to charge his cell in his old Mustang, but he knew about the call, and if she had to guess, he'd been sitting in his car waiting for them to come out. Why he was doing this type of shit, she didn't know, but Casper liked to play games, and this was his court, so she tried to keep her head down and her mouth shut. She'd been burned before, and she wasn't going through that fuckwittery again.

"Body out on the water. Was a leader of a special operations team. MSRT. We gotta go see what's what." Rutledge moved around Casper. "We'll all take our own cars if that's okay. We might be out there a while."

"God, I hope not," she murmured.

Casper winked at her. "Don't worry, it's calm today."

He turned, and she followed him out to her little BMW convertible. She slid behind the wheel, putting her coffee in the cup holder and her bagel on the seat. They were only going down the street to the jetty, but if they came back late, walking across the parking lot at night was not so fun. The container pier next door was brightly lit at all hours, but it gave her the creeps to walk alone around Sand Island at night. Too much clanging and banging from the off-loading of ships and too many weird shadows cast by all the bright lights.

Since they were only going across base, she didn't bother to put down her roof. She smiled to herself. She loved her car. It had been a splurge, but she'd decided to treat herself when she'd arrived in Oahu. She'd been through hell and was starting a new job, a new life. She deserved something fun. The car was silver and about seven years old. She didn't care; she loved the BMW, and the convertible part made sitting in traffic worth it.

She pulled into a slot by the *Aids to Navigation* building and grabbed her baseball cap off the passenger seat. She tugged her ponytail through the back and adjusted the fit. She needed to keep the sun off her face and her head. That was something that she'd learned when she moved to Hawai'i. Her scalp had burnt a couple of times. Now, she always had a hat with her.

She was about to get out but paused to eat half of her bagel, toasted with cream cheese and bacon. She needed sustenance. She took a sip of her lukewarm black coffee and mused that she also needed a break from Casper. He'd caught up with her after the meeting and asked her to talk to a couple of CIs. It had been a colossal waste of time. She had told him she didn't want to be involved in the search for the missing weaponry. Not her jam. He could go look for it while she did the paperwork he was supposed to do from their last case. He'd finally relented.

She ate one more chunk of bagel, took one more swig of coffee, and walked across the parking lot to the jetty.

Rutledge and Casper were already on board the RHIB, which would be taking them out. It had a silver cabin with seats, one captain's chair behind the pilot's steering wheel and navigational instruments. It also had a silver deck and orange hard rubber sides. It was low in the water, and Mac knew the moment they hit the throttle, the bow would pop out of the water, and they would cut through the waves. Her stomach rolled again.

After Rutledge gave her a hand getting on the craft, she immediately went into the cabin and sat down. With her blond hair and pale skin, being out on the water would fry her like an onion. She'd put on sunscreen this morning as she did every morning, but if she'd known she'd be out on the water, she would have used the SPF one-hundred sunblock.

The boat left the dock, and in seconds, they were speeding out of Honolulu Harbor. She closed her eyes but then quickly opened them again. Watching the horizon was better for her rising nausea.

"You okay, ma'am?" the man driving the boat asked her. He was tall and lean with dark hair and eyes.

She smiled at him. "Yes, Petty Officer…"

"Victors, ma'am, John Victors."

"Yes, Petty Officer Victors, I'm fine. Still trying to find my sea legs."

He smiled at her. "Took me a while, too, but you'll get used to it and, soon enough, you won't even notice when you're out on the water."

"Hopefully," she said.

"Now I tend to get land sickness after I'm out at sea for a longer period."

She blinked. "I'm sorry…what?"

"Land sickness. At least, that's what I call it. It's when you're back on solid land, but it feels like you're still swaying. Takes a day or two for that to go away, but it's all good."

She gave him a halfhearted smile and tried not to panic. She could think of nothing worse than getting over her seasickness to suddenly acquire "land sickness."

"Mac," Casper called and waved her over to where he was standing just inside the door. "When we get there, I want you to interview the guys who found the body. Rutledge, I want you to talk to the medical examiner and see what he says. It's Cadaver Dave, so he'll fight you on it, but see if you can pin him down."

He had to speak loudly over the sound of the engines and the wind, but his voice was giving Mac a headache. She groaned at the mention of the medical examiner. Cadaver Dave Mortenson. He was tall and reed-thin. His bald head was sort of egg-shaped, and his pale skin only emphasized the dark circles under his clear grey eyes. In short, he looked like he was dead, hence the nickname Cadaver Dave.

He was also not the friendliest guy on a good day. The problem was he'd asked Mac out on a date when she first started, and she'd turned him down. He'd taken it as an insult. The truth was, she didn't date anyone she worked with. She'd been down that road, and she was still trying to recover. It had cost her a career and her self-respect. She wasn't eager to ever try that again.

"What are you gonna do?" she asked.

Casper gave her one of his looks that said *don't question me,* but he said, "I want to talk to base, see how they want to handle this. I need to find out about this guy's family."

A bullshit answer for sure, but whatever. If he wanted to hide on the boat, that was fine with her.

They pulled up alongside several other boats, one of which was a larger cutter. "The body is on the *Wally,* along with the guys who found it," Casper said to them. "Someone shot Owens and then wrapped fishing wire around his neck and hung him off the anchor chain."

She grimaced. That sounded bad. Why hang him off the anchor chain? Why not just let him float away in the water? She didn't ask in case the answer was obvious to people who hang out on the water. Growing up in a landlocked state had its disadvantages.

"Got it," Rutledge said. He asked Victors to drop him alongside the *Wally* and then went over and stood on the side.

"Good luck, ma'am," Victors said and shot her a nice smile.

"Thanks," she said lightly. Victors seemed like a nice guy. She figured him to be younger than her thirty-six years. Did this qualify as working together? Probably. He was too young for her anyway, but it did point out that she needed to start dating again if she was sizing up the guys at work.

She went to stand beside Rutledge. The salt spray felt good on her skin, and the smell of the ocean always made her smile. She loved the water, loved being in it. Did not love being *on* it. A minute later, they were alongside the *Wally*.

A Lieutenant Commander named Oscar Olsen welcomed them on board, and after introductions were made, he stood straight and shook his head. "This is a bad situation. One of our own dying is horrendous, but one of our own being murdered is just not acceptable."

"Can you tell us what the situation is exactly? The details we received were sketchy at best," Mac asked.

Olsen grimaced. "At approximately oh-ten-forty-five hours a special operations group discovered a powerboat floating, seemingly abandoned." He pointed to the boat that was tethered to the *Wally*. "They boarded the boat and found a small pool of blood and what looked like drugs in the storage area. Worrying for the safety of the people who were not on board, a Guardsman went into the water. He discovered Senior Chief Craig Owens dead, floating from the anchor chain. They called it in and waited for the appropriate authorities to arrive.

"We arrived and pulled Owens out of the water." He paused. "My men have pictures of Owens in situ when you need them. The medical examiner is with the body now."

"Okay," Rutledge said. "Thank you, sir. We appreciate your insight. We'll get started if that's okay." At Olsen's nod, he turned to Mac. "Go over and talk to the guys who found the body, one at a time. I'll speak with the medical examiner and join you shortly."

She turned to Olsen. "Sir, a quick question. Where might I find the special operations team?"

He gestured with his chin to look behind her. She turned. On the far side of the deck, a group of six people lingered. They were in body armor, which should have been a dead giveaway, but she'd been so worried about being seasick, she hadn't noticed them.

She turned to thank the lieutenant, but he was gone. Sighing, she dug her notebook and a pen out of her bag. She carried a full-sized notepad tucked into a leather portfolio. The detective that trained her back in Minneapolis insisted she carry one. Said those small notepads they used in the movies were bullshit. To be a good detective meant writing down every single word, not just the highlights. She would also normally record the interview but being out on the water with the wind blowing, it would be useless. She'd learned that one the hard way one day when she'd interviewed a young officer and the whole interview was blotted out by the sound of the wind.

Walking across the deck, it struck her how hot they must be, wearing all that gear. Why hadn't they taken it off?

She came to a stop in front of the group who were in various poses of sitting or standing in the small bit of shade offered by the forecastle. The sun was getting higher by the minute, so the shadow was receding at a rapid rate.

"Excuse me, which one of you is in charge?"

"I am," a man volunteered as he stepped forward. "Senior Chief Cain Maddox."

He was tall with deep green eyes and jet-black hair pulled back in a ponytail. She wasn't sure how that was allowed, but it wasn't up to her to enforce uniform code. He was also good-looking in a mobster kind of way, but she was sure he knew that. "Chief Maddox, I'm Special Agent MacKenna Rankin with CGIS. I would like to interview each member of your team one at a time."

"Okay, but could we do this as quickly as possible? It's hot, and my people have been working their asses off."

Wasn't that just part of the job? "I'll do my best. I would—

"

"Dane!" Maddox called out.

A man who'd been sitting on the deck stood slowly, as if in some kind of pain. But once he straightened, he moved with ease and came to a stop in front of her. He was tall, taller than Maddox, and his brown hair was short, maybe a shade longer than regulation, but if she were being honest, it was his eyes that made her blink. An icy blue that made her think of a winter sky. He was damn fine-looking to boot. Wide, wide shoulders tapering to narrow hips. He looked even bigger thanks to all his tactical gear.

She gave him the once-over, and from the rumpled appearance of his uniform pants, he'd been in the water. Was that why Maddox brought him out first? She would have rather started with someone she chose, but it was a small thing, and she wanted no ill will with these people, at least not at this stage. If they were involved somehow, then it would be different.

"Your name?" she asked.

"Chief Petty Officer Dane Landry."

"Okay, Chief Landry, let's go over there and chat." She turned and walked over to the other side of the deck. They stood in the bright sunshine. She had her hat on, so she was okay. Landry was going to have to sweat it out. There was no more real shade on deck, and she wasn't going to go inside to find a room to do the interviews in.

She made a notation of his name, the date, and the time on her notepad. "So why don't you start at the beginning? Who first noticed the boat?"

"I did," he said.

His voice was deep and sexy. She had a momentary vision of him with a lot less clothing on before she managed to corral her thoughts.

She cleared her throat. "And what time was that?"

"Oh-five-thirty."

Mac looked up. "What were you doing out here at that hour?"

A small smile tugged at the corner of his mouth. "Practicing. We were running boarding drills on a container ship."

She glanced around. "Where is that ship now?"

"At the port. The captain is a friend of...someone back at base, and he lets us, and other groups, practice certain drills while they wait to dock. This was our first time using this particular ship."

"Isn't that a bit dangerous? For the crew of the container ship, I mean?"

The smirk was back. "Weapons aren't loaded, ma'am."

Well, that was interesting. She made a note to ask Maddox if he knew who the friend was, and she needed the name of the captain and the ship.

"So you noticed the speed boat at oh-five-thirty when you got out here?" At his nod, she continued. "And when did you become concerned about it?"

He paused, his blue eyes searching hers for something; she wasn't sure what.

"I noted it first thing this morning, and when we finally finished at oh-ten-thirty, or thereabouts, I pointed it out to Cain…that is, Senior Chief Maddox. I explained I hadn't seen a soul on board since we'd gotten here, and the dive flag had been out the whole time."

"What did Maddox say?"

"He agreed it was strange, so we checked it out."

She wrote everything down and then asked, "Did you recognize the boat?"

Again, he paused. "Not at that time."

Her head came up. "Not at that time… Does that mean you recognized it later?" She pinned her stare to his face.

Landry nodded once.

Interesting. "Could you elaborate?"

He caught her gaze in his. "Later, I recognized the boat. After I'd searched it and then went into the water."

There was more to this story. She could feel it. "Why don't you just start at the beginning and tell me what happened, okay?"

Landry stood in the hot sunshine and looked down at her. His face went blank as he started his account. "We pulled alongside, and I boarded the speedboat. I called out I was Coast Guard, but no one responded. I looked around, and checked out the cabin, but when it was empty, I went back to our boat. I discussed it with my commanding officer, and it was decided I should get in the water and see if I could see anything.

"I stripped down to my uniform pants and dove in. It was hard to see, and I didn't have the proper equipment. When I surfaced, I reported there was a shadow by the anchor chain, but I couldn't make out what it was. Chief Petty Officer Jace Beckett jumped on board the speedboat and searched for a mask to help me. He called over Senior Chief Maddox to show him something.

"I waited in the water, and then they announced they'd found blood and drugs of some kind. The Senior Chief called for some help from the *Wally.* I got out of the water and was sitting on deck, drying off, when it occurred to me why the boat was familiar. I'd seen a picture of it in the locker of the man who owned it. I—"

"Wait, you'd seen it in Owens's locker?" A small ripple of unease passed over her. She didn't believe in coincidences.

"Owens and I used to be on the same MRST team before I was injured and moved to this team."

Well, that explained why he seemed in pain, but she didn't like that he knew Owens. "Were you and Owens friends?"

"No."

She looked up from her notes. There'd been no hesitation in his answer, and his eyes had solidified into ice chips. His expression was no longer blank. There was active dislike there. Not only were he and Owens not friends, but she was also pretty sure Landry hated the dead man.

Her unease with the situation grew. Something was off about the whole thing, especially since the dead man was a fellow Guardsman. "So, you knew Owens and recognized the boat from a picture in his locker," she summarized. Then what happened."

"I realized that the shadow by the anchor chain was a dead body."

Narrowing her eyes at him, she asked, "Why? Why all of a sudden did you know it was a body?"

His face hardened. He didn't like answering these questions. She was sure of it.

"Because it just clicked. Sometimes it's like that. I see

something and can't figure out what it is, but with new intel, the image becomes clearer in my mind."

It was a reasonable explanation. "So, after you thought about it a bit, you realized that Owens was dead and hanging off the anchor chain."

He shook his head. "No."

"No? Isn't that what you just said?" She watched him closely.

"I said I identified the shadow to be a dead body. I had no idea it was Owens. Could have been anyone."

She made a few more notes. At this point, she wasn't sure what to ask Landry. There was obviously history between him and Owens. Was it better to ask him what it was or to investigate it first and then hit him with it later if it was relevant? She'd give him the opportunity to add anything and then go from there.

Rutledge appeared. "Hey." He nodded at Landry. "I'll start with some of the other members of the unit."

She nodded to him but focused her gaze on Landry. "Tell me, is there anything else you think is relevant or that I should know?"

Landry waited for Rutledge to walk away toward his teammates before answering. He caught her gaze again. "Nothing. We waited for the *Wally* to arrive, and then with the proper gear on, two Guardsmen brought up Owens. When they brought his body on deck, I positively identified him and then waited for your arrival."

She wanted to press him, but he wasn't likely to break. Standing him in the hot sun wasn't winning her any points with him either. On the other hand, maybe she could make him lose his temper and say something. There was more going on between him and the dead guy. Whatever it was would come out, but it was better if Landry told her in his own words because then she could gauge the level of animosity between them.

"So, let's run through this one more time." When she looked up at him, she knew she'd made a mistake. He had a glint in his eye as if he knew exactly what she was trying to do. He wasn't going to break. If anything, he was going to say even less this time. *Well, fuck.* Why was it always the hot ones that were so much damn trouble?

CHAPTER FIVE

She could make him run through his story as many times as she liked while they stood there baking in the hot sun. It didn't matter to him. He wasn't going to change anything, nor would he add more details. They'd discussed as a team what they should say regarding seeing Owens last night at the drug swap. It was decided that mentioning it at this point wasn't a good move. Cain ran Dane through the story and made a few adjustments so they didn't raise any more alarm bells than necessary. They didn't have any real information, and Cain felt CGIS could find out for themselves. The less they were told, the more they'd have to dig into Owens' life, and wasn't that what everyone wanted?

Dane couldn't help wondering if it was also because it might make him look like a suspect. He had a history with Owens. He'd spotted the boat. He'd found the body. It was as if someone was painting him into the picture no matter what he did. Better to keep that information to himself. Plus, if she wanted to know about what happened between him and Owens, then she could read the file. He didn't have to volunteer anything. It wasn't fucking relevant.

He answered her questions but volunteered nothing and studied her as he did so. She was about average height but that was the only average thing about her. She was beautiful. She had a nice curvy figure, but it was obvious she kept herself in good shape. Her cargo pants hugged her ass and her polo shirt stretched taut over her chest. Long blonde hair pulled back into a ponytail made her appear youthful. Hazel eyes peered out at him from under the brim of her Minnesota Twins baseball hat. Big, intelligent eyes that currently said she didn't believe him. Well, tough shit because he was telling her the truth. Mostly.

"And you're sure you have nothing to add?"

"Nothing," he agreed.

Except he'd like to take her to dinner or a movie. More to the point, he'd like to take her to bed, but it all seemed a bit forward to ask here. He absently wondered what she smelled like. Citrus, he decided, would be her smell. He smiled grimly, trying to focus his thoughts again.

She made another note in her big binder thing and then turned and started across the deck of the cutter. Her long ponytail was swinging back and forth as she walked. He had the urge to pull it like a kid in school. Her hips also moved back and forth with a mesmerizing sway. *Stupid.* Don't be distracted by her. She'd use it against him. That's what CGIS did. Used stupid shit against him.

Still, it was a fine ass.

He went back and stood in a small pool of shade as the two special agents interviewed the rest of the team. An hour later, they were allowed to go. He and the others followed Cain across the deck, and then they boarded the RHIB, which had been floating nearby.

"Cain," he said in a quiet voice just before they took off, "I need to talk to you when we get back to base."

Cain's eyes narrowed slightly, but he just tipped up his chin.

Dane took a seat and braced himself for the ride back. The Advil he'd taken earlier had worn off, and his back was starting to tighten up.

A half-hour later, they entered the old hangar on Base Hawai'i that was their home. The open space was always a bit on the cool side. They had the AC cranked, which was necessary since Oahu's temperature was often like the inside of an oven, but it didn't help his back at this moment.

He followed Cain as the man bypassed the two horizontal rows of desks with computer equipment on them and the whiteboard that was at the front of their makeshift office space. The back left of the hangar was Cain's office. Cain unlocked the door and flicked on the lights. A big glass window overlooked the two rows of desks and the whiteboard. They'd taken to calling it the fishbowl. No matter what, Cain was on display. The old phone on Cain's desk was attached to an even older PA system. Cain used it to call people into his office. It was like being summoned to the principal's office, and it made them all laugh.

The locker room was at the back on the right side of the hangar. It had showers, restrooms, and even some bunk beds. It was better than some of the places Dane had slept in when on duty, and he was grateful there were beds. Sleeping on the floor was a no-go for him nowadays, and sometimes they'd stayed overnight to help out with some rescues. Not his normal drill, but he was adapting.

Dane went into the locker room and wasted no time in peeling off his gear and grabbing a couple of towels. He was under the hot spray in minutes while the rest of the team was getting changed out of their tactical gear.

The steamy shower helped loosen his back muscles, along with the stretches he did while the water pounded his back.

But relief was only temporary. His doctor said because of the trauma he suffered, it would take a long while for his muscles to heal completely. His back might never function like it once did. What did he expect with a hairline fracture of the L1 vertebra? Life was never going to be the same.

Ten minutes later, he was out of the shower and dried off. He pulled on his blue operational dress uniform and then headed out. His first stop was the kitchen area, which was located between the locker room and Cain's office. There was a counter with a coffee maker, sink, dishwasher, and a fridge. Jace was standing in front of a stove, and as Dane approached, Jace turned and handed him a cup.

"What's this?"

"Soup. Tac and Cass went to get lunch, but I figured you could use something to hold you over."

He sniffed it and then took a sip. It was tasty. "Thanks."

Jace nodded.

Dane finished the soup while sitting at the table just in front of the stove. Jace and Koa joined him. "What's for lunch?" Koa asked. "Besides the soup."

Dane glanced at his teammate. Koa was the explosives expert of the group. He knew more about blowing shit up than was strictly necessary and Dane had wondered if he might have enjoyed his job a bit too much. Or at least he used to. Now he was always asking about food, specifically, their meals. He'd been shot in the gut. Damn lucky to have survived. He was officially all healed up, but unofficially, he was having issues. Some days it still hurt. Lots of times he couldn't eat. Koa never gave details, but everyone knew the gist of the story. They always tried to get food they knew Koa could stomach. It was also why Jace heated the soup. If the lunch they got bothered his stomach, Koa could eat it so he wouldn't starve.

"They went for Chinese, I think," Jace supplied.

Dane grinned. “That’s why you heated the soup.”

Jace nodded. “I love American Chinese food, but I’m always hungry an hour after I eat it.”

“Same,” Koa said as he put his cup down on the table.

“Same as what?” Cass asked as she and Tac walked in.

Koa didn’t respond, but Dane and Jace hopped up to get plates and cutlery. Once the containers were on the table and opened, Cain came out of his office, nose in the air. “Smells great.”

Dane noticed that Tac didn’t take any of the noodles even though he knew the guy loved them. His hand had to be bothering him. He had days when he couldn’t use chopsticks, or even a fork very well. It was hard on him because he was a tech guy. He spent a lot of time using a computer. Sometimes it wasn’t so easy for him. But Dane guessed the same could be said about all of them. Some days just sucked with their injuries. That was life.

They spent the next half hour eating and shooting the shit. Dane assumed everyone was thinking about what happened that morning just like he was, but no one was quite ready to dive into it yet. Finally, Cain glanced at his watch and stood up. “Admiral Bertrand is going to call in about five minutes. He wants us all on the call.”

That galvanized the team. They had the kitchen cleaned up in no time, leftovers in the fridge, and were sitting at their desks when the call came in on a secured line. Cain put it on speaker, and everyone gathered around.

“Admiral,” Cain said. “How’s the weather in D.C.?”

“Cold and rainy, goddammit. I don’t want to hear about your sunshine and beaches,” he growled. “My wife is hounding me to go south as it is. I hate sand. Gets everywhere.”

Jace guffawed, and the whole team broke out in grins.

"Please give my best to your lovely wife," Cain said. "I miss her cookies."

Dane cocked an eyebrow. Cain had cookies made by the admiral's wife? They must be closer than he thought.

"Enough of the small talk, Maddox. I was just informed very early this morning that the Navy lost some weapons and high-tech equipment. They think it might be on the way to Hawai'i. Someone heard a rumor about the location but it's not been confirmed. I need you and your team out there looking for it."

"Sir," Cain began, "could you be a bit more specific? The team is here, and we need to know what we're looking for exactly."

"There's a list of the weapons. I'll have Walsh send it to you. But the weapons aren't the worst of it." There was a pause. "The US military developed motherboards with chips that can use cell phone signals as targets. These motherboards are put into missile warheads and, once activated, target the cell phone signal. There's ground support involved, and a few other things go into it, but the gist of it is, we can use a cluster of cell signals as a target."

There was dead silence in the room. It wasn't a surprise, exactly, since it's been in the news, but Dane sure as hell was shocked that the Admiral was admitting the US had the capability.

"I'm sure you've read about it with the war between Ukraine and Russia. Both sides are using the technology, but what you don't know is that Russian missiles rely on Western chips to work. With the sanctions, they should not be able to get these motherboards and chips, but unexploded warheads have turned up, and upon examination, they contain chips and motherboards from the West."

"You think these motherboards that were stolen could be on the way to Russia?" Cain asked.

"Probably via China but, yes, it is a distinct possibility, which would be disastrous. Not only because these motherboards would be used to kill scores of Ukrainians, but it would also destroy the US's political reputation on the global stage. I cannot stress enough how urgent it is we find these."

Dane let out a breath. This was a different assignment altogether than he'd thought he'd be working on when he joined this team. He glanced around at his team members. They all looked as shell-shocked as he felt. All except Cain. He looked calm. Somehow, Dane was not surprised. Cain never said much, but Dane had always had the impression he'd been involved in a lot more than he'd ever owned up to.

"The Navy is all over this, and I don't want you to get in their way, but we need to find these motherboards. Homeland Security is working with the NSA to see if they can locate the weapons. There's an NSA outpost there on Oahu. They're working on possible scenarios. I have offered you all as help if they need it."

A sudden thought hit Dane. "Sir, this is Chief Petty Officer Dane Landry. May I ask a question?"

"Go ahead, Landry."

"What kind of case are these motherboards carried in?"

"Why?" came the quick and cautious response.

Dane glanced at Cain. Recognition flashed on his face, and he nodded. Dane asked, "Could it be a black, square metal case, about eighteen inches all round?"

"Give me a minute. Walsh!" the Admiral bellowed. Then there was silence. Less than a minute later, Bertrand was back. "Yes, that's exactly what they were in. Where did you see it?"

Cain motioned for Dane to take the lead, so he continued. "We were following up on a tip about drugs coming onto Oahu. We witnessed what looked like a drug buy take place, but the seller didn't leave right away. After the buyers left, a drone showed up. The seller put a black hard-shell case into the basket the drone was carrying, and then it flew off."

Bertrand swore prodigiously. "Find the seller pronto! I'll alert the Navy. Walsh—"

"Um, sir?" Dane hated interrupting the admiral, but he had no choice.

"What is it, Landry?" he barked.

"The seller is dead, sir. We found his body this morning."

The admiral swore again.

"The thing is, sir, he was one of us."

Silence met his last words.

"Are you saying the man who put the case in the basket was Coast Guard?"

"Yes, sir. His name was Senior Petty Officer Craig Owens. He was my former team leader in the MSRT."

Dane braced himself for a long line of swearing, but the silence was impenetrable and ominous. He glanced at Cain, who lifted one shoulder and then glanced at his phone screen with a frown.

"Okay, gentlemen—excuse me—and ladies. Chief Petty Officer St. James, I meant no disrespect." Bertrand's tone was genial and contrite.

"None taken, sir," Cass responded.

"This is what you're going to do. As quietly as possible, you're going to find those motherboards and bring them back. Not a word to anyone about seeing them. Not one word. You speak about this only to me. If the base commander, or anyone else, questions you or gives you any flack, tell him to speak with me. We have to keep this as quiet as possible."

"Yes, sir," Cain responded.

"We don't know how high up the corruption goes. Trust no one outside your team. I can't imagine a Senior Petty

Officer could arrange this on his own. You don't know who else could be involved."

"Understood." Cain frowned. "If we need resources—"

"Contact Walsh. He'll get you whatever you need."

"Will do. There's one more thing. I just got a text telling me that Senator James Weston is dropping by in the next few minutes. Do you know anything about this, sir?"

"Weston? Goddammit! That man's got his nose into everything. Just answer his questions but don't volunteer anything. Do not talk about the motherboards. Weston is not necessarily a friendly. Be careful what you say."

"Yes, sir."

"And, Maddox, for God's sake, do not blow anything up!" The Admiral chuckled, and then was gone.

Dane raised his eyebrows. "Do you have a thing about things that go boom you haven't told us about?"

Cain shook his head. "Let's just say, in the past, there have been a few explosions Bertrand would've preferred we had avoided."

Jace rubbed his face. "I gotta say, this is way different than what I thought we'd be doing."

Tac, who'd been resting his butt on one of the desks in the front row, straightened. "I worked on a few things like this over the years, usually as backup though. It will be fun to be the front line."

"I don't know about fun," Cain said and paused. Then he smiled. "No, Tac's right. It's a hell of a lot more fun than running drills. In my old unit, we used to do this type of thing all the time. When Bertrand moved me over here to start this team, it was always with the idea that he would have us on standby for just such a circumstance. The old unit is gone but not the need for it. We're here to do what Bertrand deems necessary. We're over here in Hawai'i because he wanted us to have a lower profile. Less attention. But make no mistake, this is probably just the first in many assignments that will take you outside your comfort zones. Get a coffee or whatever and let's get started. I know you're running on too little sleep, but we're gonna keep going. The Admiral wants us to find the motherboards, so let's do it."

Five minutes later, coffee in hand, Dane sat down at his desk and leaned back in his chair. His back was tired, and it hurt. The shower had helped, but what he really needed was a chance to rest and some sleep. That wasn't going to happen for a while by the look of things.

Cain stood in front of the whiteboard. "You heard the Admiral. We have to find the missing tech. Where do we start?"

Cass volunteered, "I ran the plates from the pickup when we got back earlier. You were right. They were stolen from a Honda Civic last week. The owner reported the theft. It happened downtown when he was at dinner with friends."

"So, we've got nothing on the buyer then." Cain turned to Koa. "Anything from your source?"

Koa had a hand on his gut. His face didn't give much away, but if Dane had to guess, he'd say Koa was uncomfortable. He knew discomfort when he saw it mostly because he was uncomfortable a lot of the time. It was too bad though because the Chinese food hadn't bothered him last time.

"I spoke to my source. I can find the buyer if and when we need to. He's a local gang member. My source says the drugs are meth, and they're coming from the mainland."

Jace rubbed his knee. "Not from Asia?"

"No. My source says these drugs come from the mainland. Mexico to be exact."

Cain folded his arms across his chest. "The Mexicans have gangs in Hawai'i?"

"They're working with some locals to move their product. Owens had to be a part of that."

"Koa, do you trust your source?" Cain asked.

He nodded. "He's…a friend. We grew up together."

"Why's he telling you all this?" Tac asked as he leaned back in his chair.

When Koa stayed silent for a minute, Dane honestly thought he wasn't going to answer. Koa's lips thinned into a straight line before he spoke. "He's made some bad choices, but now…he wants out of that life. If we arrest everyone, then he can make a fresh start."

Cass frowned. "It's not going to be that simple, Koa. Drugs and gangs are hard to get out of, and if he's involved, then he might see some jail time."

Koa remained silent.

Cain took the pressure off Koa by saying, "Anyone else have any other ideas on how we move forward from here? Assuming we put aside the drug thing for now."

Dane cocked his head. "I have a few questions. What the hell was Owens doing meeting with whoever it was next to the shipping lanes? It's been bothering me. Owens was a smart guy. If it were me, there's no way I would want to do business right there. Way too many witnesses."

"Dane makes a good point," Koa agreed. "It's dangerous to be right there. It would attract attention."

Cass pointed out, "But if he was picking up the drugs from an incoming container ship, it would be a hell of a lot easier to do it right there. The ship drops it over the side, and he comes along at night and picks it up."

"But he'd already made the drop." Tac put his mug down on his desk. "We saw him make the exchange for the drugs, presumably, and then he put the case in the basket, so what the hell was he doing out by the shipping lanes after that?"

"Meeting someone?" Dane ran a hand over the back of his neck. "Put yourself in his shoes. You've done your exchange and dropped off the motherboards so, realistically, you want to go home. It's the middle of the night, and you just made a lot of money. Why would you go out to the shipping lanes? He *had* to be meeting someone."

"You think he had to take the money to someone? If he was just the middleman, that would make sense," Tac suggested.

"What would a middleman's take be?' Koa asked. "If you're risking your career and your life, not to mention jail time, what number would make it worth it to be that guy?"

Dane stared at Koa. "What if that's the whole point? What if Owens felt he wasn't making enough for the risk he was taking? What if he wanted more, and that's why someone killed him?"

"Doesn't help us find the motherboards," Cain pointed out.

Dane took a sip of coffee. "I still think he was out there to meet someone. Whether he had to hand off the money or not. And I think that person killed him." He paused. "Can we get a copy of the autopsy report and any forensic evidence from the boat?"

"I'll ask Finn. He'll get us a copy." Cain leaned against one of the desks.

"Who's Finn?" Jace asked.

"Finn Walsh. He's one of Bertrand's aids. I used to be on a team with him. He's a good guy. He'll get us what we need."

Cass blew on her coffee. "Then ask him for satellite images from last night, too. Maybe an eye in the sky caught something. Worth a shot."

Cain gave a thumbs up. "Will do. What else?"

Tac spoke up. "I'm wondering if we can trace the drone. Jace has pictures of it. Maybe we can find a way to see who has one on the island."

"I've got the pictures up on my screen now," Jace said. "You want to run through them?"

"Yeah, but don't project it up on the smart board. That senator is supposed to come by. I don't want anything on the big screen if he drops in unexpectedly."

Every member of the team gathered around Jace's screen. Jace started running through the pictures from the meet one by one, starting with when the pickup driver arrived and running through to when the drone left. Dane tried to look for anything that stood out. Any little thing that might shed some light on who Owens was working with but there were no markings on the drone or the box.

"Wait." Something snagged Dane's attention. "Go back one."

Jace did as he was asked. It was a picture of Owens on the boat.

"Can you blow that up at all?"

"Sure," Jace said. "What part?"

"Owens."

Jace blew up the picture until it started to become grainy. "What am I looking at?"

Dane leaned in and pointed to a blotch on Owens's head. "See that? I think that's where he hit his head."

"The blood," Cass supplied.

"Looking at this, I'd say he fell on his own and whacked his head. Head wounds bleed profusely. He probably left those drugs behind because he didn't want his DNA attached to them in any way. That's what the argument was about at the exchange. It's why the pickup driver took out some money. At least, that's my guess." Dane leaned away from the screen.

"Makes sense," Koa said. He stood with his arms folded across his chest. "But if that happened before the exchange, then we have no idea what happened on the boat after and how Owens ended up hanging from the anchor chain."

"Maybe it doesn't matter." Tac walked over and poured another cup of coffee. "Maybe we're looking at this all wrong. The goal is to find the motherboards. If we find out who killed Owens, that's a bonus, but not really our job, is it? I think we are getting distracted by his murder. It could be linked to the motherboards, but it could just as well be linked to the drugs."

"Look, I think Tac is right," Dane said. "As much as it kills me to say it. I worked with that fucker, and he caused my injury. I want every shitty thing Owens has ever done to come to light. I want him to go down as the worst piece of shit ever associated with the Coast Guard. But that's irrelevant. We need to find those motherboards before the Russians, or the Chinese, or whoever uses them to blow up innocent civilians. I gotta be honest. I hate the idea of that tech even existing, but it's better if we at least control it. If it's up for sale, any terrorist group on earth could grab it, and then all bets are off."

Cain put his hands on his hips. "Okay then. The drone. Jace, you have the pictures. See if you can track down anyone on the island who has one that's similar. It's quite big. There can't be that many of them here. I will get the information we need from Finn. Anyone else had any ideas?"

"We should check out Owens's place," Koa stated.

"CGIS will have gone through it," Cass pointed out.

"Yeah, but that's CGIS, not us."

Dane jolted. "Candyland."

"What? The kids' game?" Jace asked.

Dane's gut tightened. "No. I'd forgotten all about it. Blocked the memory from my mind probably." He was sure he had. What else had he blocked out? He was going to have to make an effort to remember his time on the other team no matter how painful it was.

"Candyland was the word Owens used for some secret place. He and the others would talk about it sometimes before they knew I was there. Like, 'I'll be at Candyland tonight.'"

Cain shoved his hands in his pockets. "Do you have any ideas where Candyland is, or even what it is?"

Dane cocked his head. "Can we search real estate records and look for any holdings on Oahu under the name Candyland? Is there a database for that? I'm sure Owens would use the name. He'd think it was funny."

Cass rolled her eyes. "Sounds like a moron."

Tac went around his desk. "I'll see what I can pull up. You think he had a secret place?" Tac sat down in front of his computer. "That's interesting."

"I do. He was juvenile and moronic when it came to shit like that, but sly like a fox when it came to business. If he was making extra cash, he'd have to put it somewhere, and he'd want to do it without attracting too much attention."

Cain nodded. "Okay then. If we can find it—"

"Found it," Tac said. He called out an address on Waikiki Beach including an apartment number.

"Well, shit. He wasn't playing, was he?" Jace rubbed his knee. "That's seriously pricey real estate. Downtown."

"Yup," Koa agreed. "That puts him overlooking the beach next to the Hilton Hawaiian Village."

"Candyland. All those young women in town looking to party on their vacation. Easy picking for someone like Owens." Dane's stomach churned at the thought of it.

"I thought he had a wife and kids?" Cass demanded.

"He did," Dane growled. It made him sick to think of Owens out there screwing around on his wife, but it was none of his business. This was all about the motherboards.

He knew he was going to have to remind himself of that a lot during this op.

"So, we meet downtown at twenty-one hundred hours. I'll text you the address later. We're gonna take a look at Candyland and see if this asshole is hiding anything good there." Cain nodded to them. "Go home and get some sleep." He headed back to his office.

Everyone had gotten up and was gathering their stuff just as the door to the hangar opened, and Senator James Weston strode in along with two other men.

"Gentlemen," the taller, well-groomed man said. "And ladies," he amended when he saw Cass. "I am John Cross, Deputy Director of CGIS, and this is Senator Weston, and my assistant, Neil Ainsley. The senator wanted to see your setup."

Cain stood at attention. "Yes, sir." Everyone followed suit.

"At ease," Weston said. "You must be Cain Maddox." He offered his hand to Cain, and they shook. "I understand this is a new type of operation. Admiral Bertrand's baby, if I recall."

His friendly smile didn't reach his eyes as far as Dane could tell. This man was on a mission, and his gut said this didn't bode well for them.

"So, Maddox, tell me about your team," said the senator.

"What would you like to know, sir?" Cain responded.

Dane bit back a smile. Cain wasn't giving an inch. He was very loyal to Admiral Bertrand, which was nice to see. Loyalty meant everything to Dane. Especially after his last posting.

Weston's smile faltered slightly. "What exactly do you do?"

"We are essentially a special operations team. We aid

when we can with the usual Coast Guard missions: drug interdiction, rescue operations, human trafficking—"

"Yes, I know that's what the special operations teams do in the Coast Guard, but my understanding is that you are all special in some way. Explain."

Dane was glad he wasn't the one the senator was grilling because he'd probably have lost his temper by now.

"We aren't special, sir. Having team members from different operational units just lets us be a bit more flexible in how we handle situations, sir. We're all trained the same way. We just bring different bits of knowledge and experience. We're just an experiment, sir. Guinea pigs."

Weston scrutinized the team. "I've heard you were all injured at some point. Do you think you can still function? No point in having a team like this if everyone is not at their optimal level."

"My team is in great shape, sir. They are in peak condition."

Lies. That was a pack of lies. They all had injuries they were learning to deal with. Dane's gut knotted. Cain had just stuck his neck way out there. If the senator ordered them to perform a physical test of some kind, they could be done for.

"I'm sure these people have lots of work to do, Senator, and you are scheduled to speak to Base Command at Naval Base Pearl Harbor." Ainsley was trying to shepherd the senator back toward the door. "We need to get moving."

The senator grunted but started moving. "I'm sure we'll meet again, Senior Chief. Maybe your team could give me a demonstration before I leave on Sunday evening."

"Of course, sir. If schedules allow it." Cain had drawn a line in the sand and he sure as shit was not letting the bureaucrat walk over it.

Ainsley shot him a look, but the senator kept walking.

"Thank you, everyone," Cross said. "I appreciate you

taking the time." He gave them a nod and followed the senator out the door.

"Jesus, that was close," Tac said. "I can see why Bertrand isn't a fan. This guy is out for blood."

"Yeah," Cain agreed. "Let's keep ourselves busy working on finding the motherboards so we can't fit him into our schedule."

There were some murmurs of agreement. A few minutes later, they were all on their way out of the hangar when the door opened in front of them and the attractive Special Agent Rankin walked in. "Chief Landry, I need to speak with you. Could you come with me please, sir?"

Dane ground his teeth. He'd been hoping to avoid this, but he had known the chances were slim. However, he did think he'd get at least one more day before they came to question him.

"No." He stood with his arms crossed over his chest. He'd been down that road with CGIS before. He wasn't falling for that shit again. It didn't matter that they'd sent a much cuter messenger this time.

Rankin came to a stop a few feet away. "Excuse me?"

He shook his head. "No. You want to talk to me, we do it here or you can arrest me and I'll call a lawyer."

She glared at him.

He couldn't give a shit. He didn't care how good-looking she was; she was, in fact, the enemy, and he wasn't going down without a fight.

"Chief Landry, I'd just like to speak to you about Owens, at the CGIS office. That's it."

"How stupid do you think I am? A few months ago I spoke with the one they call Casper about Owens. I won't do it again. You want to talk to me in your office, then arrest me and I'll call my lawyer. Otherwise, we can talk here in front of all these witnesses. I got screwed last time, and I won't let it happen again."

Cain appeared beside Dane. "Well, Special Agent Rankin, you've got your response. My officer is not interested in going with you. If you want to speak to him, I suggest you do it here."

There was movement around him. Dane felt it. It took a second to register the fact that his entire team had surrounded the CGIS agent. Their aggressive maneuvering was making her feel very uncomfortable, if the death looks Rankin was shooting everyone was anything to go by.

"Chief," she said, trying to appeal to him directly, "we need to sort this out. If you'll just—"

"No. You want to talk? I'll talk here. Otherwise, we're done." He wasn't giving in. It had cost him too much before. Hell, it almost cost him his life.

Rankin's hazel eyes glittered. She was seriously pissed off. *Good. Join the fucking club.*

She cleared her throat. "Fine. If we can just go in the office over there, I'm sure—"

"No. I said we could talk here in front of my team. Take it or leave it. Makes no difference to me." He hadn't told them what happened yet. He'd referenced it several times, and he knew he'd have to tell them eventually, but he'd thought it would be over beers somewhere. If it had to be now, so be it. He wanted them to know. More, he wanted them to understand and believe him. He wanted that more than anything.

She clamped her lips together in a thin line and then nodded curtly. "Fine."

Dane sat back down at the kitchen table with his back to the stove. Rankin sat down opposite him. The rest of the team fanned out so they surrounded the table but at a distance. Cain came over, turned a chair around backward, and straddled it, leaning his arms on the back of it. He gave Rankin his stone face. That's what Dane called it. It made him want to smile. The whole team made his heart warm a bit in his chest. He hadn't had this kind of support in a long time.

"What do you want to know?" he asked.

Rankin leaned forward. "You filed a report against Chief Petty Officer Owens, accusing him of stealing."

"Untrue."

When she blinked, he could see the uncertainty creep into her eyes. She tried again. "We have a signed statement from you claiming you saw Owens stealing."

"False."

"Chief Landry, I've seen the report. I know you accused Owens of stealing."

He shook his head. "No. I went in and spoke with Senior Special Agent Lawrence and told him what I saw. *He* filed the report. I specifically said I didn't want to file anything. I just thought what I saw should be investigated. Lawrence, or Casper as you call him, told me that he'd write up my statement and keep it on file while the incident was investigated. Instead, he forged my signature, filed the report, and then told Owens that I'd accused him of stealing.

He was having a hard time holding his anger in check. "At no time did I give him permission to file a report on my behalf, but he went ahead and did it anyway, and I ended up in the hospital with a broken back."

CHAPTER SIX

Mac's stomach hit her feet. The moment Landry said Casper's name, she knew, *knew*, her boss had fucked this up somehow. He'd screwed over Landry, and now they were hip-deep in a homicide that might have repercussions since he mishandled the original investigation. Maybe that was why he sent her to speak with Owens's wife and then over here instead of with him and Rutledge when they interviewed the rest of Owen's team. He knew he had fucked up, and since she was the junior agent, it didn't matter what she found out.

She drew in a deep breath and then blew it out again. "Maybe we can start again." She looked up and met Landry's gaze. "In your own words, can you please tell me what you witnessed with regard to Senior Chief Petty Officer Craig Owens?"

Landry grunted then glanced around at his teammates.

It struck her that he hadn't told them the story about his injury yet. *Interesting.* It was her gut feeling that he still wasn't sure about telling them, which made it even more interesting.

"About ten months ago, I filled the place on Owens's team of a guy who'd left the service. The team didn't exactly welcome me with open arms." He tapped his fingers on the table and looked at his teammates.

He wasn't talking just to her. He was telling them as well.

"There was always an undercurrent with Owens and the others. Like something was going on, but no one wanted to include me in it. It was…weird. I tried to be friendly, but they just weren't having it." He shook his head. "Fair enough, I thought at the time. I'll just do my time and transfer when the opportunity arises.

"Then one night after shift, the guys all said they were going home. Owens had said specifically he had to be home because his kid was sick and he needed to give his wife a break. I took it at face value and left. I got home and was about to go to bed when I realized I'd left my cell phone on base. Stupid, I know. I was going to leave it until morning, but it would be my luck that I'd get a callout and not know. So, I hauled my ass back to base.

"Anyway, I got to base, got my phone, and I was leaving when I see Owens's truck. It's parked in an odd spot. It's over by the port, parked next to some containers. I knew it was his because he had a dent in the front right quarter panel and a cross dangling from the rearview mirror. I thought it was weird he was there and was just going to let it go, but I saw movement so I killed the lights, swung around, and parked by some other cars. I know it sounds strange that I would spy on my teammate, but that team, there was just something… off about it. They made alarm bells ring in my head."

She didn't want to break the flow of the story, but she desperately wanted to ask questions. She wanted to take notes, too, but she was sure Landry would stop talking if she did that. This wasn't easy for him. Telling this story. It made her want to reach out to him, and offer him encouragement, which was just ridiculous since this was supposed to be an interrogation. Was she losing her edge? Or was it just something about Chief Petty Officer Dane Landry that drove her to distraction?

"It was close to oh-two-hundred when I saw Owens coming out of a container with some sort of bag. In the end, he loaded three of them into his pickup and then left. I followed him. He went to the other side of the island, to a small beach next to one of the big parks. He transferred the bags to another pickup driven by some other guy. I got a plate and even took a picture but"—he captured her gaze—"it all turned to shit."

Mac swallowed. Landry's eyes were captivating. She was having a hard time turning away from them. They turned a deeper blue when he was angry. What color would they be when he was excited? *Jesus. Get it together.*

"Before you go on," she started, "can I ask, when exactly did you decide there was something wrong with the team? Was it from the first day or did it build over time?"

He leaned back. "I think in the beginning they were feeling me out, which is pretty normal, but somewhere along the way, maybe a month or so in, it started to change."

"Do you remember a specific event?" she pressed.

He stared at her, but she knew he didn't see her. She was pretty sure he was lost in thought. "I think it was right after we finished clearing a yacht. We'd been called out on a tip from someone. I have no idea who or any details on that. It wasn't my job.

"Anyway, it was a tip on drugs being smuggled on a small yacht. We boarded and started to clear the ship when Owens suddenly called it, said we were done. Owens let the yacht go. I asked him why later, but he just brushed me off. I think it was some sort of test, and I guess I failed because they froze me out after that."

She licked her lips as she decided how to approach her next topic. "You said you told your commanding officer about seeing Owens." At his nod, she continued, "Who was that?"

"Commander Carter Wainwright."

"Okay. Isn't he still your commanding officer?"

Dane turned to Maddox.

The other man stared at her before he said, "It's complicated."

She blinked and waited but no more information was forthcoming. *Okaaayy.* "Perhaps you could uncomplicate it for me." She was trying to keep herself reined in, but these two were pushing the limits.

Cain finally relented. "We are under Wainwright since he commands the MSRT group, but we report directly to Admiral George Bertrand, in Washington."

Holy shit. She didn't see that coming. A direct line to an Admiral. Who the hell were these people?

She looked back at Dane and decided to bite the bullet. He was already pissed off, might as well go for it. "What did Owens do when he found out about the report?" *Something that never should have happened.* Owens never should have known who lodged a report against him.

"He yelled at me. Told me I had it all wrong. It wasn't his truck."

She waited a beat, but Landry wasn't talking. She knew there was more, but he'd clammed up. She'd thought he would tell her the whole story and she was pretty sure he intended to but something stopped him. There was more to this. Maybe whatever it was linked him to Owen's death.

"That's all he did?"

Landry didn't respond, but Maddox jumped in. "Maybe we could move on. As I said, my people are tired. It's been a long day."

She was being dismissed, and that fact pissed her off, but there wasn't much she could do about it. "Where were you last night between twenty-three-hundred hours and oh-four-hundred hours?"

"I was at my place. I went to bed at around twenty-two hundred. Got up at oh-four-thirty and was here on base at oh-five-hundred."

"Is there anyone who can verify that you were home sleeping?" She suddenly realized she really wanted him to answer no. Not because she thought he'd killed Owens, although it was a possibility, but because she didn't want him to have a girlfriend. *No dating people at work*, she reminded herself. Dane Landry just had something…some sort of energy that filled her belly with excitement.

"No."

She was stupidly happy with that answer. "Right. I think I have what I need. If I need additional information, I will let you know." When she stood, he stood as well. She nodded to him and walked out of the hangar; the entire team's gaze was following her the whole way.

Once outside, she got in her car and drove the two minutes down the road to her office. The heat of the day was starting to wane. The gulls were still crying overhead but not like they did in the morning. The salt on her skin from her morning's adventure out on the water was making it dry and scratchy. She needed a shower and a snack. Another muffin? Maybe not. She hadn't had much luck today with muffins.

The issue topmost in her mind was Casper. The inaccuracy of the initial report had led her to get crushed in that interview just now. She needed to get back to her desk and review it again. There was a small chance Dane was lying, but she didn't think so. *Dane.* She should call him Landry, but somehow in her mind, he'd made the switch to Dane. Instinctively, she liked him, believed him, but her instincts had been wrong before. The fact that this group had their own hangar and answered directly to an admiral in DC meant she was going to have to move very carefully around them.

It was time to confront Casper. If he raised his eyebrows, then she'd know for sure her boss had fucked up. The only real question would be, did he do it on purpose as Dane thought, or by mistake?

CHAPTER SEVEN

"I know you're all exhausted and want to head home, but if you want, I'll tell you the rest of what happened with Owens."

He had planned on telling the whole thing to Rankin but something held him back. Maybe a sense of self-preservation. If he said what really happened in front of her, it gave him a hell of a motive to kill Owens.

The team joined him at the kitchen table. Jace retrieved beers from the fridge and handed them out, then took his seat.

Dane smiled. This was as close to sharing his story on his own terms as he was going to get. At least they'd gotten the 'over beers' part right. "After Owens found out about me filing the report, and confronted me, I asked for a transfer, but Wainwright said he didn't have anything at the moment and wasn't going to let an asset go to waste, so I had to stay put until something opened up. Owens and the rest of the team made my life miserable. They were pissed off. I got it. I didn't blame them. I would be pissed, too."

He took a swig of beer and allowed the cool liquid to

wash away the lump building in his throat. He'd never said the rest of this out loud before. He had no proof, and there was no one to tell anyway. Who would believe him?

"We were running drills on a cargo ship like today. We did that a lot more with Owens. He was big on training. Anyway, it was the first run. My job was to provide cover fire from the top of the container, only it wasn't from the top of one container. Like today's exercise, it was from the top of the third container. The drill started fine. Everyone had cleared the deck and I was coming down the metal ladder attached to the stack when my hands slipped, and I fell backward. I landed on the deck about twenty feet down and broke my L1 vertebra. Hairline fracture and damn lucky it wasn't more."

He took another slug of beer, more to avoid looking at anyone than because he was thirsty. He cleared his throat. "I banged my head, but because of the helmet, I blacked out only for a second. I had a concussion, but I've had worse playing football. The real problem was a bolt that had been sticking up on the deck was lodged in my back near my spine. It was agonizing. Anyway, the rest of the team was slow to come over to offer help. I distinctly remember the surprise on Joel Cameron's face when he saw my eyes were open. He thought for sure I was dead. He said, and I quote, 'Shit, he's still alive.'"

"Sonofabitch," Tac mumbled.

Dane nodded. "They forgot I had an earbud in. I heard them discuss the fact that I didn't die, and now what were they going to do?"

"Did you tell anyone?" Jace asked.

"Who the hell was he gonna tell?" Koa demanded. "His CO sent him to CGIS, and that's how he got in that position in the first place. He had no one left to tell."

He met Koa's gaze and nodded. Koa had gotten it in one.

"How did they make you fall?" Cain asked.

"Owens wanted me to go up on the container where we boarded and come down on the far container. I did what I was told. They greased the ladder on that one. I didn't have a hope."

Cass's face paled. "That's just bullshit. I can't believe... I mean, I believe you, but holy fucking shit."

"Yeah. It sucked. To be honest, I thought they might finish the job, but the boatswain who was driving the RHIB saw the whole thing and called in the cavalry. They airlifted me to the hospital."

Tac rubbed his hand. "Brother, I don't know why you're not in jail. I'd have killed the son of a bitch."

His heart lifted. These people, this team, got it. *Got him.* They were his people. A wave of relief swept through him that was so fierce he almost teared up. He drank more beer to calm his damn stupid emotions.

"I thought about it, Tac. I really did, but then I'd be the same type of asshole Owens was. I tried to get proof, but my gloves mysteriously disappeared and the container was long gone. The recording of the comms on the training session was also wiped clean. Owens was good. He tied up all the loose ends. I had no way to prove what he did and no witnesses who would come forward. I could say what I heard all I wanted, but he'd just claim I banged my head and wasn't thinking clearly."

"Well, someone took him out for you," Jace said. "I can't say as I'm heartbroken about it either. Fucker deserved what he got."

It made Dane feel good to know his team was with him, but even better to know that he wasn't imagining how horrifying the whole thing was. He wasn't overreacting. He was, in fact, underreacting.

Cain set his empty beer bottle on the table. "We need to find the motherboards first, but after that, we need to find out who killed Owens. He was involved in some serious shit. We need to make sure that comes to light. I don't want that asshole buried as some kind of hero."

"I agree," Dane said, and he did. "But he's got two kids and a wife. I want to find out what the hell he was into, but let's take it one step at a time. Just because he was a complete pathological asshole doesn't mean his wife and kids should suffer for it. I want everyone in the Coast Guard to know what he did. His team, as well, if they were all in on it. I want their reputations to be crushed, but I don't want their families to end up being collateral damage. You know what I mean?"

Cass looked at him with a skeptical expression on her face. "You are way nicer than I am."

A grin sparked across Dane's face. "I don't think that's saying much."

The guys cracked up as she punched him in the upper arm, but she had a smile on her face, so their joking was clear.

"Thanks for telling us what happened," Tac said. "I appreciate the trust, brother." He paused for a second and rubbed his damaged hand once more. "I know we just came together as a team about three months ago, but I have to say, this is the best team situation I've ever had, and that makes me appreciate it all the more."

"Ditto," Jace said. Koa nodded.

Cass thumped her bottle on the table. "Agreed," and then took a big swig of her beer.

"You are the first people I've ever told what really happened," Dane admitted. "I couldn't agree more, Tac."

Cain piped up, "We're a good team. Now we have to

show our worth to Bertrand by finding those motherboards and figuring out what the hell is going on." He glanced at his watch. "It's almost dinnertime. Knock off, go home, and get some sleep. We'll catch up downtown tonight and see what this fucker was hiding in his Candyland."

"Who's bringing food?" Jace called as he patted his flat stomach.

Koa shook his head. "I will. Do you ever stop eating?"

Jace patted his non-existent belly some more. "Nope. I need to keep my strength up."

The group broke up, and everyone started heading out. After Dane gathered his stuff together, he stopped by Cain's office. "Got a minute?"

"Sure." Cain gestured to the visitor's chair.

"I was wondering if we could go over the drills from this morning. I have a couple of thoughts I want to run by you."

"You sure you don't want to go home and chill?"

"I will in a bit, but like Tac said, this is a great team, and I want to make sure I'm doing my best to keep it that way." He was number two. Cain's backup. He took that very seriously.

Cain studied him for a moment. "You need to get your back working better."

"Yeah, I know. I'm doing what the doctors told me but, fuck if I can get it to loosen up."

"Harlow said to tell you to find a Pilates instructor."

Dane blinked. "Your girlfriend said what?"

Cain looked pained just saying the words. "I know, I know, but she's in nursing school with a former Pilates instructor who said your problem is the muscles around your injury. They are probably tight so the other muscles are compensating for them. You need to do Pilates to strengthen your core to take the pressure off your back muscles."

Dane fought to keep a straight face. To hear these words come out of Cain's mouth was just so…weird.

"Yeah, I know, I hated to say it, but if it'll work…"

Dane smirked. "Okay, Senior Chief."

"Fuck off," Cain shot back but smiled. "Tell me your ideas about the drills."

CHAPTER EIGHT

Mac's teeth clacked together as she dropped into her chair, finding the height, not unexpectedly, changed since she'd last sat in it. People adjusting her shit drove her nuts, but she typically bit her tongue, wanting to avoid being labeled the office bitch. Most of her co-workers were good guys and if she wasn't in the office, she didn't begrudge their use of her stuff for impromptu meetings.

She'd been looking for Casper since she'd gotten back to the office, but he was a no-show. She went through Landry's file again, from his initial interview with CGIS. And the single sheet with Owen's response to the complaint. Dane's words from her interview with him rang in her ears.

There were holes so large in the report she could drive a truck through them. Casper probably went through the motions of doing an investigation, but if she had to guess, she'd say he'd simply written up a report and filed it as closed. Without asking Owens any probing questions. "*Was your truck here? Did you steal something? No? Okay.*" That alone would've told Owens he was being investigated. It wouldn't take much for Owens to figure out who had spoken with

Casper. Hell, Casper might have even revealed it himself. "*How well do you get on with Landry?*" Yeah, she could see all that happening. Knowing Casper, he didn't do it on purpose; it was just sheer laziness.

Rutledge was coming down the aisle. "Hey," he said. "How did it go with the wife?"

"About what you'd expect. And you? How did the interviews go with Owens's old team?"

His expression pinched. "Why don't we go to the conference room and exchange notes?"

She gathered her things, including the file on Owens and Dane's complaint. She tucked them into her bag and grabbed her coffee. Her mouth already tasted like acid. What was a bit more?

The all-glass conference room was similar to the one upstairs, but the furniture was older and the windows were not as large or as clean. It felt like being in an aquarium. The smell in the room, as usual, was rank. Sweat mixed with dust, mixed with office supplies. If only they could open the windows. She walked in and took a seat so she could look out at the office. Rutledge sat at the head of the table to her left.

"So, what happened?" she asked. She wanted to hear what he had to say before telling him about Casper screwing up Dane's case.

He shook his head. "It was a shit show. I have no idea what the hell is going on, but they're all up to their eyeballs in it. Not one of them seems upset about Owens's death. More like they're terrified they're gonna be next."

She leaned back in her chair. "That's not good. What did Casper say about them?"

Disappointment beat within her chest. She was hoping this thing would be solved quickly. Not because she didn't want to do the work. She was excited to work on a big case, but she didn't want to be working on one that involved Dane Landry. The man threw her off her game. Too good-looking. Too sexy by half. If he wasn't involved in the case, then she'd be free to date him. *Oh, boy.*

"Not a goddamn thing. I have no idea what he's playing at, but he kept lobbing softballs at them. Just fucking stupid."

"You want to walk me through it?" she asked. She pulled her notebook out of her bag.

He nodded. "Joel Cameron is the second in command. He's already stepped up as the de facto head of the team. He tried to play it like he's all broken up about Owens' death, but you can see the naked ambition in his eyes. He's looking to move up and thinks now's his chance."

Mac looked up from taking notes. "Just in the team? Or do you think he wants to take over Owens's spot in the drug business? That's assuming he was in the drug business."

Rutledge grunted. "He wants it all. Don't get me wrong. He's afraid, but he's willing to give it a shot. With Owens gone, this is his opportunity, and he doesn't want to miss out."

"Sounds like he could be dangerous. Ambition always makes me wary." Her career in Minneapolis had been stunted thanks to ambition. Not hers, but someone else's. Now, it made her nervous. It was like working with a snake, and you always had to be on guard in case it decided to strike.

"Agreed. The next is Topher Grady. He's close with Cameron. He also wants a shot at moving up. He's willing to follow Cameron's lead. The two of them are tight, and I wouldn't be surprised if Cameron is selling Grady a line about being partners but ends up keeping everything for himself. It's that kind of relationship."

Great. Ambitious and underhanded were a deadly combination. "So, wait. Did either of them give an alibi for Owens' murder? What time frame did you give them?"

"I said it happened between midnight and five a.m., just to give us some breathing room. The medical examiner should get back to me today with the full autopsy results. Their alibis were non-existent." Rutledge snorted. "Both were home in bed with no witnesses. In all honesty, their entire statements were a load of bullshit. Casper was being too nice, and they were running circles around him. But I'm telling you what they're really like."

She glanced down at her notepad and then back up at him. "I really appreciate that. I mean it." And she did. Casper was not a boss she looked up to or admired. Rutledge was the only one who was giving her any kind of guidance, and she was thankful. "If we want to solve this thing, I think it's going to be you and me. Casper is too caught up in the search for the Navy's weapons. He doesn't give a shit about this."

Rutledge glanced down at his notes. "Donnie Anderson and Frankie Probert are both followers. They stick together and will do what Cameron says. They said all the right things about Owens, but I doubt either of them meant it. They seem like lightweights. Tell them what to do and they'll do it, but don't expect them to make any decisions."

He glanced down at his notes again. "Anderson said he was home with his girlfriend, Cindy Richards. I called and confirmed with her, for what it's worth. Probert was at his mom's. He moved her over here a while back to some retirement community. He says he fell asleep on her couch. I'll call, but I'm sure she'll back his story."

"I'm sure. Mom isn't going to sell her baby down the river. That leaves Ben Hestman. What's his story?"

"He's a bit different. If you ask me, he's the odd man out. He's one of them, but not. He was the only one to show genuine emotion about Owens's death. Not so much about Owens, but about the man's family. He doesn't strike me as a leader, but he isn't exactly a follower either. More like he'll do what needs to be done, but isn't big on being a part of the gang. He's got a wife and four kids. That could be why. His wife, Darinda, is a part-time Pre-K teacher. She confirmed that he was home with her when Owens was murdered."

Mac dropped her pen on the paper. She'd taken lots of notes, and she'd read Rutledge's notes later to make sure she hadn't missed anything important, but now it was time for theories. Things she wasn't going to put down on paper.

"So, what do you think? Did any of them kill Owens?"

Rutledge slouched in his chair. "I think they're all capable of it, given the right set of circumstances but, to be honest, I just didn't get that vibe from any of them. I don't think they killed their boss. Some will take advantage of the situation, but that's about it."

"Well, that sucks. I was hoping for a quick close on this one." She sighed.

"Why?" Rutledge's voice was sharp.

She blinked. She wasn't going to share the truth, that she wanted to have sex with one of the suspects, but she would share what she found out. "Casper fucked up big time with Dane Landry."

Rutledge's brows dipped into a deep V between his eyes. "What do you mean?"

She went over what Dane had told her about seeing Craig Owens allegedly stealing some crates and how he'd done what he was supposed to do, but Casper had screwed him. "Casper must've told Owens because he knew and then took it out on Da—Landry. He didn't explain it to me, but he blames Owens for his broken back."

"That could be sour grapes. Maybe Landry is just looking for someone to blame for his own mistakes."

Mac shook her head. "I don't think so. Besides, after hearing what Landry had to say, I reread the file. Casper glossed over the whole thing. He didn't even look into what Landry said. The file on Owens was one page. There's no way Casper investigated."

Rutledge's string of curses was long and impressive.

"Yeah," she agreed. "That sums it up. Casper's poor work is going to blow back on us. Now Owens is dead instead of being locked up for drug smuggling, and the situation is a fucking minefield since the press is involved." The coffee she'd had soured in her gut, and she pressed a hand to her abdomen. She would *not* regurgitate breakfast here.

Rutledge ran his hands through his red hair, making it stand up in every direction. "Do you think Landry could have done it?"

Mac paused. She needed to take the question seriously. Be honest with herself about the answer. She cocked her head. "I think, like you said, given the right circumstances, Landry could kill someone. I mean, it's sort of his job in a way. But as much as he hates or hated Owens, I don't think he'd kill him. Landry thinks Owens is a piece of shit, and if he killed Owens, then he'd be just as bad, if you follow my drift."

"Got it." Rutledge propped his elbows on the table. "Where does all this leave us?"

She shrugged. "Square one. I'm going to do some research on Owens. You guys got the stuff from his locker, right?" At Rutledge's nod, she continued, "I want to have a look, see if anything jumps out. I'll run his financials as well. If he was running drugs, he'd have to hide the money somewhere."

"Okay, sounds good. I'm going to talk to legal and see what they'd need for a search warrant for Owens' house. I don't have enough yet, but I'd like to know exactly what I'm aiming for. I'm also gonna ask about surveillance. If these guys are involved in the drug stuff, then maybe we can catch them at it."

"You really think they're all involved?"

He sighed. "I think they all wanted a piece of the action. Well, maybe not Ben. I kind of think he just went along because he didn't want to rock the boat. I want to take another crack at him tomorrow without Casper being there. And I'm not telling Casper about the surveillance either."

"Got it. I'll run the rest of the team's financials and see if anything pops. I know it's Friday night, but do you want to meet tomorrow morning and go over a game plan for the day?"

He nodded. "Yeah, but let's start a bit later. How's nine-thirty?"

"Nine-thirty for what?" Casper asked as he swept into the room.

Rutledge clamped his jaw shut.

Mac swore silently. "To meet. We're gonna go over the stuff from today and then maybe talk to some of the local vice guys about the drug trade in Oahu. Also, I think Cadaver Dave should be finished by then. We should talk to him." She looked up at Casper. "Unless you want to do that."

"No, I'm good. We chatted with the team today. Good bunch of guys. They're upset about losing their team leader. Let's give them some time off from the grilling, okay?"

"Sure." Mac struggled to keep her face neutral. "What are you going to work on tomorrow? Or are you even working this weekend?"

He tried to look insulted. "Of course, I am. I'm working with Cross on the Navy thing. I'll be in and out all day, but I'll have my phone. Reach out if you need anything. Otherwise, I think this is a great case for you two to work on your own. Get your feet wet. I'm here if you need me." With that, he waltzed out of the room.

"Asshole," Rutledge muttered.

She couldn't agree more.

They got up and headed back to their desks. Rutledge dropped by her desk about an hour later and said he'd see her in the morning. "Don't stay too late."

She nodded at him but didn't bother to respond. She had just started to dig into Owens's financials. It all looked above-board. He wasn't driving a flashy car. Didn't live in a big house. His life was modest and what she'd expect on a Senior Chief salary. But then there was the boat. That was a little bit pricey, but if he'd saved, it was a possibility.

She leaned back in her chair. What about his wife? She started digging into Alanna Owens' financials. That's when things started to trigger alarm bells.

They had two kids in private school. It was a catholic school that collected a hefty tuition fee. Alanna didn't work. She had a Mercedes SUV that was newer than Mac's own BMW. According to Alanna's credit cards, they'd booked a stay at Aulani, the very expensive Disney resort on the island and charged quite a bit in the way of food and drink, not to mention toys for the kids.

She leaned back in her chair. He was definitely into something illicit. Alanna's credit card bills were larger than they should be, and they were paid off in full every month. They were living beyond their means for sure. Not majorly, and not super obviously, but yeah, the money was there. But was it enough evidence?

Mac massaged her scalp in hopes of relieving a blooming headache. Food was a necessity, and not the stuff from the vending machines. She pushed back from her desk and took the stairs down to the café on the first floor. They were closing but the manager let her buy a sandwich and a soda. She went back up to her desk and sat down to eat.

At this point, she was the only one in the office and liked the solitude it offered her. "If I was going to risk it all and run drugs, how much would make the risk worth it?" She asked her question out loud and then took a bite of her sandwich. It was roast beef and was damn tasty.

She looked at Alanna's credit cards again, tallied up the expenses in her head, and then compared those against the man's annual salary. "Yeah, no. Not enough. Craig Owens had to have more money coming from somewhere. The amount they were spending, at least on paper, did not appear to be enough to risk everything. He had to be hiding it somewhere.

Rutledge had dropped off the box of Owens's personal items that had been collected from the dead man's locker. He'd signed them out of the evidence locker earlier to take a look and she'd signed the form saying she had received them from him. The chain of evidence was very important. She finished her sandwich and lifted the lid off the box. Clothes and toiletries, some bits of old mail, but nothing that jumped out at her.

She picked up a couple of pictures. One was of the power boat but it had no writing on the back. The other was a view of a beach and a street taken from high above, maybe from a balcony. There were people on the beach and in the water, but it was way too far away to identify any of them. It sort of looked familiar. She flicked the picture over. The word *Candyland* was written on the back.

What the hell did that mean? She studied the picture again but couldn't place it. Putting the picture aside, she went through the rest of the box. There was nothing else of any interest. She set the box on the floor and went back to the picture. It would come to her eventually but she was coming up dry at the moment.

The sound of footsteps startled her. She looked up. "Hey, Manu. What are you doing here?"

"Hey, Mac." The kid smiled. "My cat chewed my phone charger cord, so I came to get another one."

He had a cat? That was a bit unexpected. She shrugged. "Ah, well, have a good night."

"What are you doing here so late?" he asked as he disappeared behind his cubicle wall. He popped back up, charger in hand.

"Just working a case. Hey, can you come here for a sec?" Manu walked over to her cubicle. She pointed at the picture on her desk. "Do you recognize this beach?"

He gave her an uncertain smile. "Are you kidding? That's Waikiki Beach by the Hilton."

She smacked her forehead. "I must be losing it. I knew it looked familiar. Thanks, Manu."

"No problem. Have a good night," he called as he made his way back toward the elevators.

"Yeah, you, too," she murmured absently. *Candyland.* What the hell did that mean? Wasn't there a kid's game by that name? As she stared at the picture, the more certain she became that it was a clue to Owens's secret life. He kept a picture of his boat and this. Did that mean he owned this, too?

She sat back in her chair, startled at the thought. An apartment on Waikiki Beach would be damn expensive. No way could he afford it on his salary. *But.* But, if like she suspected, he had more cash on hand, then where better to hide it than an apartment in an expensive area of town? That made total sense to her.

It couldn't be in his name, though, or his wife's. She'd run both for real estate holdings as well as financials, but nothing had come up. Digging through the records she pulled both sets of parents' names. Nothing in Oahu under those names either. A company name? That could be anything.

Maybe she should look at it from a different perspective. Maybe she needed to find the address of the building and look at who owned each condo, see if any name jumped out at her. With that in mind, she started clicking away at her keyboard. Suddenly she realized she was going to have to do the same for each member of the team. Maybe they were all laundering their cash with real estate. It was going to be a long night ahead, but she had a gut feeling this trail was going to get her some results.

Fingers crossed they would be positive ones.

CHAPTER NINE

Dane leaned against the mirrored back wall of the elevator. His black T-shirt wasn't warm enough for the level of AC the building had pumping. It probably wasn't warm enough for the night itself, considering his back. A cool breeze had come up, and the temperature was dropping. Funny, he never used to think seventy degrees was cold on the east coast, but here, it was sweater weather. He was glad he'd gone for black cargo pants instead of shorts. He and his damn back hated being cold now.

Koa was beside him, wearing the same black T-shirt, but he'd opted for jeans. Probably a good thing. They looked more relaxed that way. All black tended to draw attention. He hadn't thought of that when he'd gotten dressed.

"You look like you're going to break into a place," Koa said as they rode up to the twentieth floor.

Dane grinned. "My sartorial choices were solely based on my lack of clean clothes."

Koa shook his head. "You're a grown-ass man. You need to take better care of yourself."

"Yes, Mom," Dane sniped back as the doors opened.

The carpet in the elevator was beige and so thick his soles sunk deep. *How much money did you need to buy carpet that felt like a freaking cloud?* The plush luxury continued into the hallway.

The cream-colored wallpapered walls were broken up by artwork by local artists, hanging every fifteen feet or so. The thick carpet absorbed sounds, so their steps were deadened. The whole building screamed money, but more, it stated back east money. No teals or pinks here.

"Must be nice," Dane mumbled.

"Owens is dead, so maybe not so much," Koa replied.

"You got me there."

They turned right one more time and came to a stop in front of Owens's unit. It was a corner unit, which helped with what they were about to do. Koa leaned on the doorframe, effectively blocking the view of the camera high on the wall behind them.

"You know," Dane said as he got out his lockpick tools, "it would've made more sense to get a warrant."

"I thought of that," Cain said into the earbud. "But Bertrand said to wait. He didn't want to alert anyone to this location until after we'd searched it. He doesn't want any information about the motherboards to fall into the wrong hands."

"Who are 'the wrong hands?' Koa asked.

"He didn't say," Cain responded.

Dane had the lock open in seconds and swung the door open.

"You're pretty good at that," Koa commented as they hurried in.

He grinned. "A benefit of my misspent youth."

"Good to know." Koa pulled out a cloth and wiped the outside doorknob. He closed the door and wiped the inside knob as well. Then he pulled on gloves, and Dane did the same.

"We're in," Dane announced.

"Roger that." Cain's voice sounded tinny through the comms.

"Do we chance the lights?"

Koa shrugged. "We're twenty floors up. Do you think anyone will notice?"

"Let's not chance it."

They each pulled out a penlight and bounced the beams around the apartment.

"Pulling up the schematics for the building now," Jace said. "You are in the corner of the living space. The balcony with the view of the beach is directly ahead, and the majority of the room goes to your left. Slightly forward and on the right is the kitchen. There should be a dining space in front of the windows. There is one bedroom to the left of the living room."

Dane looked and located the door to the bedroom.

Jace continued, "It has a bathroom in it. On the other side of the kitchen is the main bedroom. It also has a balcony."

"Thanks." Dane was about to ask Koa what he wanted to search first, but the Hawaiian was already moving toward the living area. Fair enough. He headed through the kitchen to the main bedroom. He could work his way back toward Koa.

As he moved through the kitchen area, he noted the stainless-steel appliances and the granite countertops. *Must be nice.* He wasn't going to sell drugs for it, but he could see the appeal. Life at the beach must be fine.

He entered the bedroom and swept the area with the penlight, cataloging the layout. Bed against the far wall. Flat-screen TV beside him. Hallway to the bathroom with closets lining the walls on the right. He started in the far corner of the room, closest to the balcony doors. Nothing in the curtains or under them. He searched the nightstand, but it was empty. Lifting the mattress, he found nothing but it must have been dusty because he sneezed. There was nothing beneath the bed either.

He went over to the chest of drawers the TV was sitting on. There were stacks of underwear and socks, a few T-shirts and a couple pairs of shorts. There were about five bathing suits as well, so he must have spent a lot of time either at the pool or on the beach. *Candyland.*

He checked the second nightstand. The drawer was full of condoms. Nice. *Asshole.* He started down the hallway, stopping only to check the closets on each side. A couple of Hawaiian shirts hung in one closet, but nothing in the other. He entered the bathroom. The toilet was directly ahead of him. To the left was the sink and across from it, a glassed-in shower stall. Between the two, on the far wall was an open doorway. He pulled out his gun and then quickly advanced, penlight and gun raised.

"Sonofabitch."

"What?" Koa's response was quick.

"There's a walk-in closet off the bathroom. It's full of designer clothes and—" He broke off as he took a step closer to a dressing table with a marble top. He moved his penlight over it. "And a shit ton of very expensive watches." There were no windows, so Dane located the light switch and turned it on.

"Shit," Tac said. "Must be nice."

The closet was a ten-by-ten square. The entire perimeter was taken up with clothes. Some areas of the closet were for longer stuff and some shorter. One cabinet had doors on it. There was also a section straight ahead that was only for shoes.

"Did you find anything *important* yet?" Cass's voice was

low but she sounded frustrated. She was sitting downstairs in a bar next door to the building, keeping an eye on the street. "I'm tired of being hit on by drunk assholes. Hurry up."

Dane smiled. He started on his left and worked methodically, checking every piece of clothing. He made it through several sections and then came to the cabinet with the doors on it. He opened them and pushed the many bathrobes aside. Hanging on the back wall were two leather crops, handcuffs, and other bondage gadgets that he wasn't even sure what they were used for. "Just found some sex toys, Cass. Does that count?"

"Fuck you," she said with a laugh.

He closed the closet doors and continued his search. A decorative wooden box on the marble-topped island held the guy's watch collection. He checked the drawers underneath. Still nothing. Owens had purchased every designer brand imaginable and then some. Versace, Dior, Zegna, Veridani, Armani—shit, there were brands Dane had never even heard of, and he knew a fair amount because his sister was into fashion and lived in New York City. He'd heard about the brands ad nauseam last time he was home for Christmas.

He continued around the perimeter of the room, even checking pockets and seams of clothing. He bent down and checked the shoes as well. Still nothing. In the last section before the doorway, he found it. "Got something."

"What?" Koa asked.

"Wall safe." He stared at the number pad. "Anyone have any ideas about the code?"

"His wife's birthday?" Jace suggested.

Koa snorted. "The man came here to party. The second bedroom is full of sex toys and condoms. It won't be his wife's birthday." He walked through the door into the closet and stood beside Dane. "I checked the kitchen. Clean. Nothing but beer and wine. No food. Must have ordered in."

Dane nodded absently. "Nothing from his family life. What about from the Coast Guard? The date he joined?"

Jace read off a date, and Dane tried it, but the diode on the keypad turned red.

"What about the date he became team leader?" Cass suggested.

Dane nodded. That one he could see. Jace rattled the numbers off, and Dane tried those, too, but the keypad turned red again.

"Trouble coming," Cain said.

"Shit! What?" Dane demanded.

"Rankin. She just entered the building."

Fuck. That wasn't good. "How did she find out about this place so quickly?"

"Dunno, but you two need to get out of there," Tac said.

"Wait," Dane said. "What's the date he bought the condo?"

Jace cursed. "Give me a second."

"Come on, come on," Dane muttered.

"He closed on September sixth."

"Oh-nine-oh-six," Dane said as he hit the keys. The keypad turned green, and the door clicked. "Yes!" Dane turned the handle and pulled it open. The safe contained a couple of handguns and a little black book. He glanced at Koa. "Any chance this has more than women's names and numbers in it?"

Koa shrugged and made a hurry-up motion with his hand.

Dane flipped the pages. There were entries of some sort, but the random letters and numbers didn't make any sense. "Shit, it's in code."

"You two need to get your asses out of there," Tac said. "She's just exited the elevator."

"Fuck, it's too late. She'll see us." Koa moved out of the closet. "I'll hide in the other room's closet. You stay here."

Dane quickly shoved the book into the cargo pocket of his pants and closed the door to the safe. He hit the lights and then opened the doors to the cabinet with the bathrobes and sex toys and climbed in. He leaned against the back wall and tried not to think about where all the stuff that was currently touching his back had been previously. He shuffled the robes back to hang in front of him. It could be worse, he told himself, but he just couldn't think of *how* at the moment.

The wait seemed interminable. "Is she by you?" he said in a low voice.

"She's been through here."

"You in the closet?"

"No, under the bed."

He grinned in the darkness. Koa hiding under the bed seemed hilarious somehow.

"She searched the closet. Did a good job tossing the room."

"Then how come she didn't find you?" he asked.

"I dragged a bunch of blankets and sex toys around me so when she looked under and pulled the blankets that's what she saw. I guess she wasn't too keen to touch them. Hell, I'm wearing gloves and I want a scalding hot shower after touching them."

Dane suppressed a smile. "Good thinking."

The lights in the closet went on. Dane went silent. Rankin did just like he did and started on her left. That meant he had five minutes tops until she reached him. Shit. Maybe he should have hidden under the bed like Koa, except he probably wouldn't have been able to get down there and up again in any kind of a hurry without destroying his back.

"We've got a problem." Jace sounded stressed.

No shit.

"What kind of problem?" Cain asked.

"There's a guy at the door to Owens's apartment. He's breaking in."

"You gotta be fucking kidding me! What the hell are the chances?" Tac demanded.

Cass said, "Is he wearing a navy hoodie?"

"Yeah," Jace swore. "He just opened the door."

"I saw him, and he's not alone. There were two of them, both in hoodies. I saw Navy Hoodie enter the building. The guy in the gray hoodie disappeared," Cass added. "I'll see if I can find where he went."

Rankin was at the section next to Dane. If he did nothing, she'd run into the guy in the hoodie. His gut said that was a bad idea. The door to his section opened and the robes moved to the side. Rankin's eyes grew wide, and he quickly put his hand over her mouth before she could say anything. She tried to fight him off, but he held it tight. "There's someone else here. Stop fighting me."

"What are you doing here?" she mumbled through his hand.

"There's someone else breaking in."

It took an instant for his whispered words to sink in. She froze. He quickly moved out of the closet, ran across the room, hit the lights, and came flying back inside. He got into the cabinet, pulling her in after him, and was just closing them in when he heard the click of the door opening. Fuck! He needed to move the robes.

He was pushed against the back wall and the sex toys. She was facing him. He crushed her to his chest with one arm as he moved the robes ever so slowly back in place.

She hissed in his ear, "What the hell are you—?"

"Not now," he whispered directly into her ear as the lights in the closet went on.

She froze. His heart was hammering against his ribs. He was sure she must be able to feel it. Ever so slowly, he pulled his gun from the small of his back. He was worried he would dislodge some of the sex toys, and make a noise somehow, so each movement was excruciatingly slow.

Suddenly, the guy in the closet was speaking. Through the doors, Dane had a sliver of a view. Hoodie was standing directly in front of the safe. *Interesting.* He didn't have to search. He knew exactly where it was.

The voice was too low for Dane to make out any words. Did he know the guy? Was it one of Owens's teammates? He wasn't sure. Still trying to bring his gun out, he shifted his weight slightly forward. Contact. His dick was now pressed against Rankin. Was it her hip? Maybe. There was no other way he could shift. He had to stay that way until his gun was free.

The smell of her hair—he'd been right about her preference for citrus—was getting to him. Her breath was on his neck. Had it just sped up? Her breasts crushed to his chest were not helping the situation. He was starting to get hard, and there wasn't a damn thing he could do about it. Running math problems in his head wasn't smart because he needed to focus on the guy in the closet with them. So his dick was gonna swell. She'd have to deal. He was human and she was sexy as hell.

He swallowed and tried to control his body, but it was no use. His gun was out from his waistband, and now he was slowly moving it down by his side.

"I did what you said! But it's not working." Hoodie was getting agitated.

Dane tried to see, but the man moved out of his sliver of view. The voice was too muffled for it to be recognizable.

Finally, Dane's gun was free and resting on his right thigh. He shifted his weight back and managed to get an inch or two of distance between his dick and Rankin's soft curves.

Suddenly, she leaned into him, and his back pressed against God knows what, something with hard beads and buckles, making him super uncomfortable. Good. Maybe that would stop him from getting hard again.

"I'm hooked on your belt," she said in a voice that was barely a whisper.

What? It took a second for what she'd said to sink in. Her belt was hooked on his. He was tempted to just stay that way until the intruder was gone but if something happened and he had to move quickly, they would both go down. Fuck. He nodded once.

"The light on the box went green." Hoodie seemed calmer now.

Dane slowly bent his knees as he tried to lift her slightly with a hand wrapped around her, but her buckle was still caught in behind his. He did the move again, but they were stuck together. This was pure torture. Now he was rubbing on her. Jesus. He was hard as rock, and there was no way to hide it.

He tried one more time to lift her. This time she brought up her hand, which ran up the length of him, as she found her way to their buckles. There was no mistaking her accidental touch on his hard-on. He was sunk. Nothing he could do. She'd just have to get over it.

She went up on her tiptoes again, and at the same time, pushed his belt down. There was a clicking sound, and then they were free. They both froze. Dane waited. Did Hoodie hear that? No, he was digging through the stuff in the safe.

Now, if only the man in the hoodie would turn around so Dane could see his face, but suddenly the door to the safe opened. Dane recognized the sound.

"It's not here...just a couple of guns." Hoodie closed the

safe. "On my way," was the last thing Dane heard before the closet went dark again.

Rankin leaned against him. Sagging with relief? He didn't know, but he didn't dare move. At this point, he was sure he'd knocked things off the hooks behind him, and if he moved, there would be a lot of noise.

"Can't find the other one," Cass reported. "Have no idea where he went."

Jace came through his earbud "Hoodie guy is coming out of the apartment. He's in the hallway. He's taking the fucking stairs."

"Avoiding the cameras in the elevator," Koa said. "We clear?"

Jace responded, "Affirmative."

Dane let out a breath and moved the robes to the side. "We're clear."

Rankin cleared her throat and pushed open the cabinet doors. She stepped out, crossed the closet, and hit the light switch. Dane came out to the main section of the closet. Rankin turned and glared at him. Her cheeks were flushed. Maybe he wasn't the only one who had been all hot and bothered in the closet. That brought a small smile to his face.

"What the fuck are you doing here?" Rankin demanded of him.

Okay, not the reason Dane had thought.

"You gotta get out of there now," Cain said. "Cameron and Grady just hit the lobby."

Dane said, "Jesus, what is this? Grand Central Station? Roger that." He focused on Rankin. "You can yell later. We've gotta go. Cameron and Grady are in the lobby."

"Are you serious?" she demanded. "You aren't supposed to be here."

He turned her around and headed out of the oversize closet, hitting the lights on the way out. "Yeah, and I'm guessing neither are you, so move your ass." They met Koa in the living area.

"Shit, where the hell were you?" she demanded.

"Later," was all he said. Then he opened the door and ushered them into the hallway. He closed the door, and they started toward the elevators.

"Too late. Take the stairs," Jace advised.

"Shit," Dane said as he redirected Rankin to the stairs.

"For twenty floors?" she said as he pushed her into the stairwell.

"Yes. Stay quiet and keep moving," he directed her. She shot him a glare, but they didn't have time for that now. "Does anyone know if the stairwell is clear of Hoodie and friends?" Dane asked, keeping his voice low.

"Sorry," Jace said. "Cameras in the stairwell don't work below the fifth floor. I've got no eyes."

Dane swore but took the stairs two at a time and moved around Rankin to take the lead, Koa took the rear. He kept his gun up just in case. He didn't want to meet Hoodie in the stairwell unprepared.

They hit floor five and peered down. "What do you think?" he asked.

"What?" Rankin demanded.

Koa ignored her. "Better than taking the elevator at this point."

Cass piped up, "Lobby and parking garage are clear. No one has entered the stairwell since you guys started down."

"Roger that." Dane held his gun up and kept going. In no time, they were at the bottom. They went down one flight farther and emerged in the parking garage. Dane and Koa tucked their guns away again but kept Rankin between them. They hit the street two minutes later and then hopped in Dane's SUV, putting Rankin in the back seat.

"You two want to tell me what the hell is going on?" she demanded angrily.

"No," Koa said.

Dane started to laugh. Koa was the absolute best at saying very little but getting his point across. He glanced at Rankin in the rearview mirror. Her mouth was gaping. She snapped it shut and narrowed her eyes. She was cute when she was angry. Hell, she was cute anytime and her curves were perfect.

"You two have a hell of a lot of explaining to do." She crossed her arms over her chest.

He sighed quietly. She was probably too pissed to ever entertain the idea of going out with him. "Probably. We're going back to Sand Island. We can talk there."

"Hey, guys?" Jace said. "We've got a problem. I went in and erased the security footage of you guys in the building, but I checked, and Hoodie didn't show his face. Not once."

"Not surprising," Tac said. "His operating seemed pretty slick."

"That's not the problem. I just checked the outside cameras. Dane, the guy in the gray hoodie, Navy Hoodie's friend, put something under your SUV."

Dane froze, his hands gripping the wheel hard. The blood in his veins iced, making his breath stutter. "Can you be more specific?" He was shocked his voice hadn't cracked.

"I can't tell if it's a GPS tracker or…something else," Jace said. "I'm trying to get a better angle on it."

"What is it?" Rankin demanded. "What the hell is going on? You two froze. I know something is up."

"McKenna," Dane started in a calm voice. "Someone put something under my SUV. We don't know what it is just yet." He'd decided to use her first name. After their time together in the closet, it seemed like they should be on a first-name basis.

"It's Mac." She frowned. "You mean like a GPS tracker?"

"Sure." No need to go into specifics.

Then her eyes got big. "Or a bomb," she added in a strangled voice.

He nodded once. Now she understood the gravity of the situation. He glanced at Koa. "You think we should pull over?"

"I think that's smart. Before we hit a bump."

Cain's voice came through the earbud. "Not a bomb. They wouldn't risk blowing up the book. Someone knew we were there and tagged your SUV. They want to follow you, or at the very least, see where you go."

What Cain said made a lot of sense. His gut relaxed a tad. He looked over at Koa, who looked slightly less stiff as well. He glanced in the rearview mirror at Mac. "We think it's a tracking device."

She sagged against the back of the seat in relief. "Do we know what kind? How far away can they be and still track us? Do they have to be close, or are they sitting at home right now?"

"All good questions but ones we don't have answers for." Dane started driving aimlessly. There was no way he was going home. He could go back to Sand Island, but the team agreed it was better if his tracker thought Dane was on his own. They settled on having him drive around Diamond Head for a bit.

Fifteen minutes later, Cain stated, "There's no tail I can see. I think the tracking is from afar."

"Shit," Koa said. "Jace, is there a way to use the device to trace it back to its owner?"

"That's above my pay grade."

Dane sighed.

"What?" Mac demanded.

"We can't find who is tracking us. We're discussing if we

can use the tracking device to locate the owner, but we don't have someone who can do that."

"I do," she said.

Dane flicked a glance at the mirror again. "You do?"

"Yeah. There's a kid in my office. If anyone can do it, he can."

"Can you call him? Can he work on this now?"

She leaned forward. "He can, but only if you tell me what the fuck is going on."

Dane cursed silently. They'd walked into that one. He relayed the information back to Cain, and it was decided they would meet back at Sand Island at the hangar. Chances were good that whoever had tagged Dane's SUV knew he was Coast Guard and his team was working on Owens's death. He also gave Mac the go-ahead to call in her guy.

Thirty minutes later, Dane parked in front of the hangar. The rest of the team was already there. Tac came forward with a flashlight and immediately crawled under Dane's SUV. A minute later, he was on his feet with a GPS tracker in his hand.

A tall, geeky-looking kid came forward. "Hi, Mac."

"Hey, Manu."

"Is that what you want me to track?"

"Yeah. Can you do it?" she asked as Tac handed him the device.

He frowned and held it up under the outside lights of the hangar. "I can, but I don't have to. It's one of ours."

CHAPTER TEN

"What do you mean it's one of ours?" Mac couldn't get her head around it.

Manu frowned. "I mean, it's the same kind we use. I'm pretty sure it's ours. See that number?" He pointed to a number etched into the side of the unit. "We put those there so we can track them better."

She squeezed her eyes shut and muttered a couple of choice curses. "Son of a—" She opened her eyes again. "Manu, can you find out who signed this one out?"

"Oh, sure." He looked around for a moment and then put the GPS device on the hood of the SUV. Then he brought out his laptop and put it there as well. He opened the screen and then started typing. Within seconds, he stopped.

"What is it?" she asked. Her stomach was already at her knees.

"That's weird."

"What?" She was very aware that the whole team was standing there listening to this. She'd prefer to find this out in private, but there was no way in hell Dane, or the rest of them, would let her. She knew that by the expressions on their faces.

"It's just..." He frowned.

"Just what, Manu?" she demanded through clenched teeth. *Just get it over with.*

"It's not signed out to anyone. It should be back on the shelf in IT. Someone took it without signing it out. That's like waaaay against the rules. Do you think someone broke in? We should call someone and tell them there was a break-in."

A break-in? *Not bloody likely.* She let out a long breath. What the fucking hell was going on? The muscles in her neck tightened. *Casper.* What if it was her boss? She pushed that thought aside. It couldn't be him. Yeah, he sucked at almost all aspects of the job, but would he really break the rules like that?

Dane met her gaze and then glanced at Manu. "You know what? Why don't we go inside? You hungry, Manu?" he asked. "There's some leftover Chinese."

"It's one in the morning. Do you normally eat at this hour?" Manu asked.

"Some days," Dane said.

"Huh. Okay then." He started toward the hangar. Jace fell in beside him and started chatting about computers with him. Cass and Tac went with them.

Cain turned and stared at Mac. "You want to tell me what the fuck is going on?"

She shrugged. "I wish I knew."

"You trust that kid in there?" he asked.

Mac thought about it for a minute. "Yeah. He's a good kid. I don't think he's involved in this at all. He does desktop support mostly. He knows computers like nobody's business, but I don't think he's that good of an actor, if you know what I mean. He's just a sweet kid."

Dane looked at her. “That sweet kid is going to have to do some hacking so we can find out what’s going on.”

She frowned. “Not sure that’s a good idea.” If it was Casper, he’d want revenge. He was that petty. She didn’t want Manu to get caught in the crosshairs. She didn’t want to get caught herself either. She’d been down that road, and it wasn’t pretty.

Dane crossed his arms over his chest. “We’re all ears if you’ve got a better idea.”

“Look, if someone inside the CGIS took this without signing it out, then there’s a big problem. I don’t want to put Manu in any danger.”

Cain blew out a breath. “She’s got a point. We don’t want the kid hurt. Let’s go inside and talk to him. Maybe he has some ideas on what we can do to find the person without putting himself at risk.”

“Okay,” Dane agreed, “but we have to get something going. If tonight proved nothing else, it said we’re sitting ducks the way things are right now. We need to up our game.”

Mac said nothing, but she agreed. Whatever was going on was not pretty, and whoever was running it seemed to know all their moves before they made them.

Cain, Koa, Dane, and Mac all hurried inside and found Manu, Tac, and Cass sitting at the kitchen table. Jace was heating up the food. He put a plate down in front of Manu as they took the last seats at the table.

Manu took a bite of his food and made appreciative noises. “This is good,” he said after he swallowed.

“I’ll get you the name of the place and a take-out menu,” Jace volunteered.

Manu smiled and then put another forkful into his mouth.

The smell of the food turned Mac’s stomach. Tension

tightened her neck muscles. She rolled her head and tried to relax a bit. She knew a headache was coming on and wanted to avoid it if she could.

She cleared her throat. "Do you have any idea how someone could have taken the GPS locator without signing it out?" She wanted to tread lightly but still get the answers they needed. She hadn't forgotten this team had been in the apartment when they shouldn't have been, but it was pretty hard to find a leg to stand on when someone in her department was illegally tracking Dane.

Manu tapped his fork on the plate. "Well," he said as he finished chewing, "the equipment is in the equipment room, and Vic is usually at the window. I guess the thing would be to wait until Vic has lunch or goes to the bathroom or something and then sneak in and take it. Unless someone asks Vic for it, he probably wouldn't notice that it's missing."

"Are there cameras in the room with Vic?" Tac asked.

"No, but there are cameras in the hallway outside. Anyone coming or going would be seen on them. We should be able to see someone if they broke into the room." He took another bite of his General Tso's Chicken and chewed slowly. Finally, he swallowed. "It would be really hard to get into the building though and, of course, you have to know where to find Vic. Also, how would they time it? It isn't like they could hang in the hallway without Vic noticing." His brow furrowed again. "I don't think a stranger could have done this."

Mac wanted to reach out and pat him on the shoulder. A big shock was coming for the kid. She said in a quiet voice, "Manu, we don't think a stranger did it. We think it was someone who works at CGIS."

He choked, then coughed. "No freaking way. It couldn't be. Who would do that? I mean, it's against the rules. Who would *do* that?"

Her boss's face swam before her eyes, but she blinked it away. "That's what we have to find out," she said gently.

Then the penny dropped. He blinked. "You want me to find out who was in the hallway? See who is on the security cameras?" He put down his fork. "Just let me get my laptop."

"Wait," Mac said. The weight of Dane's stare bored through her. He was sitting beside her. Being close to him reminded her of the closet. Seven minutes of pure torture that she wouldn't mind reliving.

But this was different. This was Manu's decision, and she wanted to make sure he had all the facts before he made it.

"Manu, we don't know what we're dealing with. If you hack into the building's security system, then you're breaking the rules. More, you're putting yourself at risk. A Guardsman is dead. We don't know what's going on. I don't want to put you in any danger."

He stared at her. "I get what you're saying, but I can also tell you what will happen first thing when I go in tomorrow, or rather Monday morning since this is the weekend. I'll tell them about the GPS unit, and my boss will ask me to go look at the system and see if the culprit is on the video. The way I see it, I'm just doing my job. I'm anticipating my boss's needs and being proactive." He gave her a self-satisfied grin.

She couldn't argue with that. "Okay, then. If you're sure."

He nodded as he pulled out his laptop from the bag by his side. Jace took away the plate of food, and Manu got all set up. "Do you think I should call my boss in the morning at a decent hour? It's the weekend, and I don't want to disturb him, but this seems like a big deal."

Mac gave him a small smile. "Let's see what's on the video, and then we'll make that decision." She said a small prayer that it wasn't her boss but knew deep in her heart it probably was. All the signs pointed to the fact that he was up to something.

"Okay, that's fair." Manu's fingers sailed over the keyboard. "Here's the feed," he said and hit the play button.

"We'll be here all night watching at this rate," Tac said. "Can you speed it up a bit?"

A few keystrokes later, the video was rushing by. He turned his laptop a bit to the right so Mac could see the video. It went quickly. People came and went down the hallway. A couple of people, including Tom Rutledge, stopped at the window and spoke with Vic. They signed out various pieces of equipment.

"What if we're barking up the wrong tree? What if someone signed this out, and Vic just forgot to write it down?" she asked.

"It could theoretically happen," Manu said. "But it's unlikely. Vic has been there for years. He doesn't make those kinds of mistakes. Or so he tells me regularly." He squinted at the screen. "There," Manu said and stopped the fast forward and reversed the feed a few frames.

Mac squinted at the screen. Dane got up and moved behind her. Cain leaned over. Cass had come around the table to their side and was looking over Cain's shoulder. "That's the guy I saw with the guy in the navy hoodie. I'm sure of it."

The man now had on a gray hoodie with the hood down. He was wearing a black beanie that was pulled low. He moved down the hallway and then stopped in front of the counter. He looked around and then produced a key. Unlocking the door, he disappeared inside.

Mac felt queasy. All her fears were coming true. She'd recognized the bracelet the man wore when he reached out and opened the door.

Two minutes and twenty-eight seconds later, the man in the beanie walked out of the room again. He locked the door behind him.

"Is there any angle where we can see this guy's face?" Dane asked.

Mac wanted to say there was no need. She knew who it was, but the words were stuck in her throat.

"Um, yeah." With a few more keystrokes, Manu had a different camera view on the screen. He started the video.

The man in the beanie turned and looked down the hallway.

"Sonofabitch," Dane said.

"What?" Tac demanded.

Mac cleared her throat. "It's my boss, Senior Special Agent Quinten Lawrence, AKA Casper."

"Holy cow!" Manu exclaimed. He glanced back and forth between the screen and Mac. "What are you going to do, Mac?"

"Nothing," Cain said. His voice brooked no argument. "Manu, I have to ask you to stay quiet about this. I know you want to tell your boss but let us investigate first. We have no idea what this means. You have to give us a couple of days to figure a few things out. If Lawrence is breaking the rules, then we need to find out why."

Manu's brow furrowed. "I guess I can do that. I think it would be better to tell my boss, though."

Mac rested a hand on his shoulder. "I will take the heat if anyone gets upset with you. I'm telling you not to say anything. It will be on me, okay?"

He took a moment but finally nodded. "I guess so. It's not like I won't be busy. They're constantly bringing me requests to look at different footage from around the city and asking me to find all kinds of data. My boss is hot to find those missing Navy weapons and tech."

Mac tensed. That wasn't something he was supposed to be discussing in front of these guys.

"What do you know about the missing Navy weapons?" Dane asked, but his voice was flat and his eyes were wary.

Manu stammered, "That is—I mean— Oh fudge. I know we're not supposed to talk about it, but I figured it was okay with you guys, right? It's okay isn't it, Mac?"

She nodded. "Just don't mention it to anyone else."

"Oh, no, of course not." Manu smiled. "Wouldn't dream of it."

Jace called, "Hey, Manu, would you like a doughnut?" He pointed to the box on the counter. "Why don't you come pick one out."

"Don't mind if I do." Manu got up and went over to peruse the box.

"So where did you learn all this computer stuff?" Jace asked.

"University." Manu leaned over the doughnut box.

Mac turned back and met Dane's gaze. His eyes were back to being ice chips. "I'll ask again, what do you know about the missing weapons?" His tone was serious.

Mac wanted to curse. It had been a long fucking day, and she'd just found out that her boss was the one who'd tagged Dane's car without permission. Things weren't looking good.

"John Cross, the Deputy Director of CGIS, told everyone this morning about the Navy's missing weapons. Everyone is all fired up to find them since he essentially said it would be a big win for the Coast Guard if we found them. People want to get into his good graces. Careers could be made on something like this."

"Fucking hell," Koa mumbled. "That just made our job a lot harder."

"What do you mean? What job?" She stared at Dane, who'd taken his seat beside her again.

He glanced at Cain, who nodded and said, "You might as well tell her."

"We were told the same thing this morning. Admiral Bertrand tasked us to find the weapons. I doubt he knew Cross was blabbing it to the world. It's supposed to be hush-hush. Anyway, that's what we were doing at Owens's secret apartment tonight. This was the first opportunity we had to search it. We think he might have something to do with the missing weapons."

"Why? Why do you think Owens was involved?"

Cain spoke up then. "That's classified as need to know, and at the moment, I'm not sure you need to know."

Heat crept up Mac's cheeks. Her hands shook, and her heart hammered into her ribs. Where did they get off cutting her out of the loop? "Wait a goddamn minute. I've been open with you. I expect the same courtesy."

Dane crossed his arms over his chest. "Mac, you have to look at it from our point of view. Your boss just tried to track me. He was, apparently, with the guy at Owens's secret apartment. We don't have enough details to know what's going on, but it's obvious something at CGIS is rotten."

"And you think it's me?" she demanded.

Dane cocked an eyebrow. "You broke into Owens's place, too, remember? You didn't show up with a team and a warrant. You had a flashlight and a pair of gloves."

She closed her eyes. *Fuckity. Fuck. Fuck.* He had her there. How was she going to explain this? She opened her eyes again and took in the room. Jace was showing Manu something on a computer on the opposite side of the hangar. "Wait, Casper showed up at the apartment after me, which means he was probably following me. Would he bother to follow me if we were on the same team?"

"If he was sending you in undercover, he might. Besides, how do we know he followed you? Maybe he showed up there randomly and recognized my SUV."

Mac snorted. "That's a line of bullshit and you know it.

You know he probably followed me." She tucked a stray hair behind her ear. "It does beg the question of how they found your SUV, though."

"I think someone was watching the security feed at the apartment building, just like we were," Cain said. "Whoever it was saw Dane and Koa enter the apartment. Probably that's how they found the SUV. Pretty sure they'd have used the external security cameras to see if anyone else, like you, came in. Then they sent their own guys down there. The two men in hoodies."

Koa frowned. "But then they would've known we hadn't left yet when they arrived. Why didn't they look for us?"

"That's a good question." Cain shook his head. "I've got no idea."

Dane narrowed his eyes. "Because maybe someone told them we were there. Maybe it wasn't a tap on the security feed but a physical person who spotted us and called someone."

Mac blinked as it clicked. "You're thinking one of Owens's team. Cameron and Grady were watching the apartment for some reason, and they made the call."

"Yeah," Dane agreed. "We didn't notice anyone, but we weren't being particularly subtle. Didn't think we had to be."

Koa shifted in his chair. "So, say it was one of Owens's team. They see us, make the call, and Casper and his co-conspirator show up in hoodies. Then the other two, Cameron and Grady, from Owens's team show up later, but why the delay?"

Dane said, "It depends on where they were on the island. Maybe they weren't close. Maybe no one was followed. A team member was there to keep watch until the guy with the passcode for the safe arrived. They saw us enter and made the call. They arrived after Mac. One guy tags the SUV. The other goes upstairs. He clears the apartment and assumes we've left. Goes to the safe to see if Owens left anything incriminating behind. Then leaves again. The other two team members show up later because they were farther away and they're a clean-up crew. Make sure to take anything that puts Owens in the apartment. Wipe it down. That kind of thing."

Mac mused about all Dane had said. So many moving pieces. This seemed more and more like a well-oiled operation.

"Still doesn't tell us why he didn't look for us. If we weren't in the SUV downstairs, then why wouldn't he search for us?" Koa asked.

"We have to figure out who the hell was in the apartment and ask him."

Dane turned to Mac. "What about you? Why were you at the apartment, and how did you find it? And what about your boss? Did he tell you about it?"

Mac gritted her teeth. They still thought she was the enemy. She decided to be honest. It was really her only shot.

"I had a feeling about Casper. Ever since Owens's body was found, he has been acting strange. But honestly, I've had my doubts about him all along. He's not very good at his job, but more than that, he seems to know everything and everyone, but lies constantly. It's…weird.

"I figured out Owens had way more money than a Senior Chief should have. There were two pictures in his personal locker belongings, one of his boat, and the other a view of the beach from an apartment. It had the word Candyland written on the back. I dug until I found it. So I went to Owens's place because I didn't want to tell Casper unless I found something. I thought… I thought he would go check it out if I told him and keep me out of it. Then I wouldn't know for sure what was going on. He did that today. He sent me here to interview you, Dane, while he and Tom Rutledge went to speak to Owens's team members. Rutledge filled me in. Otherwise, I would've been in the dark. We decided to run the investigation our way and keep Casper out of the loop as long as possible because neither of us trusts him."

Dane leaned forward and put his elbows on the table. "You can see why we're not going to show you all our cards at the moment then, can't you?"

She hated to admit it, but she did. "I get it. It just sucks. To be honest, Rutledge and I could use some help."

Dane cocked his head and then looked at Cain. He raised an eyebrow. Cain just stared at him but didn't say anything.

Koa yawned. "He's asking if we can divide and conquer. Bring her in somewhat and share what we can."

"I got that." Cain's tone was exasperated. "I guess, but Dane, you're liaison with her. Don't let her fuck us over."

Dane nodded. "Roger that."

Mac clenched a fist and breathed through her anger. Where the hell did he get off talking about her like she wasn't there? She wanted to argue and point out that she could be trusted and was a damn good investigator, but the truth was, if she pushed it, they'd just cut her out of the picture. Since they seemed to have a better idea of what was going on than she did, *at the moment*, she was stuck biting her tongue.

Cain stood. "The rest of you get your asses home. Back here at oh-nine-hundred. We'll assess and see what the plan is."

Everyone got up and started moving out. Cain called to Jace, "Take care of the kid and make sure he's cool."

Jace nodded.

Dane looked at Mac. "You ready?"

What the hell was he talking about now? "For what?"

"I have to take you back to your car unless you want me to drop you at your place, and you can pick it up in the morning. Up to you."

What she wanted to do was strangle him and his boss.

She bit back insulting words and glanced at her watch. It was going on two a.m. "Just drop me at my place."

She followed him out to his SUV, and they got in. Dane sat silently in the driver's seat.

"Are we waiting for Christmas or what?" she demanded.

He stared at her. "Checking the security footage to make sure no one else fucked with my truck."

She'd walked into that one. Once again, she bit her tongue and sat silently fuming. How had this gone so wrong?

Dane's cell sounded, and he glanced at the screen. "All clear." He started the SUV and headed off Sand Island. "Where do you live?"

She gave him the address, and he turned up the coast. In traffic, she lived about forty-five-minutes away. It should be about twenty at this time of night. Oahu sparkled in the darkness. A bunch of twinkling lights in the middle of the deep, dark ocean. Suddenly, she longed for home. For knowing her neighbors and being with her family. For not being surrounded by darkness.

Dane cleared his throat. "I think we need to divide up the tasks."

"What tasks?" She had no clue what he was on about at this point.

"Owens. If we find out anything about his murder, we'll send it your way. If you find anything out about the rest of his dealings, you send it ours."

It wasn't a fair deal, but she didn't have a leg to stand on, so she agreed. "Do you think he was killed because of the drugs or because of the weapons?" she asked.

"At this point, I think he could've been killed because he was a colossal asshole."

She smiled, which then grew into a chuckle that became a belly laugh. She gasped for breath. "Sorry, it wasn't that funny but it's so damn true. I'm just tired, I guess."

Dane grinned at her. "Don't worry, I get it. Take the laughs when you can. Working with people you don't trust is the worst thing. It disrupts your entire life."

She'd forgotten how well he would understand what she was going through. "It's a lot more stressful than I realized. And to see Casper on the video was just over the top, you know?"

"I do."

"Yeah, I guess you do."

They pulled into her apartment complex. It was a low-slung condo community. Three floors of condos with stairs in between each building. She lived halfway down on the second floor. She directed him to park in her spot and got out. To her surprise, he got out as well. "What are you doing?"

"Walking you to the door."

She arched an eyebrow at him. "It's not like we were on a date or anything."

A sexy smile curved his lips upward. "Oh, I don't know. I had more action tonight than I've had in a while."

Heat raced up her cheeks, and then she chuckled. "I guess that's fair." She turned and started across the parking lot. The lot was lit by a few streetlights and the old-fashioned lanterns along the building. Willing the flames out of her cheeks, she kept her head down until they were at the stairs.

"Sorry about that, by the way," Dane said as she put her foot on the first riser.

She shrugged. "It was a…weird situation. No need to apologize." She'd enjoyed it far more than she was willing to admit. As a matter of fact, she was quite sure she'd be having some hot and heavy fantasies tonight starring Dane Landry based on that closet experience.

She cleared her throat. "Well good— Shit."

Dane frowned. "What?"

"Sorry. Mrs. Mahelona's cat, Popoki. He must have escaped again." She pointed at the tabby cat in the bushes next to the stairs. Then she stepped down from the stair and crouched down. "Hey, handsome. Come see me." The cat came right over, and she scooped him up. She stood again and made her way up the stairs to the second floor. She knocked on Mrs. Mahelona's door.

"It's just after two. Are you sure it's okay?" Dane asked.

"Yeah. Trust me. She'll be awake all night, waiting for him to come home." She was about to knock again, starting to doubt what she'd just said to Dane when Mrs. Mahelona opened her door.

"Oh, thank goodness. Popoki, you've come home. You bad cat." She reached out and took him from Mac. "Thank you so much, dear. You know I'd be up all night worried about this little stinker."

"No problem."

Mrs. Mahelona glanced at Dane. "Is this your date? Thank you so much for helping find my cat."

"My pleasure, ma'am," he said, the picture of a hero. God, if he was wearing a cowboy hat, he could have tipped it and Mrs. Mahelona would have passed out. As it was, she was staring at him. Not that Mac could blame her. Standing there in all black, he was sexy as hell.

"Have a good rest of your night," Mac said.

"You too, dear." She winked at Mac and then dropped her voice. "So much better looking than the one here earlier."

Mac's shoulders tightened. "The one that was here earlier?" What was she talking about?

"Yes, I saw him leaving your place. Not as well built. He had strawberry-blond hair and a lot of attitude. This one is much more polite."

"Right," Mac grunted out, alarmed about what the

woman said. "You have a good night." Could she be wrong? She was old. Maybe she was misremembering the episode.

Mrs. Mahelona closed her door, and Mac hurried to her apartment across the hallway. After fumbling for a second, she found her keys and pulled them out.

"What is it?" Dane demanded.

"What?"

"You're upset. What did she say?"

Mac looked up at him. "She watches out the keyhole for the cat. You heard her say she saw a guy with strawberry-blond hair leave my place earlier tonight. No one has a key to my place except me, and I don't know anyone with strawberry-blond hair."

"Son of a bitch!" Dane swore. "Probert has reddish hair. It's got to be him."

Goddamn it. She reached for the lock, but he put his hand on hers.

"Let's think about this for a minute."

She shook off his hand. "I don't want to think about this. I want to go into my apartment and see what that asshole did."

"I know. I get it, but you're not going to be able to get anyone over here now to help unless you call in the cavalry, and I'm not sure that's the best idea. Think about it. You need to tread carefully until we know the scope of your boss's betrayal or involvement. If you call and he comes over, are you going to trust anything he says or does? Will you trust the rest of the people who come with him?"

Shit. He had a point. Would she trust the techs to process her place? Casper knew them all. Not that she thought all of them were crooked but, she had no idea if any of them were, and it would only take one who wouldn't process a print or a fiber. One who would miss a bug or a small camera.

She sighed. "I could call the police. They could come to investigate the break-in."

"Yes, you could. But the moment they ask you what you do, they're gonna ask if this has anything to do with your job at CGIS. Then they're going to poke around in things and that might make it more difficult for us. Not to mention who the hell knows if Casper knows any of them. How long has he lived here? There's no way he doesn't know some cops on the island."

She wanted to scream but, goddammit, he was right. "What do you suggest?"

"Let my team process your place in the morning. They're exhausted now, and they need sleep. Whatever is in there can wait until tomorrow. We'll come over first thing and check it out."

She hated the idea. Waiting was awful. She wanted answers now, but he was right. She wouldn't necessarily trust any answers she got so it was better to wait. As much as she loathed to admit it, she did trust his team. They wouldn't make a hash of it, and she'd have a better idea of what she was dealing with.

"Fine. Drop me at a hotel." She turned and started down the stairs.

They climbed into his SUV and then headed out of the parking lot. "You might as well take me back downtown if you don't mind. I can get a room down there and get my car."

He cleared his throat and looked out his side window and then back through the windshield. "To be honest, I think it's probably best if you spend the night at my place."

Her heartbeat ticked up. Did he say *his place*?

"I don't trust any of Owens's team members, and there's just been a lot of crap today. Plus, my place isn't far. I have a spare bedroom and…" He paused. "I'll know you're safe."

His place. Alarm bells rang in her head. Shades of what happened in Minneapolis. Or was it? He was definitely an interesting man. Maybe too interesting. She'd thought Karl, her old boss, had been interesting, too. Instead, it turned out he was just an asshole. He'd blamed her for their affair, and she had to leave. It didn't matter that he was her boss. He'd been there longer, and the other detectives had closed ranks. They'd decided she had been the problem,

Oh, she could have fought it, but what would've been the point? She'd have to work with the people who thought she'd seduced her boss. Set her sights on him to further her career. *Just look at her. Who could resist?* It was all bullshit, but that was the story he sold, and they'd bought it, hook, line, and sinker.

It wasn't like he had a wife or even a girlfriend. They had legitimately dated, but once their lieutenant found out about it, her career at the Minneapolis Police Department was over. Lieutenant Linda Holmes decided Mac had to go. Three months later, Holmes and Karl were dating. Wasn't that something? As her mother had said during a phone call, "Your uncle, of course, told Karl he was being a jerk, but there's nothing else he could do."

Mac had said nothing. She'd been hurt that her uncle hadn't backed her a bit more at the time. He was a detective with enough years in to retire, but he said he wanted to work a few more years so he didn't want to rock the boat. The lieutenant was his boss, too. Whatever.

In the end, she was happier in Hawai'i.

She chose her next words carefully. "You don't think I'll be safe at a hotel?"

He glanced over at her. "I think there is more opportunity for them to get to you at a hotel. I think you'll be safer with me."

"I see. What makes you think they haven't broken into

your place?" She stared at him, but he just kept looking at the road ahead.

"Because I have a security system that would've alerted me. I have other things in place that I will check when we get there, but I'm pretty confident my place is clear." He finally glanced at her again. "Look, I just have a bad feeling in my gut about all this, and I don't want to leave you on your own. I'll drop you at a hotel if you want, but then I'm just gonna have to take the room next door, and I would rather not do that. I like to sleep in my own bed. Plus, I need to feed my cat."

She burst out laughing. "Well, by all means, let's feed your cat. I'll try not to be insulted by the fact that you think I can't handle myself. I will chalk it up to us both being tired and you wanting to keep an eye on me because you don't trust me. Those are reasons I can live with."

He said nothing. What she'd said was true, but what she didn't say aloud was she had a feeling in the pit of her stomach, too. It was fear. She was afraid. A storm was coming, and there was nothing she could do. She was already caught in it.

CHAPTER ELEVEN

Dane pulled into his driveway and parked the SUV in his garage. He got out slowly. His back, already stiff from the events of the day, had frozen on the drive over.

"You, okay?" Mac asked.

"Yeah. It's just been a long couple of days, and my back needs a bit of a break." He hit the lights and studied the door that led into the house.

"What are you looking for?"

"Just some things I left so I know if anyone has opened the door." Since Owens and the team tried to kill him, he'd taken extra precautions for his safety. He didn't believe for a second those assholes wouldn't try to finish the job. He looked closely and found that the tiny thread he'd left was still in place. He used the key to unlock the door and then walked into his kitchen, flicking on the light as he went.

"Nice place," she said as she came in behind him.

"Thanks." He liked his little house. The kitchen, although small, had enough room for a small island in the middle. A counter on the left side separated the kitchen from the dining area. "I'm just going to check the other doors." He went to the front door and did a check and then cleared the sliding glass doors to his back patio. "Everything is good. No one has been in here."

Mac had taken off her shoes and was standing in his kitchen.

He walked toward her and then jumped. "Seriously, Beans? I'm not that late." The cat had bitten his ankle.

"What?" She turned and stared at him.

"Beans."

"Er, no thanks, I'm not hungry."

He cracked a grin. "No. Beans." He pointed down at his cat. "He's hungry and mad at me because he can see the bottom of his bowl. He bit me to tell me he's pissed off."

Mac looked at the cat and then at the bowl, which was on a mat with a pet drinking fountain, next to the door to the garage. "I see. He still has food, but he doesn't like it when he can see the bottom of his dish?"

Dane nodded.

"I had a cat like that growing up." She squatted down, and Beans prowled over to her.

He was a short-haired tabby cat with a couple of rings of long hair around his shoulders, which made him look very odd.

"I found him on my doorstep one day. He's a little wonky looking but super friendly unless he can see the bottom of his bowl. Then he bites."

"I can see he's got quite the coat." She scratched Beans under his chin and then petted his head. He started to purr, and she said, "And a loud purr."

"Yeah. He's like an engine revving. You get used to it."

Dane walked over and grabbed the cat food from the cupboard. After filling the dish and setting out a couple of treats, he straightened and leaned against the sink. "Can I get you anything?"

Mac stood. Beans was busy eating. "No, I'm fine."

She wasn't fine. She was upset, as she should be. He could see it in the fine lines of her face and the jerky way she moved. If he told her not to think about it, she'd probably just think he was being a dick. "You want some tea or something?"

She shook her head. "I'm set, thanks."

This wasn't going to work. She was wound tight. There was no way she would sleep like that.

"I know you're upset about what happened tonight. You're in a tough spot, and I would imagine you're feeling pretty much alone. You aren't."

She crossed her arms over her chest. "Can we skip the pep talk? I just want to go to bed."

Fine. He wanted to help her because he knew what it felt like, but some people just couldn't be helped. At least not in the moment anyway.

"Okay. Follow me." He crossed the dining area and walked down a hallway. "Your room." He pointed to a door on the left side of the hallway. "Mine is there." His was on the right. "The bathroom is here." The door was opposite her bedroom. "Yell if you need anything."

She nodded and disappeared into her room.

So much for trying to extend the olive branch.

"Whatever," he groused and went into his room, closing the door behind him.

He peeled off his T-shirt very slowly. His back was on fire. The Advil was in the kitchen and he needed a double dose of it. He opened his door and started down the hallway, only to come face-to-face with Mac as she exited her room.

"Er, sorry," she said.

He just nodded and moved around her, continuing to the kitchen. He grabbed the bottle and shook out a couple of pills. He downed them with water and then started back to his room.

Mac was leaning on the doorjamb of her room. "Um, do you have a T-shirt or something I can sleep in?"

"Sorry, I should've thought of that." He went back into his room and pulled open one of his drawers. He pulled out a black cotton shirt and turned around, almost running her over. He hadn't realized she'd followed him into his room. He swore as he reached out, wrapping an arm around her, and braced his other arm on the doorframe to stop them both from falling. "Sorry. I didn't see you."

She'd flattened her hands on his chest, and he couldn't lie, he liked the way the heat of her palms seeped into his bare skin. Her hair curled around her shoulders. He hadn't seen it down yet and he found it was a spectacular style on her.

She looked up at him, her eyes wide. "My fault. I should've warned you I was there."

Was her voice a little breathy, or was that his imagination? "No problem."

Except it was a problem. He didn't want to let her go. He liked the fit of her body pressed against his. He'd noticed and relished how nice her curves felt while they were in the closet, even though it was highly inappropriate. He was enjoying it now, too, and if he didn't let her go soon, she'd be able to feel just how much.

"Sorry," he mumbled again as he removed his arm from her waist. He bent down to grab the fallen T-shirt and pain speared across his back. "Fucking hell!" He didn't straighten immediately, pressing a hand against the center of his spine.

"I got it." She bent down and picked up the T-shirt. They both straightened. "Your back still hurts that much? Didn't the vertebrae heal?"

"I had a compression fracture of the L1. It healed a while

ago, but the soft tissue damage around it is going to take time, or so the doctor says. Mostly the muscles just get tight, and it makes it hard to move without pain shooting in one direction or the other."

"You need to do Pilates."

He blinked. What the hell? Is it a conspiracy? "You're the second person to tell me that today."

"It really works."

He put a hand on his back. "Do you do Pilates?"

"Oh, sure. Been doing it for years. It makes all the difference." She smiled at him.

"Maybe you could show me some moves, or whatever, sometime."

"Sure." She took a step back and held up the black tee. "Well, thanks for the shirt."

"No problem."

She went down the hall to her room and closed the door behind her.

Dane looked down at the cat who was sitting at his feet, looking up at him. "Yeah, I know, Beans, but we're working together. Work and play don't mix."

The cat stalked by him, jumped up on his bed, and curled into a ball on one of his pillows. Dane let out a long sigh and headed to the kitchen for his Advil. He carried a glass of water back to his room, set it on his nightstand, and then finished getting ready for bed. As he removed his pants, something clunked against his thigh.

The book.

He'd forgotten all about shoving the little black notebook into his pocket, thanks to the whole closet incident and the possible bomb. It had been a hell of a day.

He propped up his second pillow, turned on his bedside lamp, and got into bed. He flipped through the book. There were lots of entries, but they were all written in some sort of code.

Each page had three columns. Every entry had a combination of letters and numbers. The first one seemed like maybe it could be a date. It was six digits. The next one varied in digits. Maybe amounts of money or drugs? The last one had random numbers as well, but they all had a dash and two letters after each entry. What the hell did that mean?

He studied the pages. The middle column sometimes had two lines per entry but not always. The last one always had the dash followed by two letters. Initials maybe? A key to who had made the deal? The numbers and letters swam before his eyes and he yawned widely. He put the book under his pillow and turned out the light. He'd bring it up tomorrow when Mac wasn't around. Maybe the team would have better luck figuring it out.

Two hours later, he sat bolt upright in bed. His heart was pounding, and he was bathed in sweat. He'd had the same nightmare he'd been having since his fall. He was on top of the container and he knew the ladder was greased, but he had to go down anyway. He tried to hang on but couldn't get a grip. It was just like what happened in real life, only in his dream, the deck was a hundred feet below.

He glanced at the clock. Oh-four hundred. Five hours before he had to be at work. He rubbed his face. Going back to sleep now was out of the question, but maybe if he had a hot shower, it would help. He rolled out of bed and headed down the hallway. It didn't hit him until after he was in the shower that he probably should have brought something to wear when he got out. In the fog of his nightmare, he'd forgotten Mac was here. At least, she hadn't caught him walking around in his boxers. The last thing he wanted to do was make her feel uncomfortable.

The hot spray cascaded over his back while he did a few

stretching exercises. Exhaustion overwhelmed him. His body craved sleep, but his mind wouldn't stop spinning.

As the water turned cool, he cranked off the faucet and grabbed a towel off the rack. Five minutes later, towel cinched around his waist, he opened the door and came face-to-face with Mac. "Shit," he said as he backed up. She'd scared the crap out of him.

"Sorry, I didn't mean to startle you." She gripped the doorjamb with one hand. "I just heard you up and wanted to make sure everything was okay."

"Ah, yeah. Sorry. I didn't mean to wake you. I just… Sometimes… Everything is fine." It had taken him a moment to realize what she meant. "Nothing new happening. Just couldn't sleep. Sorry if I woke you."

She shook her head. "I wasn't asleep either." She tucked her long blond hair behind her ears.

"Can I get you anything?" He was wracking his brain to think what might help her sleep, but seeing her in his T-shirt was giving him all kinds of thoughts, and none of them involved sleep.

"No." She hesitated and then asked, "Do you have any decaf tea?"

What had she asked for? He was seriously distracted by her legs and the way the T-shirt clung to her chest. He was sure she wasn't wearing a bra. "Um…" What was it? Oh, yeah, tea! "Let me check." When she backed up to let him pass, he left the bathroom and headed toward the kitchen. Walking around in a towel wasn't ideal, but he was kind of stuck with it now. She was making him discombobulated.

He pulled open the cupboard where he kept things like tea. "I have lemon and, uh, some tea that's supposed to help you sleep. Do you want some of that?" He turned as he asked her the question.

She was directly behind him. "Sure, that sounds great."

He pulled down the tea and a mug and started making her a cup.

"You have hot water on demand?" she asked as he held the button and filled up her cup.

"Yeah, it was here when I bought the house." He set her cup on the counter to let it steep.

She pulled out a stool from under the island and sat down. "I didn't realize that you'd had surgery on your back."

He frowned. Surgery? What was she talking about?

"The scar. It looks fresh."

"Oh, right. There was a rivet sticking out of the deck. It went into my back. The scar is where they sewed up the hole."

She blanched. "I had no idea. It wasn't in the report."

"A lot of things weren't in the report," he said before he could stop himself. "Shit. I'm sorry. I didn't mean—"

"No, it's okay. You're right. There were a lot of things left out of the report." She flattened her palms on the table. "I was hoping you could help me fill in some of the details. I actually have the report with me. I'll show it to you if you will help me understand how everything happened."

Did he want to do that? He wasn't sure, but he did want to see the report on his accident. "We can look at it but not tonight." She needed sleep, and him bringing up her boss wasn't going to help. He turned to take the teabag out of her cup. "Here. I don't think milk and sugar go in this one," he said as he set it down in front of her.

"Maybe you should have a cup, too. Maybe we'll both get some sleep then."

It wasn't a bad idea. His mom had sent the tea, and he'd never tried it. "Worth a shot." He turned to get another tea bag and let out a grunt. He'd turned too fast, and pain went across his back.

"You okay?" She'd gotten off her stool and was directly behind him.

"Yeah. Just…my back."

"May I touch it? Your scar?"

He grunted. She apparently took that as a yes.

Her touch was feather-light, but it sent all kinds of signals all over his body. "You were so lucky." He didn't move. Didn't even want to breathe.

She dug her fingers into the tissue around his spine and began to massage his muscles. "I can feel the knots. You need to stretch this out. A massage once a week for the next few months would help tremendously. You don't want this to be permanently knotted if you can avoid it."

Her fingers were giving him relief in his back but excitement shot through his body and he was getting hard. What was the protocol here? If Mac were any other woman, he'd turn around and kiss her. But she was, for lack of a better word, *the enemy*. At least for now.

Her palms and fingertips were warm as she moved her hands over his back. "Your muscles are really tight. We need to sign you up for a regular Pilates class." Her touch flitted over his skin, then disappeared, then came right back. She was running her fingers over his scar. The destroyed nerve endings didn't feel a thing as she skimmed the actual scar.

"I just can't imagine…" she breathed as her fingers repeated the here-gone-here sensation.

He was doing his best to be still, but his dick missed the damn message. It was going to be pretty damn obvious when he turned around, and there wasn't a fucking thing he could do about it.

"Ah, Mac, I'm not sure what…" He turned slowly.

She stood, looking up at him. "I'm sorry. I know I've crossed all kinds of boundaries here. I just had the urge to touch your scar. I'm…" She cleared her throat. "To have a broken back and now you're back on a spec-op team. That's incredible. Your scar just looks so red and angry. I…I had the urge to try and smooth it out. Soothe it somehow." She shook her head. "Sorry, I am losing it." Her cheeks were tinged pink as she pressed her hands to them. "And now you must think I'm a total nutcase. Here I'm touching you. God, I'm so sorry. It was just instinct."

When she started to move away, he touched her arm. He bent and captured her lips. They were warm and soft. She opened them under his touch, and he slid his tongue into her mouth, pulling her against him. *What was that they said about keeping your friends close but your enemies closer?* She wrapped her arms around his neck, bringing her hips against his. Their tongues danced as he ran his hands over her butt, grinding her against his hard-on.

Suddenly, she gasped.

"What?" He looked to see what had captured her attention. Beans was on the island. He had one paw up like he was getting ready to scratch.

"Um, your cat pulled my hair."

"Oh, God, I'm sorry. Dude's got a mind of his own."

She chuckled and took a step back. "It's all good." She cleared her throat and went around the island. Picking up her tea, she said, "I'm just gonna go to bed. I'm…I'm sorry about…" Her cheeks turned pink. "I don't know what came over me. It… I won't… Er, goodnight." With that, she was gone.

He stared at his cat. Should he give Beans a treat for saving him from doing something stupid? Or should he put the cat outside for interrupting the best kiss he'd had in a long time? He cursed as he grabbed his tea and headed back to bed. Life was getting interesting. Too bad 'interesting' always had a funny way of blowing up in his face.

CHAPTER TWELVE

Mac leaned against wall next to Mrs. Mahelona's door and watched as Dane and his teammates got ready to enter her apartment. She had wanted to be the first one through the door, but Dane pointed out that this type of thing was what they were trained for. She wasn't actually a Coastie. Most of the CGIS Special Agents weren't. Her job required a background in law enforcement. She was trained to investigate, not breach doors. Back in Minneapolis, they had SWAT for that. While she understood why they excluded her, it still burned that she couldn't participate. It was *her* apartment.

She tensed, shoulders tight, as they got into formation. Dane had called out his team this morning after they'd gotten up and he made coffee. Four hours sleep was better than none, but it wasn't much especially after the very hot kiss they'd shared. Thinking about that wasn't helping her tension and the nervous leaps and pirouettes happening in her gut. Neither was watching Dane in his ass-hugging faded jeans and a blue T-shirt that matched his eyes. The fact they put on their tactical gear and strapped on several guns just made him all the hotter while boosting her internal thermostat. *Damn him.*

Using her key, they unlocked the door but didn't open it. From where she was standing her line of sight was obscured. Too many strong, hot bodies between her and her apartment door. She slid along the wall until she was almost directly opposite her door.

"On three," Cain called. He was at the back.

Dane was crouched low on the right side of the entry point, and Tac stood upright and poised to breach on the left. Dane would turn the knob and then push the door open with his hand while staying crouched. Tac would go through once it was open. They would all pour in and clear her place in seconds. Then the real work would begin. She had to find whatever Probert—if it was him, although Dane seemed pretty damn sure—had left behind. A bug, something incriminating. Or maybe he'd been looking for something, but for the life of her, she had no idea what it would be. She'd puzzled over it while she'd been lying in Dane's guestroom but had come up empty.

"One," Cain counted. They tensed and got ready to move.

"Two," said Cain. Dane put his hand on the knob. At "three," Dane turned the knob and pushed open the door.

The explosion smacked her hard against the wall. The boom was deafening. She was on her back, staring at the ceiling in the hallway. The loud, high-pitched buzz in her ears muffled all other noise, and her head hurt. It took her a second to work out what had happened. *Dane.*

She tried to get up, but the world tipped sideways, so she flopped back. She turned her head. There was a boot not too far away, but she couldn't tell if it was attached to anything.

"Dane?" she called. "Dane?" But with the ringing in her ears, she couldn't be sure she was making sounds.

Someone groaned.

Someone else started to laugh. "That sucked," Jace said. "Everyone alright?"

"Motherfucker," Cass said. "I got a hole in my favorite jeans."

Mac blinked. Something was running into her eye. Water? The explosion must have set off the sprinklers. Was she getting wet?

"Tac, you, okay?" Cass started taking roll call.

"Yeah. Had my bell rung pretty good, but I'm okay."

"Cain?" As she called the roll, Cass's voice seemed to be coming from so far away.

There was a string of curses, and then Cain appeared at the edge of Mac's vision. He was leaning against the wall. "I'm okay."

"Koa?"

"Yo," came the echoey response.

"Dane?" Cass finally called.

Mac waited for the response. Her heart hammered against her ribcage. He had to be okay. He couldn't have gotten hurt because of her. She closed her eyes for a second and said a prayer. *Come on, Dane, say something.*

"BP's a little high, but she should be fine. Slight concussion." Dane's voice reached her ears. He sounded strong. That's when she realized she was moving. She opened her eyes. He was walking next to her. She was on a stretcher of some kind. She tried to sit up.

"No. Stay down. You have to go to the hospital and get checked out."

"You're…" What did she mean to say? Concentrating was hard. Oh yeah… "You're okay?"

He nodded. His clothes were dusty, and a blood smear marred the sharp edge of one cheek, but he seemed to be moving okay. She blinked to clear her head, but even that sent a stabbing pain through her brain. She left her eyes shut. Whoever was carrying her moved her to a gurney and then the sensation of rolling along dizzied her. Her body stopped, and she cracked one eye to find she'd reached the back doors of the ambulance. The strobing blue light was too much, and bile rose up her throat. She gave herself a stern talking-to. *You are* not *going to be sick. Don't you flipping dare.*

"What happened?" *Good Christ, was that weak, limp voice hers?*

"I'll explain later. Now you're going to the hospital. Cass is going with you." Dane laid his hand on her arm. "We've alerted your people. I'm sure they will meet you there. You need to tell them that Cass isn't leaving your side. She's your protective detail. Got it?"

She started to nod but stopped as pain erupted like Diamond Head. "Yeah, got it."

Cass appeared next to Dane. "I've got her."

"Don't leave her side for anything. I don't give a shit who orders it, copy?"

"Roger that. I've got her." Cass hopped in as the EMTs pushed Mac into the ambulance.

"Wait," she said, but no one listened. She wanted to stay. What the hell had happened? Why would Probert want to blow her up? None of it made any sense. "Dane," she called, but they closed the ambulance doors. "Shit. I need to be there."

Cass stared at her. "You need to get checked out. You took a hell of a knock. Your head must be killing you. Don't worry. The guys are on it. I'm here to keep you safe." She patted her hand on Mac's arm. "We've got you."

Mac glanced up and saw the seriousness of what Cass was saying. She took a deep breath and tried to relax. Dane was okay. She was okay. It would all be okay. Cass was there to protect her. *But why did she need protecting in the first place? Who would want to kill her?*

Dane fisted his hands as he watched the ambulance pull out of the parking lot. He'd almost lost it when he found Mac lying under a bunch of debris with blood pouring out of a head wound and dripping into one eye. His heart stuttered as he recalled his terror at the first sight of her.

"It's not your fault," Koa said as he came up to stand beside Dane. "You couldn't have known."

"She was in the wrong spot. I should've moved her."

"Bullshit. She was standing by her neighbor's door when we got into position. She must've moved so she could see better. It was stupid, and a mistake, but it wasn't yours."

Koa could preach that all he wanted, but it didn't make Dane feel any less responsible.

Cain walked over. "She's gonna be fine. Come on, let's check out what's left of the apartment. The fire department just gave us the all-clear."

They took the stairs two at a time. It was hard to believe he'd walked up those stairs only a few hours ago. They'd come so close to going into Mac's apartment. They would have been dead, both of them, if they'd opened the door at that moment.

"We don't have much time before CGIS comes and takes over. Tell me about last night," Cain said.

Dane stood next to the blown-out and blackened doorway. "We were coming up the stairs but stopped because the neighbor's cat was loose. Mac picked it up and returned it to the lady."

"Mrs. Mahelona," Koa supplied.

"Right. She mentioned to Mac she'd seen another man

coming out of her apartment earlier. Said he had strawberry-blond hair."

"Earlier when?"

Dane cocked his head. "Ah, good question. Don't know. You're going to have to ask her."

Koa walked over and tapped on Mrs. Mahelona's door. It opened immediately. He spoke quietly to the elderly lady, who smiled up at him. She was holding the cat, which Koa petted while she spoke. Koa nodded and then came back to the group assembled at Mac's apartment doorway.

Koa tipped his head back toward the neighbor's apartment. "Oh-one-thirty to be exact. She was looking through her peephole, keeping an eye out for her cat. Some soap opera she likes reruns at that time. It had just started."

"Here's what I don't get; how did they know Mac wasn't home?" Tac said as he entered the huddle.

"All kinds of ways," Dane answered. "Think about it. What would we do to figure out if someone was home? Track their cell, check security cameras, and look for their car. Her boss was part of the group that put the GPS tracker on Dane's SUV. If he'd followed her to Candyland, he could have easily seen her get in the SUV. Plus, her car is down there. Maybe he has a tracker on her car as well. They could have assumed she was still in downtown Oahu."

Cain let out a breath. "Let's check that out immediately. That would answer a lot of questions, but mostly how much we can trust her. Although, after this, I think it's safe to say she's not involved in whatever is going on."

Tac shook his head. "This is the craziest shit. I'll head downtown and check out her car."

"You're not wrong, brother," Jace agreed. "We haven't really begun any kind of operation, and people are already trying to kill us."

Dane shook his head. "Not us. Mac. This was meant for her."

"Why?" Tac asked. "What the hell does she know that would get her killed? Is she holding out on us?"

Dane had been asking himself that same question for the last hour. Had she played him? Maybe she'd seduced him to get more information or keep him occupied so he didn't pay attention. Was she part of the group selling the motherboards? No matter how hard he spun that idea around in his brain, he just couldn't make it work. Definitely a case of one and one not equaling two.

He remembered back to them kissing in the kitchen. There was no dishonesty in that kiss. No, she was being truthful with him. He was certain. But then, she might be a good liar. Cops usually had to be to get the bad guys to open up, but she would have to be a Meryl Streep-level actress to pull off what she did last night, and he didn't think she was that good of an actress.

He cocked his head. "What if she doesn't know that she knows something?"

Koa stared at him. "You mean she's seen something or heard something that could expose someone, but she doesn't know it."

"Exactly. Whoever did this is playing for all the marbles. They tried to kill a CGIS agent. That's not something you do just for fun. This isn't just about a drug shipment."

"You think it's about the other thing," Cain stated.

He wasn't going to risk saying anything about the stolen motherboards in public, but Dane knew exactly what he meant. "I do. I think we're missing something. Hell, we're missing the whole damn puzzle, but the sooner we figure this out, the better it is for Mac and everyone else. And here." He pulled the black book out of his pocket. "I forgot about this last night. I took it from Owens's safe. It's in code."

Cain took the book and flipped through the pages.

"I couldn't figure it out, but I'm guessing it can't be too difficult. The first column might be dates."

"Agreed." Cain pointed to Jace. "You said there's a drone flying competition today."

When Jace nodded, Cain instructed, "Go. Dane, you and Koa go with him. I want you three to try and find whoever flew that drone. We need to find those…uh, items as soon as possible. That drone is our only real lead." He turned to Tac. "We're gonna sort this mess here. Maybe figure out what the end goal was besides killing Rankin. Way too many explosives for her to be the only target, but we have to do it fast. I figure we have twenty minutes tops before the big guys show up and take over. When we're done here, Tac and I will go downtown and get her car. Once we're back at the hangar, we're gonna dig into this book."

"Sounds good," Tac said. He turned to walk into the apartment but pivoted back. "Be safe guys. Keep your heads on a swivel and cover your six. This shit is weird. It could come at you from any angle."

"Roger that." Jace started toward the stairs, and Koa and Dane fell in step behind him.

An hour later, Dane was standing next to a bunch of teenage girls who were yelling and screaming while flying some kind of small drone. The sound was ear-piercing. He wished wholeheartedly that he had some pain meds with him. "Jace," he said, "do you have any Advil? These kids are giving me a major headache."

"Sorry, I left them in the car."

Dane debated for a full minute and then decided it was worth the ten-minute walk back to the parking lot. "I'm going to get some. I'll be back. Keep your eyes open. Yell if there's a problem."

Koa swore. "Bring me some, too. My fucking head feels

like it's about to explode. All these things buzzing around and shit. It's making my nerves raw."

Dane smiled. Koa wasn't one for loud noises. If Dane was finding it hard, Koa was finding it excruciating. The ear-splitting explosion at Mac's apartment had probably triggered a massive headache.

"Don't forget me," Jace chimed in and then swore. "All these kids on top of all the adults. It's a madhouse, and my knee is killing me."

"Roger that." God, they were a bunch of misfit toys. Broken and put back together not quite right. Shaking his head, he walked to the edge of the field and crossed the road. The drones were on one side in a huge open space, organized by group. Small drones all the way up to the big suckers. A field on the opposite side of the road had been converted into a parking lot.

He was glad today was moderate in temperature. He loved the Hawaiian sun, but she could be harsh at times. A coolish breeze stirred the grassy area and made it all bearable. He reached Jace's Jeep and reached into the glove compartment. Jace didn't have the doors or the roof on his vehicle so there was nothing to lock. He could lock the glove, but he only kept a bottle of water and some Advil inside. He just didn't see the point, and neither did anyone else. The Jeep was twelve years old. Who the hell would want to steal it?

He grabbed the Advil and downed two pills with the water. He put the pill bottle in his pocket and started walking back across the field to the road. The sound of a buzzing off to his left made him turn and look. The drones were supposed to be flown only on the other side of the road.

A large drone came over the field and then swung back. It did a weird little dip and then landed. Dane immediately pivoted and walked in that direction. He'd seen that little dip before. *On the beach.*

"I think I found our drone. I'm in the field across the road, the one with the parked cars."

"Roger that. On the way," Jace answered.

"Coming," was all Koa said.

Two young Asian guys were standing next to the parked drone. One had the iPad to fly the drone and the other had a can in his hand. They looked to be in their early twenties. Not the hardened criminals he'd been expecting.

He smiled as he approached. "Hi. Nice drone."

The two men looked up at him. "Thanks. You into flying?" the shorter of the two asked. He was wearing a light blue T-shirt and what looked like board shorts. He was drinking a soda.

"This is all new to me. A buddy of mine just got started so we thought we'd come to check it out today. Have you two been flying long?"

"A couple of years," the taller one with the iPad said. "It's fun."

"Can you do tricks? I saw some pretty cool things over there. It kind of blew my mind how hard these things are to fly, and then to get them to do tricks…it's just awesome."

The shorter one grinned. "Dude, we can do all the tricks. I'm Chan and this is Paul."

Dane came to a stop beside them. "Jeff," he said and offered his hand. They shook, and then Paul launched the drone. He spent the next five minutes showing off, doing all kinds of tricks. Dane pretended to be impressed. Drones were annoying to him, but he had to admit, this kid knew his shit.

"On your eight o'clock," Jace's voice crackled in his ear.

"On your three," Koa added.

"On my count." Dane kept his voice low. Paul was bringing the drone in to land it. "One," Dane murmured.

The drone did the little dip thing. "Two," Dane said. Paul landed the drone and clicked the screen to turn it off.

And finally, Dane called out, "Three."

Jace and Koa were on the kids in an instant. They had them, hands behind their backs with no room to move.

"What the hell, dude? What's going on?" Paul demanded. "Are you stealing the drone?"

Dane walked in front of him. "I don't want your drone. I want to know where you took the package you picked up the other night at the beach."

"I have no idea what you're talking about," Paul said and tried to look tough, but he was failing miserably. His eyes darted around, and he kept shifting his weight from one foot to the other.

"What about you, Chan?" Dane asked, fixing him with a hard stare.

"Dude, the drone's not mine. I don't know what he did with it the other night."

Dane crossed his arms over his chest and stared at the two kids. "I'm going to give you one chance. You tell me who you gave the package to the other night, and I won't destroy the drone. Otherwise, I will crush that thing with my Jeep. Are we clear?"

Both young men avoided looking at him, Paul gazing out over the field and Chan down at his feet.

"You've got to the count of three, and then the drone is destroyed. "One…two… Okay," he said and started walking back toward the Jeep.

"You didn't say three," Paul called. "You said you would count to three."

"I lied," Dane called over his shoulder.

"Fine. Fine! I'll tell you!" shouted Paul.

Dane turned and came back. "Okay, Paul, who did you give the package to?"

"I don't know," the kid whined. Dane rolled his eyes and turned to walk away. "Wait, wait. I swear I don't know. That's the beauty of the drone, man. I picked up the package, and the guy used the video feed to verify that it was picked up. He told me where to leave it, and I did. He viewed the feed and then paid me the money. Fastest grand I ever made."

"You have no idea who the guy is?"

Paul shook his head.

"How did you meet him?"

"We didn't meet. I got an email, and he laid out what he wanted. Was I willing to do it? Sure. I mean, it's a few minutes of work for a thousand bucks. It's a no-brainer."

"I'm going to need to see the wire transfer. I need the number of the account it came from."

"Dude." Paul frowned like Dane had shit for brains. "Bitcoin."

He should have known. Fucking cryptocurrency was the bane of every law enforcement branch. "Do you know anything about the guy?"

Paul shook his head.

"What about you, Chan?"

"He went by the name TigerKing. That's it. That's all I got."

He nodded to Jace and Koa. They let the guys go.

"Here's the deal. If this guy, this TigerKing"—he scoffed —"contacts you again, you're gonna text me right away. Do you understand? Because if I find out you didn't, I will take your drone away and report you. Are we clear?"

"Yes," Paul mumbled.

"Sure," Chan agreed.

Dane gave them his cell. He also took their full names and their cell numbers. "I mean it, guys. Stop being stupid."

They both nodded, and Paul moved forward and picked up the drone.

Dane, Koa, and Jace watched them move quickly across the field and climb into an old beat-up minivan. "We need to get back to the hangar. Maybe we can track down the name," Jace said as they watched the minivan drive off.

"I kinda wish we had grabbed them." Jace put his hand out to Dane.

Dane frowned, but when he figured out what Jace wanted, he dug the Advil out of his pocket and tossed it to him. "I know what you mean. At least then we'd know that they weren't going to email TigerKing and tell him we're on to him."

"Sometimes being on the right side of the law sucks," Koa stated and then took off toward the Jeep.

Dane sighed. "He's not wrong." His gut tightened.

There was more trouble brewing, and they were going to be right in the middle of it. He could only hope things went their way, but with what had happened so far, he wasn't counting on it.

CHAPTER THIRTEEN

"I'm fine. It's just a headache." Mac wasn't lying. It *was* a headache, the biggest, baddest one she'd ever had, but still just a headache. She needed to get out of there so she could get on with her investigation.

Rutledge sighed. "Mac, just see what the doctor says. I understand you passed out at the scene."

"For a minute. I think that was less about the bump on the head and more about the shock of the explosion." She swallowed. "I didn't expect the place to blow up." Her stuff. All of it was gone now. Shit. She closed her eyes.

"Sorry, am I tiring you out?" Rutledge asked.

She opened her eyes. "No. I was just thinking about my stuff. Did any of it survive?" She looked around Rutledge at Cass.

Cass shifted in her chair. "I'll ask." She pulled out her phone and clicked away at the screen. A second later, it went off. Cass stood and walked over to the door. "I'll be in the hallway right outside." She sent a look at Rutledge. It was a warning if Mac had ever seen one. Cass was fierce with her different colored eyes and the ability to make her face go steely, scary cold. She was glad Cass was there to protect her. Mac did not like the odds if she had to go up against the other woman.

Rutledge dropped his voice and moved his chair closer to her bed. "What's with her?"

"What do you mean?" Mac shifted so she was sitting a bit more comfortably. She was realizing it was more than her head that hit the wall. Bruises were starting to appear all over. She was a hot mess.

"She won't let you out of her sight."

"Maddox assigned her to stay with me."

"Why? What's it to him? This is CGIS business. Not whatever the hell his team does." Rutledge narrowed his eyes. "Unless you're not telling me something."

Mac weighed what she could say and what she couldn't. She wasn't ready to tell him about Casper yet, nor about Owens being involved. "Dane and the team are working the drug angle on the Owens thing. We're working the murder. I'm sharing resources a bit since we only have the two of us and they have a whole frickin' team," she said in a voice just above a whisper. "I was with one of them last night when I found out that someone had been in my apartment. We think it was one of Owens's team. We went back this morning to see what the situation was and that's when the whole thing blew up, quite literally."

"Why the hell didn't you call me?" Rutledge demanded. His eyes flashed.

She immediately felt guilty. In reality, it had never occurred to her to call Rutledge. Dane had been there and had a logical course of action. Calling Rutledge could have opened up a big can of worms better left sealed up.

She could beg off and say she had a headache and didn't want to talk anymore, but that wasn't fair. "Because calling you would have meant calling the forensic guys, which would have meant calling Casper." She sighed. "I don't trust him. I don't want him anywhere near this. He already screwed up once. Plus, it was a good thing I didn't call you. If we'd opened that door, we'd both be dead."

He paled slightly when that sunk in. "I guess, but still. I thought you trusted me."

"I do." And she did. *Mostly.* "But they"—she angled her head toward the door and immediately regretted it when pain shot through her temples—"don't, and we want their help. Or, at least, I do. I think they know more than they are saying, and I want some answers."

Rutledge gave a grudging nod. "Have you found anything out so far?"

She grimaced. "I haven't really had a chance to get any questions answered. The only thing I know for sure is Owens was dirty. He had way too much money for being in the Coast Guard. He had a secret apartment on Waikiki Beach. I saw it last night, but then I hit a bit of a snag. A lot is going on. The list of who would want to kill him is growing. Drugs? Maybe his team members? It could all be about money."

The doctor breezed in the room. He was a tall, thin bald man with frameless glasses and a serious bedside manner. "How are you feeling?" he asked as he read her chart.

Mac glanced at Rutledge. "I'll fill you in more later."

Rutledge nodded and stood. "I want to hear about this apartment."

"The info should be on my desk."

He nodded. "Well, I will leave you to it. I'm glad you're okay." He gave her a pointed look, and she knew he meant it. She'd given him the apartment. That should keep him happy for a while even though it would piss off Dane. Couldn't be helped. She had a job to do, too.

The doctor came around to the side of the bed. He

checked her eyes and took a look at the cut on her head. "I think you should spend the night in the hospital." She started to protest but he cut her off. "I know it's inconvenient and you have things to do, but trust me when I tell you death is even more inconvenient. We need to make sure there's no brain bleed or any other underlying issues."

"Listen to the man," Cass said as she re-entered the room with a small paper bag. "I promise to keep you up to speed."

Mac wanted to argue, to fight and say she was fine but, in truth, she was pretty beaten up and exhausted. A night in the hospital wouldn't be so bad. She could use the sleep. Besides, it wasn't like she had a home to go to. "Fine," she agreed.

"Good." The doctor gave her a pinched smile. "I'll have a nurse get you some meds for your headache, and I'll be back to check on you later." She nodded again and he left.

"You hungry?" Cass asked.

She was about to say no when the smell hit her nose. "Cheeseburger?"

A wicked grin lit Cass's face. "And fries. I figured you could eat a horse right about now. I love *Uber Eats*." She placed the bag on Mac's rolling tray. "Let me shut the door so we don't get yelled at for starting a riot. If the other patients catch a whiff, all hell will break loose. By the way, your car is now in the parking lot."

Mac smiled back. "You rock. This is awesome. Wait, how did you get my car?"

"I had Tac drop it off."

"But he didn't have keys…" She frowned. "You know what? I don't want to know. Sometimes, it's better not to ask."

Cass smiled. "Ain't that the truth." She laid the food out in front of Mac and helped her get comfortable. "Enjoy."

Mac dug in and finished her meal in record time. She

leaned back on the pillows and relaxed. "So, what did the guys say about my stuff?"

Cass packed up all the garbage and moved the tray out of the way before answering. "Um, some might be salvageable."

"Bullshit," Mac spat. "You're trying to be kind."

Cass met her gaze. "Yeah. Sorry. They said it was probably a total write-off. Your bedroom might have some salvageable stuff, but it doesn't look good. What the explosion didn't get, the fire department drenched with water afterward."

Mac let out a long breath. "But I'm still here so that's the main thing. No one got hurt."

Cass nodded. "Good attitude. That'll help."

"Yeah. This is going to truly suck." A good attitude wasn't going to cut it.

"Did you have insurance?"

Mac nodded.

"That's good. Look at it this way. You get to go shopping to replace your entire wardrobe. That's not all bad."

Mac raised her eyebrows. She hadn't pictured Cass as a big shopper. "I never thought of that. I don't even know where to go really. I brought all my stuff from the mainland."

"Oh, I can show you. I know all the best stores." Cass blushed. "Shopping is kind of my thing. Don't tell the guys. They'd never let me live it down."

"I won't tell your secret if you promise to help me with the shopping. I needed a new wardrobe anyway. I'm not good at that sort of thing."

"Oh, we'll definitely go. We'll have a great time. Promise." With that, Cass went back to checking her phone.

Mac settled on her pillows and closed her eyes. Casper. Where the fuck was Casper? He should have shown up by now.

When there was a knock at the door, Mac opened her

eyes. John Bishop Cross stood in the doorway. "I hope I'm not interrupting." He was wearing a white shirt with the sleeves rolled up and gray suit pants. The white shirt showed off his tan and made his blue eyes pop. The man had charisma to match his good looks.

Behind him was Neil Ainsley, looking disheveled as usual. His brown suit pants looked like he'd slept in them, and his light blue shirt had a coffee stain on the sleeve. He'd probably spent the night at the office with everything that was going on. Cross would have fresh clothes to change into and a chance to shower. Ainsley would never be given that kind of consideration. It was as if Ainsley was the storer of all the bad, stressful stuff and Cross was the face of everything else.

Mac was suddenly conscious of how she must look. Who was she to pick on Ainsley's appearance when she must look like a truck hit her? Fuck it. She really didn't care. Cross was a political animal. She doubted he even knew her name before almost getting blown up today, and she didn't care about Ainsley at all.

"Can we come in?" Cross asked.

"Of course." She shifted gingerly into a sitting position.

"Oh, please don't move on my account. I just wanted to see for myself that you were okay." He turned to face Cass, and she stood.

She was taller than the average woman, about five-foot-ten if Mac had to guess, and with her long blond hair and striking eyes, she was a knockout.

Cross took notice. "CGIS Deputy Director John Cross." He offered his hand. "We didn't have a chance to meet when we were with the senator at your hangar yesterday."

She looked at the hand and then looked at him. "Cass," was all she said. She barely touched his hand before dropping it. She did the same with Ainsley after he offered his name. Cass crossed her arms over her chest and stared at the deputy director. Mac's heart soared at the exchange. She'd never seen anyone put Cross in his place faster. It was heavenly.

Cross's smile wobbled as he turned back to Mac. "Is there anything I can get you?" He waved to Ainsley, who was hovering at the end of the bed.

He meant *tell Ainsley what you want.* She suddenly felt bad for the man. It had to be tough being the never-really-seen assistant. "I'm fine, thanks." She included Ainsley in her smile, which she immediately concluded was a mistake since his features brightened.

He reached out and touched her foot on the bed. "I'm so glad you're okay."

She forced a smile while she squirmed inside. "Thanks."

This was about to get awkward fast if Ainsley kept talking. Cross seemed to sense it as well and looked like he was about to say something, but Ainsley's cell went off.

"Sorry, have to take this," he said and then gave her another smile before walking out of the room.

Saved by the bell.

Cross drew in a deep breath. "I have had preliminary reports from the scene. It sounds bad. I am so glad you weren't seriously hurt. The senator was not thrilled to hear someone had tried to kill one of my agents on the heels of losing a special operations team member."

What the hell was she supposed to say to that? It wasn't like she planned it. The senator could just suck up his unhappiness. "Not so thrilling for me, either."

"Do you have any ideas who might have been behind this?"

Mac hesitated. She had a good idea, but she didn't want to say anything just yet. She didn't have anything concrete. Cross was known for killing the messenger. If she said something, and it was wrong, he'd make her pay. "I have no clue. The only thing I'm working on is the Owens murder."

Cross frowned. "Have you discovered anything?"

How did she answer this one? He was the big boss. Blowing him off wasn't an option.

"We think Owens was definitely into supplying drugs." She wasn't going to mention that the guys thought he might have been involved in the Navy weapons thing, too. Cross would swoop in and cut her out of the loop. Hell, he'd probably try to cut Dane's team out of the investigation, too. Yeah, she was not getting involved in that political quagmire.

"What makes you think so?"

"He had way too much money flowing in that couldn't be accounted for. I discovered he had a secret apartment. Tom Rutledge, my partner, can supply details." She hoped Rutledge got a chance to look at the files before Cross showed up.

Cross narrowed his eyes. "So, you think selling drugs got him killed?"

"I would say it's a possibility. We need to do more digging."

"Do you think maybe you were getting too close and someone decided to take you out of the equation?"

She frowned. "But I'm not close."

Cross studied her. "But they don't know that. I think it's best if you sit the rest of this one out."

"Sir, no. I want to be part of the case."

"I understand that Mac, but obviously it's dangerous, and you've gotten hurt. You are officially on leave. With Senator Weston here, I can't be shown to be playing favorites. He's gone Sunday night, but I know he'll be checking, so you have to be sidelined on this one, Mac." He offered her a smile. "Take a few days when you get discharged from here and sort out a place to stay. Call Ainsley if you need help with anything. I'm sure he can help you track down a new place, or at least get someone to help you." He reached out and touched her arm. "We need you to be one-hundred percent. I don't want any of my agents hurt on the job, but especially someone so new."

Asshole! Did he just imply that it was her fault because she didn't have much experience as a CGIS agent? "I was a cop for seven years before I moved here. I know how to handle myself. Please let me continue working the case."

"Sorry. The decision is made." He offered yet another quick smile and then nodded to Cass as he started out of the room. "I'll coordinate with Tom Rutledge. You rest up, Special Agent Rankin. We'll check in with you in a week or so." Then he was gone.

"Sonofabitch!" she spit out.

"Mac," Danny Collins said as he entered the room. His partner, Rick Nelson, was directly behind him. Collins had short red hair and freckles. He was stocky with brown eyes and a bit of a gut. His partner Nelson was the opposite, tall and thin with a shaved head. They looked like the odd couple.

"Hi, guys." She had no interest in having visitors, but it was nice of them to come so she swallowed her anger at Cross and made an effort to be friendly. "How's it going? What are you doing here on a Saturday?"

"How are you feeling?" Collins asked as he approached the side of the bed. Nelson went to the foot.

"Got a headache, but otherwise fine."

"Good. Glad to hear it." Nelson smiled. "Sorry about your place. We were just there. Quite a mess."

"Yeah, so I've heard." The last thing she wanted to talk about was the fact that she was homeless. When Collins glanced at Cass, Mac introduced everyone. "Oh, sorry. Cass is a friend." It just seemed easier to leave it there.

"I see." Collins smiled at her. "Do you think, Cass, you could maybe give us a few minutes? We need to ask Mac some questions about what happened."

So…not a social visit. They were here to question her. The heat crawled up her neck to her cheeks. It was hard to keep swallowing her anger. Did no one give a shit that someone tried to blow her up? "Where is Casper?" she demanded. It came out of her mouth before she even thought about it.

"No idea. We've been trying to reach him," Nelson admitted. "But you know Casper. He loves to go fishing on the weekend. He goes out Friday night and doesn't come back until Sunday afternoon. No one can reach him."

He had the decency to look slightly embarrassed, which he should. Her boss should be here. He'd made a point of telling her he was going to work all weekend. So much for that, but she wasn't really surprised.

"So, um, Cass could you give us a few minutes?" Collins asked again.

Cass looked up from her phone. "No."

They both looked incredulously at the agent who'd nonchalantly returned her attention to her phone. Mac had to bite the inside of her cheek to keep from laughing. It got better every time. Hilarious. No one ever expected her to say no. It made Mac feel infinitely better for a moment.

Nelson shot Mac a look. "I'm afraid I'm going to have to insist."

"I'll save you the trouble," Cass said, looking up. "I'm Tactical Law Enforcement. My clearance level is way beyond yours. Anything you have to say to Mac, you can say in front of me. If you recall, someone just tried to kill her. Nope, not leaving her side. You have a problem with anything I've just said, take it up with my boss." Cass went back to browsing her phone.

The two men looked at Mac and then at each other. Collins stammered, "Er, well I...guess...that is—"

"Let me make this easy, guys," Mac said. "I'm tired, and I have a headache. If you want to know what happened, now is your moment. Assistant Director Cross just put me on leave for a week. Once I'm out of here, I'll probably head back to the mainland."

Nelson got out his notebook, and Mac told her story again. There was nothing new to add. No new revelations. She didn't mention that she spent the night at Dane's. She didn't even mention his name, just that she'd been with a friend, which she was pretty sure they assumed was Cass.

Collins closed his notebook. "Okay, we'll be in touch if anything else comes up. We'll leave so you can get some rest."

Mac just stared at them; her lips pressed tightly together so she wouldn't sound off. They not only were working on the bombing of her apartment, but would probably get her case, too, the murder of Senior Agent Owens, the one she'd just been relieved of, the one that had caused her to get blown up in the first place. She was beyond pissed about all of it.

"You take care, Mac," Nelson said as he and Collins started toward the door.

"You, too," she croaked and then collapsed back on the pillows as soon as they were out the door.

"You okay?" Cass asked.

"Just tired. I have a headache." She closed her eyes.

Cass glanced at her phone screen. "The guys want to know if it's okay for them to come by."

She opened her eyes. "Sure. That would be good. Tell them to bring dinner. I'm starving again. What time is it?"

"Dinnertime. I'll get them to bring food."

"Also"—Mac adjusted herself on her pillows—"no one seems to have heard from Casper. Can you ask the guys to see if they can locate him? He told me he was working all weekend, but he might have decided to blow it off and go fishing, which is probably more likely. I would just feel better if we knew for sure."

Cass's thumbs flew across the screen. "Will do. You rest until they get here."

That sounded like a great idea to her. The last twenty-four hours had been a roller coaster, and she was exhausted. Kissing Dane had kept her up all night. It was stupid, but the electricity between them was a live wire; dancing and arcing, drawing her closer.

It didn't hurt that he was also smart and sexy as hell. The fact that he liked animals and was obviously crazy about his cat was just the icing on the cake. Too bad he still saw her as the enemy.

Too bad someone else saw her as the enemy as well. They'd tried to blow her up. she just needed to figure out why.

CHAPTER FOURTEEN

"Mac asked if we could locate her boss before we go to the hospital. Anyone got any ideas?" Tac asked.

Dane, Jace, and Koa were on their way back to the hospital, Jace was driving. The team was having a quick check-in via speakerphone.

Tac continued, "Apparently, people have been calling him, but he's not answering."

Dane shifted uncomfortably in the Jeep's passenger seat. When they took off the doors they must have removed the extra padding in the seats. "Does Mac think Lawrence is in trouble?"

"Not sure." Tac asked, "Where are you guys?"

"We're not far from Sand Island," answered Dane. "We were headed there until you told us to meet at the hospital. Where are you guys?"

"We're grabbing dinner," Cain cut in. "Do me a favor and run over to Sand Island to CGIS and check on Manu. I sent him over there to see if he could track down Lawrence, and now I'm having second thoughts. I don't want the kid to get into any trouble."

"Do you think he's in danger?" Jace asked.

"Most likely not, but just to be sure. I wanted to keep the kid busy. I'm worried he'll tell the world that we know Lawrence broke in and stole the GPS. So I asked him to see if he could hack Lawrence's cell."

"We're pulling onto Sand Island now. We'll call once we talk to Manu." Dane disconnected just as Jace parked, and they all got out. They started across the parking lot as Cain's text with Manu's number arrived.

Dane called immediately. "Hey, Manu, it's Dane. You're on speaker, pal."

"Hi. I just got in. I'm running a triangulation on Casper's phone. Give me a minute and I'll..."

Manu trailed off and silence took over the line. "Manu?" Dane's heart rate ticked up. "Manu? Are you still there?" He increased his speed and approached the doors to CGIS.

"I think..."

"What? I can't hear you. Are you in trouble?" Dane glanced at Jace and Koa.

"I think this thing is broken." Manu sounded shocked.

"Why? What's broken?" Dane paused his hand on the door.

"The coordinates place Casper's cell at the port. Right next door."

Dane's stomach clenched. "Can you tell where exactly?"

"I can probably narrow it down some for you. Are you going to check?"

"Yeah." As much as he dreaded it, he was going to go check.

"Do you want me to come?" Manu asked.

Jace smiled. "No, kid, it's fine. You stay here and guide us if we need it.

They all went back across the lot and hopped back into the Jeep. Dane held on to the roll-bar as they headed to the next port over. Three minutes later, they parked and got out. They were walking toward the offices when Jace asked, "What kind of car does Lawrence drive?"

"Good question." Dane sent a text to Manu and got a reply immediately. "Old blue Ford Mustang."

"Like that one over there." Jace pointed.

"Yeah." Dane pulled his gun from the small of his back and held it down by his side. Jace and Koa followed suit. In the farthest corner of the lot, next to a stack of containers, sat a vintage blue Ford Mustang. Parked well away from any foot traffic and in the shadow of containers that appeared not to have been moved in months.

Jace commented, "It looks like a nineteen-ninety-eight model. That qualifies as old. Was Manu even born then?" As they approached the car, he pointed and asked, "What the hell is that?"

Dane squinted just as the breeze kicked up. His stomach rolled. "Brains."

"Shit." Jace blinked.

"He's been here a while," Koa mused as they approached the Mustang. "The smell is intense."

Dane approached the left side of the car while Koa went right. Jace stayed at the rear. All of them had their weapons drawn. Dane crouched low and peered into the window.

"Nothing here," Jace called. He was checking out the backseat.

The brain matter and blood were splattered against the driver's seat and windshield. The window was blown out, presumably by the bullet. The dead man's head hung forward, but his white ponytail was sticking up. There was a small hole on the right side of his head and a larger one on the left side. Someone had shot him from the passenger seat, or at the very least, leaning in the passenger window.

"It's definitely Lawrence, although I can only tell because

of the ponytail." Dane took a step back. The smell was getting to him. "How long do you think he's been here?"

Koa shrugged. "Sitting in the sun with the rest of the windows up has gotta speed up decomp, but I'd still guess he's been there a while. Overnight maybe? What do you want to do?"

Dane swore. What he wanted to do was forget he saw this and head to the hospital to see Mac. He'd been trying to keep thoughts of her out of his head all day, but this just brought it back like a sucker punch to the gut. This so easily could have been her.

Dane told Koa, "Call Cain and fill him in. I'll call Manu and get him to put me in contact with one of the CGIS agents."

Koa nodded and pulled out his phone.

Jace frowned. "Manu is about to get a hard lesson in life if he has to see this one. Let's keep him away if we can."

Dane nodded. "He doesn't need to be involved." He hit redial on his cell. Typical of Jace to think of Manu. Jace had a big heart and tended to want to take care of the world. "Manu," Dane said. "Yeah, we found him."

"Is he okay?" The anxiety in Manu's voice was palpable.

"Give your phone to one of the special agents. I know it's Saturday and everyone isn't in, but pick whoever you think is good."

"Is he dead? Ohmygosh. How'd he die?"

"Manu," Dane said in a calm but firm voice. "Just do as I asked."

"Yes, sir."

He heard all kinds of rustling noises and then the sound of the stairwell door. The echo of footsteps and panicked breathing was next, and then the sound of another door opening. There was another thirty seconds of silence and then a few murmurs.

"Hello? This is Special Agent Danny Collins. Who is this?"

"Collins, this is Chief Petty Officer Dane Landry. We found Quinten Lawrence. He's parked over at the port."

"What the hell is he doing there? We've been trying to reach him."

Too late. Dane tried not to sigh. "He has a good excuse for not picking up. He's dead."

"Shit." There was a beat and then, "Where are you exactly?"

He gave Collins their location and told him they'd wait. He hung up and looked at Koa. "What did Cain say?"

"He cursed a lot and then said get to the hospital ASAP. They'll have dinner, and we can discuss our next move."

Within seven minutes a half dozen cars pulled up and screeched to a stop about forty feet away. A squat redheaded guy got out of the first car and hurried forward. "Which one of you is Landry?" he asked.

"I am." Dane stepped forward.

The redhead came over and offered a hand. "Collins." He let go of Dane's hand and walked around to the front of the car. "Shit," he said and got pale underneath his tan.

"By the looks of things, someone was in the passenger seat when they shot him."

"Yeah," he said, but he was distracted by checking over the scene.

Dane, Jace, and Koa stood back for about twenty minutes and let the agents get on with their work until Dane had had enough and moved forward. "Collins."

The agent looked up and walked over.

"We have places to be. Can you take our statement so we can go?"

Collins' brow pinched in irritation at being directed, and Dane was sure he was about to say something about not caring how long Dane's team had to wait, when another car pulled up and Cross got out. He was wearing the same look as when he came to the hangar. A white shirt with rolled-up sleeves. Everyone stopped and looked.

"Deputy Director Cross," Collins said as he walked over to the other man.

Great. Now they'd be here forever. Dane turned on his heel and walked back over to Koa and Jace. "Let's go."

Jace raised his eyebrows. "But they didn't take our statements yet."

Koa snorted. "They'll keep us here for hours at this rate. I'm with him. Let's just move away slowly and get in the Jeep and split. It's not like we can tell them much anyway."

Jace flashed a grin. "Is that what you're going with? We don't know anything. Seriously? We know a lot more than they do."

"Yeah, but they don't know that, and it will take them a while to figure it out. The longer they're working, the longer they stay out of our way."

Jace shrugged. "Fair point."

They moved back a bit at a time, making it seem like they were getting out of everyone's way. Then they just turned and walked to the Jeep. A minute later, they were headed off Sand Island. Dane knew there would be hell to pay but he needed to see Mac. Needed to know she was alright.

"The food smells good. I'm starving," Jace said as they entered the room.

"Fish and chips," Tac called.

Koa walked over to Tac, who handed him a container. "Salad with baked white fish. Should go down okay."

"Thanks." Koa took the food and grabbed one of the extra chairs someone had brought in.

Dane had stopped at the doorway, the anxiety washing away had planted his feet. Mac looked good. A hell of a lot better than when they'd put her in the ambulance. He wanted to go over and give her a hug but knew that was a bad idea.

He settled for offering her a smile. "How are you feeling?"

"Much better," she said. "My head doesn't hurt as much, and Cass has been keeping me safe, so I'm all good."

He nodded. He knew it looked weird that he was still standing at the door, but his relief at seeing her was so great he was having a hard time getting his knees to work. Stupid, but there it was.

"Cain," he called.

The other man got up and walked over to Dane. "What's up?"

"So, I might have caused a problem."

Cain cocked an eyebrow.

"No one wanted to take our statement and then Deputy Director Cross showed up, so we weren't going to be getting out of there anytime soon. I made the decision that we leave. They can track us down later. We don't know anything about the murder, so there was no point in hanging around."

Cain smirked. "Let me guess. You had other things on your mind." He cut his eyes toward Mac.

"Maybe." Was it that obvious?

"Don't worry. I'll run interference. We didn't tell Mac about Lawrence. You up for it?"

Dane gave a curt nod. He hated doing this kind of thing, but someone had to, and he'd rather she heard it from him. He walked over and took a seat by the bed. "Mac," he said quietly.

The others in the room sensed what was coming so they all stepped away, giving him and Mac a bit of privacy.

Mac frowned. "What is it?"

"We found Lawrence. I'm sorry, there's no easy way to say this. He's dead."

She stared at him owlishly, chewing her lip for a beat, then, "Huh. I guess I'm not surprised. It's not like him to completely disappear when there's action. He likes to be in the middle of things. Where'd you find him?"

"At the port, next to some containers. He'd been shot in the head while sitting in his car." He tried to gauge her reaction, but she seemed neutral.

"He loved that car. Always said he wanted to be buried in it. I guess he sort of got his wish."

Dane cocked an eyebrow. "You okay?"

She met his gaze. "I wasn't Casper's biggest fan. I don't think he deserved to die, but at the same time, I won't be crying over his loss. He was involved in this thing up to his ears. It caught up to him."

The rest of the team seemed to understand that Mac was fine, and they all got settled in chairs around the room once again. Dane went over, closed the door, and then took the chair closest to the bed. Tac handed him his meal.

"So, what do we know?" Cain asked as he waved a French fry.

"Someone is cleaning house." Dane popped a piece of fish into his mouth, chewed quickly, and swallowed.

Mac was lifting her soda but halted halfway to her lips. "What do you mean?"

"It's really the only thing that makes any sense." Dane stared at his Styrofoam container. "Owens does something, and someone kills him. It seems to have kicked off a chain reaction. We know Casper was involved, and now he's dead. Someone tried to kill Mac. Loose ends."

"But how am I a loose end? I don't know what the hell is going on." Her forehead wrinkled, and the small lines around her eyes looked much deeper than they had yesterday.

Getting blown up will do that to you. Dane shook his head. "I'm not saying you're involved. I think someone believes you know something, or *could* know something, and they don't want to take any chances."

"But I really don't know anything." She looked around the room.

"Dane's right." Koa threw his empty container in the trash can. "You probably don't even know you know it, but someone cleaning house is the only thing that makes sense. I also think it's probably because of the last deal."

Cass frowned. "How did you leap to that conclusion?"

"Those motherboards will be worth a fortune. Whoever sold them made a killing, pardon the gallows' humor. He's cleaning house and shutting down his operation."

Mac asked, "What motherboards?"

Cain glared at Koa, who immediately froze.

Dane swallowed his food. *Shit.* He'd totally forgotten Mac wasn't in the loop on that one. He winced.

Cain sighed. "Part of what was stolen from the Navy were motherboards for missiles." He went back to eating his fish.

Mac looked at Dane and raised an eyebrow, but he sure as shit wasn't taking the bait. No details would come from him.

So she asked instead, "Do you think we should warn Tom Rutledge? He's part of the team. Maybe they think he knows something, too."

Dane shook his head. "Someone would have already tried to take him out if they saw him as a threat. Look at the timeline. Owens is killed Thursday night. Friday night they set up to take you out, only you don't open the door. Lawrence wasn't so lucky. I would guess he's been dead since last night. So, if Rutledge was on the list, they would've taken him out by now, or at least tried to. Besides, I'm sure your friends at CGIS have thought of this and will be all over him."

"They aren't here trying to protect me," Mac pointed out.

"True, but people have been in and out all day, and Cass has been here. If they were going to make another try for you, it would be tonight." That thought clanged like a claxon in Dane's head. What were they going to do about that?

"Which means we need to move you," Tac said. "It's the smart play."

"Agreed." Cain stood and stretched. "We'll sort that out in a second. First, Finn Walsh sent satellite images. Jace, can you bring them up on the laptop?"

Jace dropped his empty container into the trash and hauled a laptop out of a backpack that Cain and Tac had brought. A minute later, they were all gathered around Jace and the laptop.

"Excuse me?" Mac called from the bed. "Are you going to share?"

Cain studied her.

"You should know that Deputy Director Cross kicked me off the case. He actually put me on leave. I didn't have a choice. I can't help you with anything officially, nor can I say anything to anyone else officially either."

Dane knew immediately she was angry. He'd be pissed too. Being taken off the case made logical sense, but it hurt. Some asshole wants her dead. She didn't want to be out of the fight. He knew exactly what that felt like.

Cain nodded to Jace. He moved the laptop over to Mac's bed, and they all moved to surround Mac. Jace pulled up the satellite images.

"There's Owens," Jace said.

"Can you zoom in at all?" Cain asked.

Jace zoomed in as much as he could. "Owens is on his boat and alive at oh-one-forty-five." He continued to click through the images.

"There." Dane pointed at the screen. The bow of a boat could be seen. In the next shot, the second boat was beside Owens. "Jace—"

"I'm zooming." The image of the second boat got bigger. "Two people," Jace confirmed.

"I can't make out any details. No way to recognize them." Dane cursed under his breath. He had been hopeful this would have given them something to work with. They flicked through the pictures. The two men boarded Owens's boat. The next image showed all three of them together. The shot after that had only one man on Owens's boat. Then there were two people and a lump. Dane said, "Must be Owens, already dead on the floor of his boat."

"Yeah. Looks like it," Jace agreed.

In the last shot, there was just one man on the boat again and nothing else. "There are no more. The satellite moved out of range."

Koa grunted. "That was disappointing."

Everyone moved back to their seats, Jace taking the laptop with him. "At least we know we were right. A second boat came, and we know there's two people involved."

Dane knew by the way Jace was moving that his knee was hurting him. Dane dug into his pocket and brought out what was fast becoming the community bottle of Advil. He tossed it over. Jace caught it and nodded his thanks.

"Two people," Mac murmured. "It could be members of Owens's team but, honestly, I don't think they would have done it. According to Rutledge, they're all afraid of being next."

"Do you trust Rutledge?" Dane asked.

She paused. "I… I don't know." She sighed. "Regardless,

what I was going to say was, they would've known better than to hang him on the anchor chain by the shipping lanes."

"She's right," Cain said. "If it were us, what would we do?"

Dane stretched his legs straight out in front of him and crossed his ankles, trying to find a more comfortable position. The hard hospital chairs sucked balls. "I would meet him, kill him, take the boat much farther out, and then wrap him in chains with weights and drop him over the side, making sure that the currents weren't heading toward land. Then I would scuttle the boat."

"Exactly," Mac said. "And remind me never to be alone on a boat with you," she added with a tight grin. "That was pretty fast. Been thinking about that for a while, have you?"

He shrugged. "Let's just say I might've imagined it a time or two." He winked at her.

"What does the ME's report say?" Cass asked.

Jace pulled it up. "Finn Walsh is super-sonic fast."

Cain nodded. "He's good people."

"Uh…he was shot. Nine-millimeter. Dead before he was in the water. Throat was slit after death, so were his wrists, and there was a slash across the chest as well," Jace read.

"So why the anchor chain?" Cass asked.

"The two on the boat can't be trained killers or spec op either," Koa stated. "My guess? They slashed him and hung him there thinking it would attract sharks and other predators, thinking he would get eaten."

Dane nodded. "Only once the heart stops, no blood gets pumped. It would have pooled in his feet. Only a small bit would be released into the water. Plus, we found him way too soon. If he'd have been much farther out, it could've worked. Or, at least, he would have possibly decomposed before anyone found him.

"Owens wasn't stupid. I think he knew his partners, or

bosses, or whoever didn't know about the shipping lanes and how busy they are. He probably thought there would be more traffic so when he met whoever, there would be more protection. If it did go sideways, he knew he had a better possibility of being found sooner rather than later."

Mac frowned. "You think he planned for his death?"

Dane ran a hand over the back of his neck. "I don't think 'planned' is the right word. I think he thought he had the situation under control, but he was hedging his bets in case he didn't."

"All this gets us no further in the investigation into the motherboards," Tac said. He flexed the fingers on his right hand.

Dane caught Jace's eye and nodded toward Tac. Jace offered Tac the Advil, but he shook his head. Dane knew Tac's right hand bothered him sometimes, but he didn't know the extent of the injury.

"Did you guys learn anything today at the drone festival?" Cain asked. "We've all been a bit distracted."

Dane filled them in on what the two young dudes they'd found had said. "So, all we really know is that he goes by TigerKing."

"You mean like the guy who collects exotic animals?" Mac asked.

Dane shrugged. "I guess. I have no idea what it refers to, just that it's the name he used."

"Is there any way to track that down?" Cain asked.

"The payment was in crypto." Jace shrugged. "So…no. I can try and track his online presence, but I think it's a long shot."

Mac took the last sip of her soda. "Do you want me to ask Manu?"

"No," Cain said. "Let's leave the kid alone for now. I'm guessing he's going to tell his boss about finding Casper on the equipment room video now, and that's going to lead to all kinds of questions for all of us. Let's not involve him any more than necessary. We have more pressing matters to deal with."

"Like?" Tac asked.

Dane answered, "Like protecting Mac. She's our only lead at this point. We can't let anything happen to her."

Cain stood. "Exactly. Tac, go talk to the doctor, and the nursing staff and let them know we don't want anyone in the room all night. Threaten them if you have to. We need this room locked down."

"Roger that." Tac got up and left the room.

"Cass, can you go get Mac some clothes? Make sure you get receipts, and you'll get reimbursed."

Cass nodded. "Leave it with me." She shot Mac a smile. "I know just where to go."

Mac frowned. "Um, I just need some underwear, jeans, and T-shirts. Er, maybe some shoes."

"I got you. No worries," Cass said and started across the room.

"Don't you need my sizes?" Mac asked.

Cass tossed her head back and laughed as she walked out.

"Somehow I do not feel reassured about Cass shopping for me," she grumbled.

Dane grinned. "Could be worse. Could be one of us."

Mac chuckled then winced. "Valid point."

"When Cass is back, we're going to move you." Cain glanced at his cell. "Jace, secure a hotel. I think the Kahala will work."

"Roger that," Jace said and left the room.

"I've gotta go make some calls. See what I can find out. I'll be back shortly." Cain strode out of the room.

Dane looked at Mac. "How are you holding up?"

She started to say something and then shrugged. "Surprisingly well, to be honest. Mostly, I am just pissed off. Cross taking me off the case is so damned annoying. He blamed it on Senator Weston's presence, but he did it to cover his own ass. It's beyond frustrating to know someone is out there trying to kill me, and there's not a damn thing I can do about it." She shook her head.

"Tell me about it," Dane said. He knew exactly what she was going through.

She met his gaze. "Shit. Sorry. I forgot."

"No apology needed."

"The file on your accident is in my bag still. I guess we'll have lots of time to go over it now. Fill in the blanks. I hate having loose ends."

He smiled. "Thanks." He was glad she'd trusted him enough to bring it. Mostly, he was just glad she was okay. Seeing her lying there covered in debris had just about done him in. He didn't want to think about what could have happened. Not just to her, but to all of them.

He cleared his throat. "Why is Weston really here? Did Cross mention it?"

She shook her head slowly, as if afraid she'd scramble her brains. "According to Ainsley, it's an unofficial visit before he goes to Asia on an 'official' visit. I have no idea what that means."

"It means," Jace said as he walked back into the room, "Weston is here for some free publicity before he heads to Singapore. He's holding some talks there with other Asian countries, ostensibly to discuss the whole Taiwan issue, but it's just a PR stunt. Singapore backs China on the one-state thing, so they won't support the US view on Taiwan. Weston is up for re-election. He's just trying to get into the news."

"Look at you being all up on politics," Dane said.

Jace grinned. "Had lots of time to read when my knee

was healing. Kinda got hooked. Anyway, the hotel is set. I'll go see how Tac is doing." He walked out again.

"Let's make sure we get you organized. Where's your bag?"

She glanced around the room. "That's a good question…"

"Where is the last time you saw it?" he asked.

"It's in your SUV. I left it in there when we went to my place this morning. I should've given it to you last night. I guess I just got…distracted."

He liked the way her cheeks turned pink when she said it. "Yes, last night was a bit…distracting." He gave her a wicked smile. "When this is all over—"

The door burst open, and Cain stormed in. "We need to move her now. There's a whole contingent of CGIS agents in the parking lot, and they're on their way in. We'll never get her out of here if they get a hold of her. There are going to be questions about last night's search and about Casper. They might even think we're crooked as well since we didn't share anything."

Dane was on his feet. He looked at Mac. "It's up to you. Us or them?"

Cain arched a brow. "Tom Rutledge is in the lead."

Mac tossed a look between Dane and Cain. "Find me some clothes."

CHAPTER FIFTEEN

Tac walked into the room amid all the chaos. "What's happening?" he demanded.

"CGIS are on their way in. We need to get her out of here pronto." Dane opened the closet door, looking for any clothing to put her in. "Nothing."

"I'll get her some scrubs." Cain hustled out.

"Is there any way to slow them down?" Dane asked.

Tac shrugged. "The doc agreed to put her on a no-visitors list. It might slow them a bit."

Mac racked her brain, but no quick solution was coming to her. Her headache had lessened, but honest to God it hurt to think. "We might just have to make a run for it," she offered.

Dane nodded. "Tac, bring your truck to the side entrance. We'll go down the stairs and meet you. Text me when you're in place."

"Got it," Tac said and hurried out of the room.

"Are you sure about this?" Dane asked.

"Yes. There's no point in staying and talking to them. I have a feeling it will just jam me up. I'd rather apologize than ask permission. Cross made it clear I was on leave so, technically, I'm on vacation."

Cain burst into the room with a set of scrubs. Mac got off the bed a bit too quickly and almost fell over.

Dane grabbed her and pulled her to his chest. "You okay?"

"Yeah. Just moved too fast after lying around all day. I'll be fine." She took the scrubs and hustled into the bathroom. She leaned against the closed door for a second. Did she really want to do this? It could be the end of her career at CGIS. On the other hand, who could blame her for trusting the team that had kept her alive when members of her own team were dropping like flies?

She got out of her hospital gown and pulled on the green scrubs. She didn't have shoes but hopefully no one would notice. She glanced at herself in the mirror and squeaked. She looked like shit. Her hair was sticking up in all directions from her ponytail. There were still smudges of dirt on her face, and her skin was nearly transparent. *That's what they mean when they say pale as a ghost.* She desperately craved a shower but that would have to wait. She took a towel off the rack and wet a corner under the tap. Thirty seconds later, she'd scrubbed her face clean. She fixed her hair as best she could and then went back out into the room.

"Let's go," Dane said.

Cain opened the door and checked the hallway. "Clear."

The trio exited the room and turned right. They moved swiftly along the hallway until they came to the stairwell. Cain hit the door and then started down. They were halfway down the first flight when a door below them opened.

"She's on the fourth floor."

It was Rutledge's voice. She wiped her slick palms on her scrubs.

Dane grabbed her arm and swung her around and then

helped her back up the stairs. They went past the fourth floor and got out on the fifth. They stood in the hallway while Cain kept watch on the heavy fire door.

There was a quiet buzz and then Dane said, "Tac is in place downstairs. Side entry."

Cain gave a slight nod. He had the door open just a crack. A minute later, he said, "Now," and they raced down the stairs again.

She went as fast as she could but knew it would have been faster if Dane had just picked her up. They hit the bottom and burst into the hallway. "The emergency room is closer," Dane said and immediately sent a text to Tac with the change in plans. They moved swiftly past the nurses' station and out through the doors to the ambulance bay. As they neared the end of the driveway as Tac pulled up. Dane helped her in and followed her into the back seat. Cain was riding shotgun. Tac took off before the doors were even closed.

They were out of the parking lot and on the highway in what seemed like seconds. Tac settled lower in the driver's seat, trying to look casual, not at all like they were stealing her away to keep her safe.

"Now what do we do?" she asked.

Cain was typing furiously on his cell. "We're going have to ditch all cell phones. Cass will pick them up and take them back to the hangar before meeting us. She'll grab a few burner phones on her way to meet us." He pulled the pillowcase off the pillow. "Turn 'em off and put them in this. We'll leave it in the stairwell and Cass can get it there."

Dane did as he was told, and Cain added his own and Tac's.

"I have no idea where my cell even is," she said.

"I picked it up. It's in my SUV," Dane said.

"ETA is about forty minutes in this traffic," Tac informed them.

Mac's head hurt a bit. "Where are we going?"

"The Kahala. It's a nice hotel. There are dolphins," Dane supplied.

"Why do we want a hotel with dolphins?" she asked.

Dane smirked. "We don't care about the dolphins. We care about the families and the lovely family rooms. They have suites with two bedrooms attached to one foyer. The outside door opens to the hallway, but we can open or close the bedroom doors as we need. It gives us space to work that's not far from downtown but far enough away from Sand Island. We have stuff to figure out. No one is going to look for us at the Kahala."

She leaned back against the cushiony seat back, overwhelmed by the last ten minutes. *Had it only been ten?* Her recall of the rush to clear the hospital room strobed like old-school flash bulbs…jarring, jerky and bright. She blinked hard to clear the sensation and focused on the next forty minutes of her life.

It made sense to be where families were. Not that they wanted to bring danger to anyone else, but chances were excellent no one would look for them at a family hotel. She wasn't even sure why they were running. *Rutledge.* He just wanted answers, didn't he? She'd told him about the apartment. He must have seen the stuff she'd confiscated from Owens' locker. She'd left it on her desk, so it should be fine. She shouldn't have broken into Candyland, but considering what was going on with Casper, she figured she'd be forgiven for that. And she'd been blown up. Surely, she would get a pass on a ton of shit just for that.

She hadn't told anyone about Casper and the GPS tracker because…well, in truth, doing so would call a lot of attention to the fact that she broke into Owens's apartment.

She sighed heavily. She was spit-balling, making sure she could cover her ass, which was sad. She should have stayed in the hospital room and waited for Rutledge.

But did she want to answer any questions? Who could she trust? That's what it came down to. Rutledge was on her team, and she *thought* he was a good guy…but she didn't trust him completely. No, truth be told, she didn't trust anyone in CGIS at this point. No one tried to blow Rutledge up, so maybe he was one of them. Maybe he'd been on that boat when Owens was killed. Maybe he'd done the dirty deed. Likely, he wouldn't know anything about shipping lanes. Then again, he was a scuba diver, so there was that as well.

She ran a hand over her face. Almost anyone fit the bill at the moment. TigerKing. Seriously. Who would— She jerked upright.

"What is it?" Dane asked as he stared at her with narrowed eyes.

"TigerKing."

"What about it?"

"Deputy Director John Bishop Cross graduated from Princeton University. He was the quarterback on their football team. The Princeton *Tigers*. He has pictures on the wall in his office."

Dane stared. "You think Cross could be the TigerKing?"

"It fits, sort of, at least, the name does. He wouldn't know where the shipping lanes were, but he'd certainly know how to get stuff smuggled into Hawai'i."

"But didn't he tell all of you guys about the Navy's missing weapons? Why would he do that if he was the one smuggling them?" Cain asked.

"Cover?" She thought back to his little talk. "And a way to control the flow of information. He brought us all upstairs and told us that the Navy thing was a big secret, so big that he didn't want anything done in writing. Everyone was to work on it but only tell him if they found a lead. He said that emails weren't secure enough. He even had the floor swept for bugs and took all our cell phones to a separate floor before the meeting."

Dane leaned back in the seat. "That does sound strange."

"Sounds like someone is definitely trying to control the narrative," Cain agreed. "He could be the one we're after, but we need proof. We have to find the motherboards."

"Do you think they are still on Oahu?" Mac asked. "Wouldn't they be gone as quickly as possible?"

"Maybe," Dane said. "Or maybe not. Depends on who he is selling them to. If it were me, I'd want to make the sale as quickly as possible, then the buyer has to get them out, and it's no longer the seller's problem."

"Coming up on the hotel," Tac said as they drove down a quiet, tree-lined street.

"We're not going in through the lobby." Dane smiled at her. "You'll look a little out of place. You and I are going through the restaurant and will enter from the back side."

She looked down at her scrubs. They weren't wrong. "Okay."

Ten minutes later, she was sitting on the bed of a large room that had a window overlooking the dolphins' pool. The beach and ocean lay just beyond the man-made lagoon. The king-sized bed was decorated with a comforter with large colorful flowers. There was enough space for a sofa at the other end of the room along with a chair and a coffee table. The furniture was done in shades of blue that matched the pictures on the wall.

The bathroom was off to the left of the bed. She'd used the facilities as soon as they'd gotten into the room. The massive, marble-tiled bathroom featured a separate shower and a whirlpool tub. Under other circumstances, she'd have been thrilled to be here. A weekend getaway with Dane… She swallowed. *Stupid idea.* What happened to never getting involved with someone she worked with again? She needed to keep reminding herself of that, but the kiss had just been so…good. It had been a while since she'd kissed someone like that. She couldn't even remember the last time.

"You okay?" Dane asked.

"Wh—what? Sorry, I was daydreaming."

"I asked if you want to take a shower."

"Love to, but I need clothes to put on." She wasn't getting out of the shower, only to spend a lot of time wearing nothing but a bathrobe or, worse, a towel.

"Cass is going to be here in about fifteen minutes, so if you want to hop in, you'll have clothes by the time you're getting out."

"Thank God. I am desperate for a shower." She stood up and wobbled slightly.

He was there immediately, steadying her with his hands on her waist. "Are you sure you're okay?"

She winced. "Yeah. I'm just a little woozy. I think I'm dehydrated. I'll drink some water and be okay. Do you happen to have any of that Advil left?"

"Do you still have a headache?" Concern was written all over his face.

"A touch, but it's more the bruises. My shoulder and arm hurt from being smacked into the wall."

"Right. I'll get them from Jace. Why don't you get in the shower, and I'll bring them when you're finished?"

"Sounds good. Thanks." She stared up at him, reluctant to move. She liked his hands on her waist. Having him close made her feel safe.

He finally dropped his hands and moved away. "Let me know if you need anything," he said as he walked toward the door. "We have the outside door to the hallway double-locked and bolted. The two rooms share a foyer. I'm going to close your room door, but we're right next door and I'll leave our door open. You don't even have to go out into the hallway to get to us, okay?"

"Thanks." She smiled at him and then faced the mirror and grimaced. She really needed a shower, for more reasons than one.

The hot spray stung as it sluiced over the abrasions on her back. She winced but stuck it out. The heat relaxed her back muscles and she let the spray continue to soothe her body. Dane popped into her mind. It must be tough having his back seized up all the time. Just this bruising was killing her. She couldn't imagine having a broken vertebra and dealing with the fallout of it.

She gently lathered the shampoo into her hair and steered her thoughts away from the sexy Coastie and back to the bigger issue.

Why? Why kill her? What did she know that she didn't realize was important? She could not come up with one thing. Owens sold drugs and some sort of motherboards to someone. Then he went out to sea, specifically to the shipping lanes and got killed. How was she supposed to know who did it?

She rinsed her hair and then worked in conditioner. Could it really be Cross? She let the spray wash down over her face. Yeah, it could be Cross. He was ambitious enough to want more and cutthroat enough to kill Owens if he thought the man posed a threat. Yeah, she could easily see that happening, but then why kill Casper as well? Was he just Cross's lackey? The painful thrumming in her head accelerated as she continued fretting.

And how did Cross end up here? A Deputy Director in Oahu? Wouldn't it be better to be where everything happened? So why had Cross been sidelined to Hawai'i? Or was it a more important posting than she thought?

She rinsed off one last time and stepped out of the shower. While toweling herself off, she discovered a few more aches and bruises. Black and blue were going to be her colors for the next while. She put on the robe that hung on the back of the door and wrapped her hair in a towel. After opening the bathroom door, she stepped out into the room. The bed was covered in clothing, all different colors and styles of tops and bottoms.

"Whoa! Cass knows her stuff." Mac picked up a pair of light sweats that were gray and a deep green T-shirt. A bag beside the bed held underwear sets. She pulled out a lacy deep green bra with a matching thong. They were soft and clean and just what she wanted.

Mac quickly got dressed and then found toiletries at the bottom of the bag of underwear. She combed out her hair, and then walked into the bedroom next door.

Dane looked over as she entered. His eyes roamed over her as if checking to make sure she was okay. She gave him a little nod then checked him out in return. He was still wearing his jeans and T-shirt from earlier today. The T-shirt set off his eyes. He was incredibly sexy even when he was tired. She needed to rein in her overactive libido and focus on something else. "Anyone have a tea bag? I could use a cup of tea."

Koa flicked on the kettle on the desk next to him. "I just made a cup. There's still water in the kettle."

"Thanks." She looked at the bed where the laptop was open. "What are we looking at?"

Cain gestured. "The autopsy on Casper."

"It's back already?" she asked as she approached the bed. "Wait, how did you get it?"

No one said anything.

"Right. Forget I asked. Does it tell us anything important?"

"No," Dane said. "Nothing we didn't know. He was killed by a bullet to the head. Nine-millimeter, same as Owens. Time of death was somewhere between midnight and oh-two-thirty."

"He was killed this morning then." She let out a breath. "Where does that leave us?"

"No-fucking-where," Koa groused as he poured water into the mug with a tea bag. "We've got nothing. No lead other than the name TigerKing. And you."

"And me." Her stomach knotted. "I've been thinking about it, and I just can't come up with why they would want to kill me. I've got nothing." Her shoulders sagged. She hated that she couldn't supply an answer. She was an investigator, after all. It was her job to find answers.

"Don't worry about it. It's been a long day for all of us," Cain said. "I think we all should get some sleep. Mac, you'll stay here with Dane and Cass. Tac, Jace, Koa, and I will alternate keeping watch. We have another room that gives us a view of the front of the hotel, and someone will watch the beach as well. We'll sleep in shifts."

Mac nodded absently. Even though she'd been lying in bed most of the day, her body was exhausted. It was only eight o'clock, but she still thought she could go to bed and sleep. "I think I'm gonna head over to my room. Thanks, guys." She smiled at them. "Seriously, you guys saved my life today. I owe you."

"Forget it. Part of the job," Koa said and then headed out of the suite.

"What he said," Tac mumbled as he and Jace followed Koa. Jace gave her a little nod.

"Well, I'm not shy. Damn straight, you owe me. Shopping isn't for the weak!" Cass said with a wide grin splashed across her face.

"I owe *you* big time." Mac ran a hand down her new gray sweatpants. "Great choices."

"I know my way around clothes." Cass yawned suddenly. "I'm gonna grab a shower and then sleep for a few hours. Dane, are you okay taking the first shift?"

He nodded. "No worries. Rest up, Cass."

"'Night, Cass," Mac said as she went to the foyer. Dane and Cain were behind her. Dane had her cross-shoulder bag. "Thanks for getting my bag."

"No worries. I did take your cell though. We left all the phones at the hangar as a precaution."

Mac nodded. It made sense but it also reminded her that she was in a serious mess. "I can't thank you guys enough," she reiterated. "I'm not sure what kind of trouble you're gonna get into, but I appreciate everything you've done to keep me safe."

Cain snorted. "We haven't done much. We got you blown up. Besides, we're not the ones who are going to get into trouble. By siding with us, you put yourself in the crosshairs of your department. I can't imagine your partner, Rutledge, is going to take too kindly to any of this."

"No, I suppose not. But when you look at it from my point of view, how do I know who I can trust?"

"Agreed," Cain said. "You're between a rock and a hard place. The most you can do is try to get some sleep. We'll take a fresh run at everything in the morning. Hopefully, something will pop then. I have Jace working on a special project that, with any luck, will result in a solid lead. See you in the morning." Cain exited the foyer to the hall and Mac went into her room. Dane leaned on the door jamb to her room.

She held up the bag.

"It's weird to think this is the only thing I own that hasn't been blown up or soaked with water."

He touched her arm. "Don't worry, you'll be able to replace everything. It's just stuff."

He was right but, for the time being, her whole world was reduced to one cross-body bag. It made her heart lurch in her chest. "Wanna stay for a bit? I'm not sure I'm quite ready to sleep." Yes, her body was exhausted, but her mind was buzzing.

Dane winced as he sat down on the sofa.

"Your back again?"

"Yeah. It's just been a long couple of days. I was mostly covered today, so I didn't bear the brunt of the blast like you did, but it was enough to inflame things."

"Stand up," she said. He needed some help, and she was going to give it whether he liked it or not.

He narrowed his eyes at her but stood slowly.

"Come over here." She pointed to the floor in front of her. "I want to show you some stretches."

He reluctantly came and stood in front of her. She turned him around and then pointed to the mirror in front of them that was over the sofa. "See how your right shoulder is slightly higher than your left? It's also slightly more forward." She turned him sideways and kept her hands on his waist. "Your ear should line up with your shoulder and hip." She met his gaze in the mirror. "You are out of alignment."

A slow, sexy smile spread across his face. "In all kinds of ways, I'm sure."

The smile made her pulse tick up a bit. "You need a foam roller to roll your back and loosen up the muscles. You should also do some exercises to loosen your pelvis. You're tight." She was trying to focus on his body to help him with the pain, but the feel of the firm muscles under his clothes was exciting her. She itched to touch his skin. Maybe this wasn't such a good idea.

She took a step back. "So, one of the stretches you can do is to roll down and up, one vertebra at a time." She bent forward at the waist, putting her hands on the floor, and almost groaned out loud. Her body was tight, too, and it did not appreciate the speed at which she dropped her head. She wobbled.

Dane twisted around and caught her hips.

She came back up slowly, still slightly woozy.

"Maybe you should wait a little while to show me this stuff. You've been through a lot today."

He still had his hands on her hips, and she was leaning into him. Her hands went to his chest as if they had a life of their own. She met his gaze and parted her lips. She really wanted to kiss him. She wanted more than that, but she'd start with a kiss. She leaned up and brushed his lips with hers.

"Mac," he breathed. "Not sure this is a great idea."

"It's not, but like you said, I've been through a lot today. I can blame my poor decision-making on being blown up."

She went up on her tiptoes and brushed his lips again with a little more force this time. His eyes had turned a deeper blue as his hands tightened on her hips.

"What do I blame my poor decision-making on?" he asked as he studied her lips.

"You were being chivalrous and giving the lady what she wants." She ran her hands up his chest and around his back. He had such broad shoulders and strong arms.

"What do you want, Mac?" His voice was low, and it sent shivers across her skin.

She met his gaze once more. "You."

CHAPTER SIXTEEN

Dane struggled to draw a calming breath. He'd wanted Mac from the first moment on the deck of the cargo ship when he'd spied her swinging hips and ponytail. She'd been front and center in his fantasies. And now she wanted him.

It was wrong.

Bad timing.

Stupid timing but, damn, if he didn't want her too.

He'd give her an out.

"Mac, this is...not...good." That wasn't what he meant to say. This was fucking fantastic, but it wasn't smart. "I mean not smart."

She smiled at him. "I know. Seriously, Dane, I know. I've done stupid, and this is it, but I got blown up today, and when I came to on that stretcher, you were there, and I promised myself if I got out of this, I was going to have you, if for no other reason than I want you. I don't want a relationship. I've dated at work before, and it ended in a nightmare. I don't want to walk down that road again, but I cheated death today—*we* cheated death—and I think that requires a bit of celebration."

He wanted to be the kind of man who was strong enough to turn her down for moral reasons, but…there was just no way he was missing the opportunity to have Mac. She was smart, funny, and sexy. But more than that, he admired her greatly—her strength, her perseverance, her courage over the last couple of days. *God, was that how long he'd known her? Felt like she'd always been in his life.* She was everything he looked for in a woman.

He tangled his fingers in her hair and kissed her hard on the mouth. She answered by wrapping her arms around his back and bringing her hips to his. Their tongues danced, creating the best kind of friction. He cupped her ass and brought her closer, rubbing his swelling hard-on against her pelvis.

She let out a soft moan and ran her hands under his shirt. Her touch burned like fire, but he wanted it everywhere all at once. He reached back with one hand and pulled his T-shirt over his head. He dropped it onto the floor and pulled her in again, recapturing her mouth in a scorching kiss.

Mac ran her hands over his chest and then dropped them to his belt buckle. She undid his buckle and his jeans' button.

"No," he growled. "Not yet." He spun their bodies around and walked her backward to the bed, where he laid her down.

She pulled off her T-shirt and dropped it off the side of the bed.

He stared at her breasts in the lacy deep-green bra. Unbelievably perfect. "You are so fucking beautiful." He brought his weight slowly down on top of her as he pulled the cup to the side and covered her left nipple with his mouth.

She arched beneath him as he drew the taut peak deep.

He swirled his tongue around her nipple again and again until she speared her fingers into his hair and whispered his name. It sounded like heaven on her lips, and it touched a part of him that he hadn't realized existed. A fierce wave of protectiveness washed over him. He'd do everything he could to keep her safe. To make her happy. To make her his.

He took off her bra and nipped at the right nipple, causing her hips to jerk hard. He kissed down her chest, along her belly, as he pushed her sweatpants over her hips. She wiggled out of them. He sat back on his haunches to relish the vision before him of Mac lying there, her blond hair splayed over the pillow, her full breasts like beautiful mounds with pebbled peaks, and the dark green thong against her tanned skin. She was so captivating and sexy.

"You are stunning," he said in awe before lowering his mouth to hers.

She fisted his hair and deepened the kiss before she reached down and lowered his zipper. Then she stroked him through his underwear until he broke the kiss and cursed.

Her hands cupped his ass as she rubbed against him. "I want to feel you inside me."

"Not yet." He wanted to be inside her, but he wanted other things first. He bent his head to suck her nipple again just as she touched him again through the fabric of his underwear. He hissed. He couldn't help it. He wanted her touch badly, but he knew if she started, he wouldn't have the power to stop her. And he had so many things he wanted to do to her first.

He traced his mouth from one nipple and then the other. Slowly, he left a trail of kisses down her stomach to her thong. He got harder still as he ran his fingers across the lace.

When he reached the middle, he dipped his fingers lower to caress between her folds.

"Dane." Her voice was breathy, and he doubted he'd ever heard anything as sexy.

The sound of his name on her lips again created a tidal wave of fierce desire, and he quickly yanked off her thong. He blew on her clit gently. When she whispered his name again, straining her hips to reach him, he dropped a kiss on her core.

"Dane," she said again and then bit her lip. Her fingers fisted in his hair as he slid his hands under her hips to bring her to his mouth.

He used his tongue to tease and suckle her, taking her to the brink before stopping. "Say my name, Mac." He wanted her to remember who made her feel so good. He wanted it imprinted in her brain.

"Dane." It came out almost as a curse, and it made him smile. He teased her some more with his tongue, then put his fingers inside her as he blew on her clit. When she moaned, he did it again, adding more fingers. Her hips bucked. He drove his fingers inside her, faster and faster until she was breathless and begging him. He sucked her once more as her body tensed and arched, and he tasted the rush of her climax. He felt incredibly powerful and insanely protective of her. None of it was going to help him if this didn't work out, if she didn't want to see him after all this was over. Did he want to date her? He didn't know. His life was way too complicated at the moment. But none of that mattered now. He still had her at the moment, and he meant to enjoy every minute of it.

Mac had wanted Dane from the moment she'd questioned him on the deck of the cargo ship. The second he'd given her that smirk, she'd wanted to screw it off his face. And it had been better than she'd imagined. She guided him on top of her and then kissed him hard. The rugged planes of his chest against her curves fit perfectly. This man was made for her body. Those eyes were made to read her soul.

Their gazes locked as she reached down to push off his jeans and black boxer briefs. But he rose quickly off the bed and pulled them off himself, then came back to lay on top of her. He swore as she stroked her hand over his engorged dick. She loved that he was so hard for her.

She rolled him over and climbed on top of him before raining kisses down his jaw. As she ran her hands across his chest, she sucked on his nipple and then blew on it. When she did the same with the other nipple, he groaned. She loved that she had the power to make him lose control.

Her need for him was fierce, but more, it was primal. She needed him like she needed air to breathe. He was giving her sustenance. His strength, his determination, his stamina. He'd come through so much, and now he was giving her what she needed to keep going. Letting her take what she wanted with no expectation of anything else.

It made her want more. Want it all.

She knew. *Knew.* Dane Landry had somehow gotten under her skin and one time, one night, was not going to be enough.

But it had to be. She shut off her mind. Now was all about feeling. And she wanted to feel it all.

She shifted her weight until she was straddling his hips. She slowly rubbed her wet core over his cock, and he flexed up, grinding his heat against her slick folds. She raised her hips and then lowered herself down onto him. First, she just let the tip enter her. Teasing him, she pulled back.

He swore. His eyes were a midnight blue.

She lowered herself again. This time, she took in more of him. She started to pull back, but he grabbed her hips with a growl and brought her down hard on top of him. He filled her up completely, and she let out a moan. He felt so damn good inside her.

He gripped her hips to guide her to his rhythm. She rode him, picking up the pace. The way he filled her was pure pleasure. Her breath puffed out in small, sharp gasps. She was going to come. She said his name and urged him on, her hips rushing to meet his thrusts. She teetered on the brink and had to bite her lip to keep from screaming.

He drove deep inside her, and she crashed over the edge, euphoria filling her every cell.

Dane cried out as he came, "Mac!"

Her body kept squeezing him as wave after wave of her orgasm washed through her.

She fell on top of his chest, sweaty and out of breath. That had been fucking amazing. "Again," she demanded.

Dane gave a slow, sexy chuckle that rumbled out of his chest. "Absolutely. I'm here for you as many times as you want."

He rolled her over onto the bed and started kissing her neck when the sound of a cell phone filled the room. "Shit." He was off the bed and reaching for his jeans in a fraction of a second. "Landry," he said as he answered the phone.

"Yeah." When he looked at Mac, her heart stopped in her chest. His entire body stiffened slightly and his mouth firmed into a straight line. "I'll ask. Give me five." He ended the call.

"That was Cain. Tom Rutledge called Admiral Bertrand. He wants to sit down with you. The admiral passed along the message."

She stared at Dane. He was still naked. All she wanted to do was spend the rest of the night in his arms, go back to where she felt safe and secure. Happy. She swallowed. "When?"

"Now. Cain is supposed to call him back and give him a location."

She sat up, suddenly conscious of her nakedness. She dragged the coverlet over her torso. "What do you think?"

Dane clamped his jaw shut and gave a slight shake of his head. "I can't advise you on this one. It's your career. If Rutledge reached out to the admiral, then there's got to be a lot at stake."

She sighed. "So, you think I should do it."

"Hell no! I think I should take you and run like hell. Get the first plane off this rock and get you somewhere safe. But it's not up to me."

Her heart squeezed tighter in her chest. Dane cared. It was stupid for that to matter, but it did. A lot. She should be determining her future but instead, she was acting like a high schooler asked to the prom. Still, he cared, and she immediately felt stronger because of it.

"Okay, I'll meet him. But only him. Pick a spot you think will work. He'll have all the CGIS resources on his side, so choose wisely." She clambered off the bed and laid a hand on his waist. "In case you're wondering, I have no idea where that would be."

He picked up his cell and hit a button on the screen.

She dropped her hand lower and stroked him. "I want a rain check," she murmured and then headed for the bathroom.

Thirty minutes later, they were sitting at a restaurant in downtown Honolulu. The popular seafood place was packed to the gills. Mac had no idea how they managed to get a table, let alone in a quiet corner in the back.

The whole team was there, some outside to watch the street and some inside to watch the crowd. Dane and Cain sat at the table with her. She'd asked them both to stay. One, she really did feel stronger with Dane beside her, and two, she wanted Cain as a witness. If it ever came out that she was sleeping with Dane, then his statement would be discounted, so Cain had to be there as well.

"He's here. Walking in." Jace's voice sounded in her ear. He was sitting at the bar. Tac had remained out front, monitoring who came and went. Cass was renting a different SUV and then was to come back to watch the street with Tac. Mac refrained from touching her ear as she was having a bit of an issue getting used to the earbud. It wasn't something she'd used before. It was like her Air Pods only flesh-colored, and they fit differently.

Rutledge entered by the hostess stand. He asked for them presumably because the waitress pointed him back toward their table. He looked tired. Older somehow. She must look the same. Amazing what a couple of days could do.

He was wearing a T-shirt and jeans. As he approached the table, he held his hands up, making sure they were in plain sight. He wasn't a fool. She'd give him that. But what was he?

He pulled out the chair opposite her and sat down. "How are you?"

"Fine. Alive."

He stared at her. "Why did you run when I came to the hospital?"

"Seriously? Someone had just tried to kill me and you showed up with a whole team. What was I supposed to do? Sit there and wait to see if it was going to happen again?"

Rutledge reared back and held up his hands. "You're right. Sorry. I guess I was…a little heavy-handed. But Mac, I thought you trusted me."

Did she trust him? A bit. "I trusted you to a point, but then Casper was involved with Owens, and I knew you were keeping secrets of your own. It didn't seem prudent to trust you anymore."

"What do you want?" Dane demanded.

Rutledge glared at him and then refocused on Mac. "Look, I need to go over stuff with you."

"Like what?"

"The apartment. I found Owens's locker contents on your desk. I took a team over to the apartment by Waikiki Beach, but it was empty."

"Owens is dead. What did you expect to find?"

He shook his head. "No, I mean empty. Like there was nothing in it. Not one scrap of clothing, not one bit of food. Only the furniture was still there, and even then, everything had been vacuumed. There wasn't one fingerprint anywhere."

"What?" Mac stared at him. "Are you lying to me?"

"No, I swear it, Mac."

She looked at Dane. He and Cain exchanged a look and Cain shrugged. "Someone cleaned it up."

"No shit," she said. "But who?"

Dane tapped his fingers on the table. "Had to be Owens's team. It would take more than one person to clean a place that size in a short period of time."

"Wait. You were in there, too?" Rutledge demanded.

Dane didn't bother responding to the question. Instead, he asked, "Did you pull the security footage?"

"Yeah. It's been erased. The whole night was gone." Rutledge narrowed his eyes at Dane. "I assumed that was you guys."

Cain shook his head. "We erased some of it but not all. Why would we bother?"

Rutledge counted off his fingers. "Oh, I don't know, breaking and entering, theft. You didn't have a warrant or permission to be there."

"Those things don't concern us," Cain said. "At least not at this moment. What did you come here for?"

"I need to know what Mac knows. What you know."

"And why would we tell you?" Dane asked.

"Because we're not enemies. Because"—he ran a hand through his thinning hair—"I'm with NCIS."

"The Naval Criminal Investigative Service? You're a Navy cop?" asked Mac. *What the hell?*

He leaned in over the table. "My name is Dalton Sinclair, not Tom Rutledge. I've been with NCIS for four years. What I am about to tell you can go no further." He stared at Dane and Cain. "I'm authorized to tell you because your admiral has sworn to my boss that you can keep your mouths shut."

Both men nodded.

Mac was still trying to process what the hell was going on. "What the hell, Rut—Sinclair?"

"About eight months ago, some guns went missing from Naval Base San Diego. It was the third time in as many months. My boss sent me undercover to see if I could figure out who was stealing the weapons and how they were doing it."

The waitress arrived at their table. "Aloha, how are you this evening? Is this your first time here?" She was in her early twenties with a big smile pasted on her face. When they all stared at her in silence, her smile faltered. "Um, would you like to see menus?"

"Just bring us four Big Swell IPAs," Cain said.

"Alrighty then," she said and walked back toward the bar.

"You were saying?" Mac prompted.

Sinclair picked up his story again. "Anyway, I went undercover and found one guy who helped get the weapons out, but he didn't know anything about what happened to them from there. He had no clue who was in charge or even who was next up the ladder from him. He was paid to drop the weapons in a certain spot on a certain date and keep his mouth shut. The only thing he did know was that the weapons were headed for Hawai'i, and he only found that out because of sheer happenstance.

"He was walking along a pier, picking up some stuff that he'd ordered for the Navy, and saw the crates he'd dropped off being loaded into a container. He asked the guy where it was going, and he said Honolulu. It was just blind fucking luck."

"So how did you get in with the Coast Guard?" Mac asked. This whole thing was blowing her mind. What the hell had she fallen into? Was her life always going to be such a mess? Her stomach churned, and her head started to bang again.

"My partner and I came over and tried to track what happened to the crate, but there was no paperwork. It was like that crate didn't even exist. We asked around but got nowhere. Then we asked other agencies for help. The DEA told us they were aware a drug smuggling ring was operating in Honolulu. Drugs were being brought in by ship but then disappearing before they got into port. The searches they'd conducted, looking for the stuff, had gotten nowhere. They knew meth was coming from Mexico, but once it left San Diego, like the weapons, it seemed to disappear into thin air.

"Who figured out it was Owens and his crew?" Dane asked.

"No one. We realized the only way the drugs and stolen weapons could disappear like that was if they were taken off the ship at sea, but it's a huge friggin' ocean, and how were we going to track when the stuff disappeared?"

The waitress arrived to deliver their beers.

"Thanks," Mac said. She knew she shouldn't drink with a concussion but with everything that was going on and now Rutledge AKA Sinclair's revelations, it was too much. She took a deep swallow of hers. This day was just full of surprises. The way things were going, she was going to need a lot more beers.

"We decided to track the next shipment. We got the information from the clerk for the next drop. We'd left him in place so we could maybe figure out what was going on. We watched the guns, saw them get picked up and loaded onto a container ship. A smaller one. We watched it via satellite as it made its way over here. When it got to port, we had the DEA board and look for the container. They found it, but there was nothing in it except the toys that had been loaded in California. The guns only took up a small part of the crate. But here's the kicker. The only thing that happened on board that ship was a visit from a Coast Guard vessel."

"That's what made you suspicious?" Mac asked.

"It was the only logical answer. My boss reached out to someone high up in the Coast Guard, and the plan was born. I was to come over here and work for CGIS. See if I could get wind of what the hell was going on."

Mac took another sip of beer. Sinclair being undercover made sense when she looked back. The hushed phone calls and the stopped conversations when she entered the room. The disappearances on occasion and the constant searching of containers at the port.

"But something happened back in California," Cain said.

Sinclair nodded. "Yeah. Three months ago. The guy we initially found, the clerk, was killed."

Mac broke out in a cold sweat just hearing those words. "Oh, my god,"

"Yeah." Sinclair took a pull of his beer. "It was bad. Hit and run. They left him to die in a ditch."

"Shit," Dane mumbled.

"We lost the trail at that end, but the shipments kept coming. We knew because stuff was still going missing. The agents in my office tried to figure out who was doing the stealing now, but it was impossible. It wasn't one guy in the warehouse anymore. It was all done by computer. Things were being re-routed, and by the time someone realized they were missing, they'd vaporized. Deleted out of the system." He took a swallow of his beer again. "Anyway, by that time, I suspected Casper was involved somehow."

"How did you know?" Mac demanded. "What did I miss?" That was the crux of the situation for Mac. Not only had she missed that Casper was crooked, but she'd missed that Sinclair was Sinclair and not Rutledge.

Sinclair shook his head. "You didn't miss anything. You knew something was off with Casper, just like I did. The only difference was, I had the resources to track it down. Casper was a gambler. That's where he would disappear to all the time. He would say he was out investigating a case and take off to see his bookie, and since Hawai'i is one of only two states where all gambling is illegal, it's done in bars and parks and all kinds of underground places."

Mac tapped her beer glass. "So are you saying he didn't screw cases up on purpose? That he was just trapped by his addiction?" Guilt hit her hard in the stomach. She'd been so quick to condemn Casper. What he'd needed was help.

"Don't go feeling guilty just yet. Casper has been blackmailing people to feed his habit for a while now. He also ran a couple of hookers to make some cash. He had a problem, but his moral compass was crooked long before gambling got its claws into him. Besides, we think he killed Owens."

That stopped her cold. Her lungs refused to inflate. Casper killed Owens? She blinked in shock. That thought had just never occurred to her. The possibility hadn't remotely entered her brain. Which begged the question, had she lost her edge? Maybe all the shit in Minnesota with Karl had affected her ability to do her job. She stared at the table. How could she have not seen Casper as Owens's killer? Dane squeezed her thigh under the table. She covered his hand with her own, drawing strength from it. The hits seem to be coming hard and fast. She needed an anchor. "Why would Casper kill Owens? Besides, he didn't dive. He said he was claustrophobic, and being underwater freaked him out."

Sinclair nodded. "We think he had a partner who did the diving. We think Owens was killed because Casper's partner wanted Owens dead. Somehow, he'd become a liability."

Because of the motherboards? Were they worried that he knew about the motherboards and he was a loose end to tie up or was it because he was greedy and wanted a bigger piece of the action? Either one would fit his personality.

"And you think the partner killed Casper," Dane stated.

"That's the theory," Sinclair said. He looked across the table at her. "I'm sorry, Mac. I wanted to tell you. I knew from day one you weren't involved, but I just couldn't blow my cover. I'd worked too hard to establish it. You understand, don't you?"

She nodded but didn't bother speaking. What could she say? She folded her hands on the table and let out a breath. "So, what do you want from me?"

Sinclair took another quick sip of his beer and then put it down on the table. "I need to know what you know. Obviously, something's making Casper's bosses nervous. I need to know what that is."

She crossed her arms over her chest. "Yeah, me, too."

Sinclair frowned. "What does that mean?"

"It means I have no clue why those assholes tried to kill me. None."

CHAPTER SEVENTEEN

Dane finally removed his hand from Mac's leg. He could tell she was struggling by the tension in her expression. The revelations were coming fast, and she was getting knocked sideways, not unlike being blown up earlier, only psychologically.

"I don't understand," Sinclair said. "How can you not know?"

She snorted. "Shocking, isn't it? You can imagine how I feel about it."

Dane stared into the depths of his beer. This wasn't going the way he'd expected. He wasn't prepared for the idea that Casper had killed Owen. It hadn't occurred to him. He still wasn't sure about it, but it made sense.

"There's nothing. I don't know anything. Less than you do." Mac shrugged. "To be honest, we haven't been able to figure it out at all. I don't know anything about Casper and his shenanigans. I haven't done anything or been anywhere that you haven't been, or that I haven't told you about. It's just one big mystery."

Dane's heart contracted just a bit. She was really at a

loss, and having this hanging over her was brutal. The fear in her eyes ate him up inside. He did not want her to be afraid. To feel fear. He'd been there. He'd lived in a constant state of fear after his fall. Would Owens try to finish him off? It had crushed his soul. He did not want that for her. He needed to figure this out so she could go back to living a normal life. He wanted to see Mac smile and laugh; carefree and not sad.

Sinclair stared at Mac. "Seriously? You really don't know?" He looked at Cain and then Dane.

"She really doesn't know," Dane confirmed.

"Well, shit. I was hoping you could shed some light on this for me," Sinclair said.

Mac grunted. "The feeling is mutual. I would love to know what's going on."

Sinclair lifted his beer toward Cain. "What can you guys tell me? I know you know more about Owens. Your admiral said as much to my boss, but he couldn't get into it with me. Said to ask you to explain."

Cain gave a curt nod to Dane. It was okay to share the story, but Dane wasn't too keen to just start blathering away. How did they know this guy was legit? How did they know he wasn't crooked like Casper?

"Because the admiral vouched for him," Cain said.

Dane wanted to growl with frustration, but he knew Cain was right.

Sinclair looked back and forth between them. "Oh, you're worried about me?" He cocked his head. "Fair point. I am who I say I am." He swallowed. "I need you to trust me and tell me what you know, if for no other reason than I got that kid killed, the one who was working in the depot in San Diego." He swallowed a couple of times. "I told him it would be fine, and no one would know. I gave him my word he would be safe, and now he's dead. That's on me. I want to know who killed him, and I want that asshole strung up for his murder." He rubbed his face.

Dane got it. Guilt was a tough nut to crack. He felt guilty about not pushing Casper to investigate Owens more. If he had, the motherboards might not be missing. Owens's operation might be shut down and there wouldn't be all those lives in danger.

He knew it wasn't directly his fault, just like he was guessing Sinclair knew the kid's death wasn't really his fault. But Dane also knew he would carry the guilt of Owens's death with him for the rest of his life and by the look on Sinclair's face, the kid's death would haunt him as well.

"We were on a stakeout on a beach on the North Shore," Dane started. He told Sinclair what they saw and what they knew. It took a while, and when he'd finished, Sinclair immediately flagged down the waitress and asked for another round.

"So, where do we go from here?"

"If you can locate Probert, maybe we can figure out who's behind all this. He's the guy that set up the bomb in Mac's place, or at least we think he is," Dane suggested.

"Agreed. I've got my NCIS colleagues looking for him, aside from myself, and a couple of CGIS people. The problem is no one can find him. He's gone to ground. And for a small island, there are a shit ton of places to hide on Oahu, not to mention all the other islands. If he hopped a boat, he could be anywhere by now."

"Try Kauai," Dane offered.

Sinclair stopped lifting his beer for a sip. "Why?"

Dane leaned forward and put his arms on the table. "I'd forgotten, but when you said about the other islands, a memory popped into my brain. When I was on Owens's team, Probert used to talk about a shack he and a friend shared over in Kauai where they'd go hunting wild boar."

Sinclair brought out his notebook and made a note. "Do you have the friend's name?"

Trying to remember, Dane blew out a long breath. "Charlie. Charlie…Helm I think."

"Well, it's a place to start. Thanks." Sinclair looked up. "What are you going to do?"

Cain narrowed his eyes. "We're going to keep Mac safe and take a fresh look at things in the morning. There's got to be more loose threads to pull. We just have to find them."

Sinclair frowned. "Look, I know you don't want to let me know where you're staying. At least, take my cell number so if anything comes up, you can reach out. I want to solve this. Casper was an asshole, but I still need to catch his killer. I think it's the boss of the operation, and I want to nail his or her ass to the wall."

Dane pulled out the new burner cell Jace had gotten him and programmed in Sinclair's number. "We'll reach out if there's anything."

Cain stood and put money on the table. He rattled off a phone number. "Got it?" he asked Sinclair.

"Yeah. That's not your number, though. It's a D.C. area code." Sinclair stood as well.

"It's someone who can reach us in a hurry if you need us. We'll be in touch."

Dane and Mac stood. His back twinged but nothing like it had been hurting earlier. Sex seemed to have released some of the tightness. He bit back a smile. *Good to know.* Mac, on the other hand, seemed to be stiffening up. She was moving a bit more gingerly than she had been earlier.

They left the restaurant and waited on the street. Cass arrived driving a different SUV. Must be a rental. Dane had opened the door when Jace's voice reverberated in his eardrum. "Gun!"

Dane grabbed Mac and spun so he hit the ground beside

the SUV, taking the brunt of their fall on his back, and then rolled to cover her with his body.

The shots came in one long burst. Glass shattered. They shot up the SUV and then the tires. The sound of a motorcycle revving and taking off ricocheted around them. People were screaming.

"I'm on him," Tac said, and then there was the sound of another engine revving and tires screeching.

"Are you okay?" He looked into Mac's eyes. They were wide with fear, and she was having a hard time catching her breath. "Just breathe slowly. Take deep breaths," Dane instructed.

"Sitrep," Cain demanded.

"Cass, you okay?" Dane called.

He was met with a string of curses, long and loud. "Fuckers tore a hole in my jacket."

"She's good," Jace said. "Me, too."

Dane pulled Mac into a sitting position and, at her nod, hoisted her to her feet. "You, okay?"

"Yes," she croaked. "That was just so unexpected."

"Sonofabitch! I lost him." Tac's voice sounded in his earbud. "He got away in traffic."

Cain said, "Don't worry about it, just head back here."

"Holy shit!" Tac yelled.

"What?" Dane demanded.

"Koa just shot past me on his Ducati. He's still after the guy."

Cain was standing next to Dane and Mac. He looked at the two of them. "I don't like him on his own."

Cass came around the SUV. "Do you want me to go after him?"

"No, he's got too much of a head start. Go grab another set of wheels. This one isn't going anywhere."

"Roger that," she said and trotted off down the sidewalk.

Neither did Dane. "Koa," he said, trying to raise him on the earbud. It was no use. He was too far away.

The sound of sirens reached them. "This is going to go downhill fast," Dane said.

Cain nodded. "Are there any injuries?"

They looked around. People had scattered. Dane didn't see anyone who looked like they'd been harmed. "Where's Sinclair?" A groan came from behind a planter on his right. He moved in that direction, but Mac was still holding on to him. Her eyes were wide, and she seemed to be having a hard time letting go. "Jace, check over there." He pointed off to his right.

He put Mac in the back seat of the SUV. "Mac, honey, I need you to snap out of it." She still had a far-off look in her eye. Had she hit her head again? He'd done his best to make sure he took the hit on the sidewalk. His back was screaming because of it.

"Mac," he said again and gave her a little shake.

She blinked, and finally, her gaze came into focus. "What?" She looked around. "Sorry, I was just… Sorry," she said again.

Jace was pulling someone to their feet. It was Sinclair. "He's okay," Jace said.

Sinclair limped over to them. "Jesus, they aren't playing around."

"No, they aren't," Cain agreed. "Did anyone get a look at the shooter?"

"It was Cameron, Owens's second in command," Sinclair supplied. "I assume Topher Grady was the shooter."

"Are you sure?" Dane asked. "I can't imagine these guys being so stupid. Why would they shoot at us? They have to know we'd recognize them."

Sinclair nodded and then winced. "You're right. I recognize the bike. Saw it when I went to interview Cameron. He had it tucked under a tarp in the back of his garage with all kinds of stuff in front of it."

Mac cocked an eyebrow. "Then how did you see it?"

Sinclair looked a bit sheepish. "I had to use the bathroom and got lost."

She grinned.

Dane's stomach unknotted slightly when she turned that smile his direction. He'd been worried about her there for a minute. Hell, he'd been worried about her one way or another since they'd met. His heart had damn near stopped when the bullets started flying. He tucked a finger under her chin. "Glad you're feeling better."

"Yeah." It was her turn to look sheepish. "I…I almost had something, a thought—a piece of the puzzle that we need. It was right there, as if getting shot at knocked it loose, but then it was gone again." She let out a long sigh. "You're right though, why would they take the risk? What are they so afraid of?"

The sound of a motorcycle approaching had everyone reaching for their guns. There hadn't been time earlier to get off a shot, but now Dane was prepared. He drew his weapon only to realize it was Koa. He rolled to a stop at the curb just as several police cars pulled up behind him.

Dane raised an eyebrow, but Koa shook his head. "Lost them when they off-roaded through a park. Too many kids and families. I wasn't taking the chance."

"No worries. Sinclair says it was Cameron and Grady."

Koa nodded. "I recognized Grady. We did a course together before I got injured. He was the shooter."

Sinclair had started speaking with the cops. He had his badge out and was doing a lot of gesturing. Cain went over to join him. Five minutes later, he came back. "Jace and Tac will stay and answer questions. The rest of us are heading back to the hotel."

Cass appeared with Jace's SUV, and they all piled in. Koa followed them on his Ducati.

"What do you think?" Dane asked. "About Sinclair."

Cain shrugged. "He seems to have skin in the game now, so that helps. He took charge back there and got us cleared to leave so I think he's on the level."

Mac sighed. "I'm not sure he believed me that I have no idea why they tried to kill me."

"It doesn't matter what he believes. It's the truth. You just have to go with it." Dane's gut told him the whole thing with Sinclair was bothering her. If it were him, he'd be asking: *How could I have missed it? How could he be right under my nose like that and me not see it? Does that mean I'm not very good at my job?* Self-doubt was a bitch. He wanted to comfort her, but that urge would have to wait.

They arrived back at the hotel and went to their rooms. Mac walked into the foyer and then headed toward her door. It was late, and her posture and the dark rings under her eyes were a clue she was exhausted. She seemed to have stiffened even more on the drive over, and she had repeatedly rubbed her temples like she had a headache. The pinched skin around her eyes hadn't been there earlier, despite the concussion.

Damn, it had been a hell of a day.

She opened her room door and then turned. "I'm going to crash. What time will we move in the morning?"

"Oh-eight-hundred seems early enough," Cain said as he walked into the other room. "Night," he called.

Dane leaned against her doorjamb. "Are you okay?"

"Yeah." She sighed. "Just been a long day. I've got bruises on top of bruises now."

"You want me to get you some Advil?"

She laughed. "You guys are *always* taking them."

"We're a group of misfits and broken toys. It takes all kinds of things to get us through the day."

"Broken toys, huh?"

He shrugged. "Pretty much."

"I'm good, but thanks. See you in the morning."

He nodded and stepped back. She started to close the door then stopped. "Hey, Dane? Thanks for saving my life."

He just nodded. He couldn't get the words out through the lump in his throat. He'd seen her almost die twice today. He couldn't take much more.

When she closed the door, disappointment rocketed through him. What did he expect? A repeat of earlier? An invitation to share her bed, with her snuggled into him? Not a chance. That little interlude was over. He'd known it as soon as Sinclair announced who he really was. Mac had been taken for a ride, and nobody was getting in after that. At least, *he* wouldn't let anyone in. He got it and didn't blame her for a second.

And then being shot at again after that? Yeah, she needed some time to process everything. He should keep his distance. Probably for the best anyway. He had to concentrate on other things, namely getting himself back in the best shape possible. It hurt like a son of a bitch at the moment, and if he stayed in this condition, his spot on the team was in serious jeopardy.

He walked into the other bedroom, sat down on the sofa, and leaned his head back against the wall, closing his eyes.

"Misfit toys, huh?" Cass said.

He opened one eye and looked at her. "What would you call us?"

"I think broken toys sums us up. The Island of Misfit toys, isn't that what it was called?"

He chuckled. "Yeah, and we live on an island. Maybe we're misfits. Maybe that's better than broken."

"Nah," Cain said as he came out of the bathroom, "you're all broken."

"Asshole," Cass said without heat.

Cain sat down on the other end of the couch. "But I was broken once, too. This team will put you guys back together. You won't be the same, but you'll be better. Stronger as a team than you ever were on your own."

Dane had a sneaking suspicion Cain was right. Dane already felt much better about life since he'd joined the team three months ago. Things were coming together. If his team leader said, "Do Pilates," then who was he to argue? Cain had done right by him so far.

"I'm gonna take the first watch," Cass said and left the room.

Dane stayed on the couch. He knew he should get up, but he was somewhat comfortable, and his give-a-damn was too busted to make the effort.

Jace hit Dane's foot. "You want coffee?"

He opened his eyes and blinked.

"Wh—what time is it?"

"That's right, rise and shine, princess. You've been there all night."

"Shit, why didn't someone wake me?" He took his feet off the coffee table and straightened up with a groan. His back responded like it was a two-by-four: stiff, rigid. No, it was beyond stiff. Every muscle was bruised.

"Cain said to let you sleep."

Dane cursed. "Sorry, guys. I should've—"

"Drink this," Jace said as he handed Dane a cup of black coffee, "and shut up. You needed the sleep. We all saw you take that fall with Mac. You took the brunt of yours and

Mac's weight on your back. That shit had to hurt. Bet it still does."

Dane wanted to deny it, but there was no way they couldn't tell how much pain he was in.

Tac put the Advil on the table in front of him and went back to his chair at the end of the coffee table. "We all know this case is personal for you."

Dane blinked. Shit. Did they all know about him and Mac? Hell, that would be bad. "Well, I…"

"Owens was an asshole and caused your accident," Tac continued. "There's a lot wrapped up in this for you. We're all here for whatever you need."

Dane didn't quite know what to say. It was true. This case was personal for all kinds of reasons. "I… It's been a long time since I had a real team. So, thanks. It means a lot."

"No worries. Get some breakfast." Tac pointed to the plates of food on a room service cart by the window.

Dane stood and then bent at the waist and reached for his toes to stretch out all the aching muscles. The pull was harsh on his hamstrings.

Koa walked in and headed straight for the food. "I'm starving."

"Do I have time for a quick shower?" Dane asked.

Tac nodded. "Cain and Cass are outside on watch. You're good."

Dane took a shower. It wasn't as quick as it should have been, but he needed the heat on his back to help him loosen up. Twenty minutes later, the room was empty, and he was just standing by the curtained window rushing through breakfast when Cain and Cass walked in.

"Shit. Sorry, I'm moving," Dane said as he set down his fork.

Cain waved him to stand down. "No rush. Tac and Jace

are already out there. I want you to stay and run through things again with Mac. She up?"

"I am," she said as she walked into the room. She was wearing a pair of black cargos and a Kelly-green T-shirt. Her hair was pulled back in a ponytail, and she was carrying a file folder in her hand.

Dark shadows ringed her eyes, but she was moving okay. Probably not much sleep, but her body rested at least. Dane pointed to the food, and she nodded.

"I spent the night thinking about the whole situation and still didn't come up with much." She helped herself to some juice. "But then when I pulled out the file I had in my bag on Owens and the one on Dane's accident. I found it."

"Found what?" Dane asked.

"The reason they want me dead." She turned to Cain. "At my place, where was the bomb set up? By my computer?"

He nodded as he chewed on a piece of bacon.

"Thought so. Lucky Rutledge—I mean Sinclair—didn't see this file, otherwise they'd want him dead, too."

Dane narrowed his eyes. "You're not making much sense."

Cass handed Mac a coffee. "Thanks," she said and put the file on the table. "Come check it out."

They gathered round the table, and she opened the file. She set out the pictures, lining them up in order on the table. "Casper took these pictures by himself. In the report, he said no one was available to help since CGIS was down a few members. Everyone took that at face value. Rutledge… Sinclair started the following week, and I started the week after."

Dane took a deep breath. He hadn't seen the pictures before. He'd asked to see them, but Casper had refused. He had been airlifted to the hospital before these were taken. There was debris on deck from the medics who had given him an IV and saw to his wound. The first few pictures showed the debris and a pool of his blood where the bolt had gouged his back. The next group showed the ladder he'd come down. He looked closely. The rungs looked normal until the third picture in that group. It was a close up of three of the rungs. Two glistened in the sun. The one below it didn't.

"Sonofabitch. Casper knew. Had proof they greased the rungs." Dane's heart pounded as adrenaline flooded his veins. He fisted his hands. It was a damn good thing Casper was dead. After seeing this, he wasn't sure he wouldn't have killed the man himself.

Koa squeezed his shoulder.

Dane closed his eyes for a second and took a deep breath and then eased it out.

"I'm sorry, Dane. I didn't think." Mac started to reach for the pictures, but he stopped her with a shake of his head.

"I asked to see them at the time. Now I know why he wouldn't show them to me. I'm okay. I'm glad I'm seeing them. Proof that I wasn't making it up. This shit wasn't my fault. It wasn't an accident."

"No," she agreed, "it wasn't."

The next group of pictures were shots of the deck from different angles. He let his gaze roam over them, but nothing stood out to him, but then he took another steadying breath and made himself focus. He went back over each picture again. "Holy shit," he said and leaned over one of the pictures.

"What?" Cass said.

He pointed. The picture showed containers on the top of the cargo ship. One of the doors was open, and inside, a set of hands was loading a black square package, with a skull and crossbones surrounded by the sun, into a backpack.

"Sonofabitch," Koa said. "They did it right there, and he took pictures."

"Casper wasn't stupid. He knew he had them. Knew he had proof. If he was a gambler like Sinclair said"—she blew out a breath and pointed to the image—"this was his meal ticket."

"So, who do you think killed him? Someone from Owens's team?" Cass asked.

"No. I think whoever runs the whole operation saw him as a threat and took him out. Casper probably got paid a bit here and there. Not enough to make a serious dent in the profit but enough to keep him happy. They needed him to make sure no one was on to them. I'm coming around to the idea that Casper killed Owens, too. It makes sense. Use one asset to kill the other. This stinks of someone cleaning house."

Dane stared at the picture, and another piece of the puzzle snapped into place. "Cain, how come we haven't practiced on the ship before the other day?"

Cain ground his teeth. "I've been asking since I got here, but the other day was the first time they said yes."

"Who? Who said yes?"

"The people in Cross's office."

"Why would Cross have anything to do with it?" Dane asked.

Cain shrugged. "Because he is the one who set up the relationship. Or, at least, it goes through his office. Why all the questions?"

Dane paused before answering, and did a fast gut check, but got the same result. He knew he was right. "Because that's how they get the drugs, and now weapons, here," Dane said. He was sure of it. "When I was on Owens's team we used the cargo ship to train all the time. At least once a month. We'd go out and train and while no one was looking, they take the opportunity to move the drugs and weapons into their bags to take it off the ship. No one is the wiser. Even me. Anything Owens and his people bring into port is just their gear on their boat. They can walk it right out to their cars or his boat or whatever, and no one thinks twice. It's fucking brilliant."

Koa grunted. "Shit."

"Yeah. So Sinclair was right, but he thought it was just random searches. Training makes a much better cover." Cain narrowed his eyes. "They let us use it this time because the ship was held up an extra day. A crane broke down in the port, and they had to wait. Owens and his people had it first. That's why he had the drugs and the motherboards. He picked them up that day."

"Exactly," Dane continued. "It also means the ships' captains are in on it too. They aren't going to let just anyone open a container. Even if we are the Coast Guard, there's no way they wouldn't be suspicious after a time or two."

Mac said, "Should we call Rut… Sinclair and tell him what we know?" She tapped her fist to her forehead, as if trying to beat Rutledge's real name into her memory banks.

Dane shook his head. "Not yet. We only have this picture, and you can't tell who it is. I think we go talk to one of them."

"Yeah, but which one?" she asked.

"Ben Hestman," Jace said over the earbud. "I cracked the code last night. You were right, Dane. The first column was dates. The second was the amount of drugs and the third was money. The dashes had initials after them. Ben Hestman had the fewest entries. He had some at the very beginning, and then they stopped altogether. I think he probably wanted out."

"Wait, what code?" Mac demanded.

Dane had forgotten that they hadn't shared finding the

little black book with Mac. "We found a book in Owens' safe. It was written in code. We've been trying to crack it."

"What do you think? Should we go with Ben Hestman?" asked Cain.

Dane cut in, "That makes sense. Of all the guys, he was sort of the odd man out. He was the most…neutral toward me. Not friendly, but not full of animosity either. Ben just kept his head down and did his work. My guess is he didn't want to be involved anymore. He had to agree to keep his mouth shut, but he didn't want a cut of the pie. What do you think, Mac?"

She hesitated. "I didn't talk to them myself. Sinclair did, but if I had to guess, then yes, Ben seems to be the one that has the most to lose, so probably the most likely to flip."

Cain touched his earbud. "Jace, Tac we're heading out. I'll explain on the way. Bring the SUVs around front."

"Roger that," they said, one right after the other.

Cain stood. "The team is still officially on leave so we should find him at home at this hour if he's not on the run like the others."

Dane's adrenaline surged. They were on to something. He could feel it. If Ben knew about the drugs, then he might also know about the motherboards. They might actually be able to do what Bertrand needed them to do but, more importantly, with this information out there, Mac was no longer in danger. That was his end goal. Above everything else, he needed Mac to be safe. Fingers crossed this would make that happen.

CHAPTER EIGHTEEN

Mac got out of the SUV and fell in behind Cain. Dane brought up the rear. They walked down the path to Ben Hestman's door. His house was a small bungalow on a quiet cul-de-sac. The front yard was littered with tricycles and balls, a soccer net, and even a hockey stick.

"Everyone in position?" Cain asked softly.

Mac heard the other members of the team confirm in her earbud.

Cain knocked on the door. A minute later, a small woman in her mid-thirties answered. She had on black shorts and a flower-patterned shirt. A splotch that could have been a baby puke stain on one shoulder, and her hair was sticking up on one side. Frazzled didn't cover it.

"Can I help you?" she asked in a wary voice.

"Ma'am, I'm Cain Maddox. This is Mac Rankin and Dane Landry. We'd like to speak to your husband."

She'd looked at Dane when she'd heard his name. There was recognition there for sure. She hesitated and then gave a little nod. "Wait here." She closed the door again.

"Be alert. He might make a run for it." Cain uttered the

warning, but Mac fervently hoped he was wrong. She wanted this to be over. The whole drive-by yesterday had changed something. Dane had saved her life, and judging from the way he was moving this morning, at great cost to his back. For some asinine reason, the bomb had seemed less personal. It wasn't. She'd still been the target but blowing someone up was less directed than searching them out in a car and shooting at them. She shook her head at her reasoning.

The way Dane had covered her with his body, putting himself in harm's way to make sure she was okay; it was all too much. She couldn't deal with it. Deal with the fact that he could have died, and it would have been her fault. She needed this to be over. She wanted another fresh start. Maybe even leave Hawai'i. Everything here felt tainted by this whole mess, even Dane. Especially her relationship with Dane. *God, did they have a relationship?* She snuck a peek at him, but his posture was rigid and his expression blank. He didn't look back at her or give her a reassuring smile. That really would have helped her mood.

They waited three interminable minutes, and just as she ran out of patience the door opened again. Ben Hestman was slightly shorter than both Cain and Dane. He was broad but not as big as the other two either. His dark hair was cut in a buzz cut and he had multiple tattoos on his arms. He was in good shape but mostly what struck her was that he looked exhausted. His face was gaunt and his eyes sunken. He had a haunted look about him. She understood that perfectly. He wasn't the only one haunted by these events.

"Darinda said you wanted to talk."

Cain nodded. "May we come in?"

Ben hesitated but then stepped back and let them into his living room. It was small and crowded with toys. A small boy sat in the middle of the carpet, playing with blocks. Mac guessed his age around maybe two. Darinda came around the corner from the kitchen, carrying a small baby, maybe six months old, if Mac had to guess. The pink blanket the child was wrapped in made Mac assume the baby was a girl.

Ben waved them over to a dining table that was just off the kitchen. They walked through the living room to get to it. The house was small, and other than the blocks, it was tidy. Mac's heart went out to the woman. It could not be easy with four kids under the age of six. Mac's sister Natalie had two kids, and Mac couldn't babysit for more than an hour or two without being exhausted.

"What are your children's names?" she asked.

"Connor and Jason are the two older ones. They're at a playdate." She nodded toward the little one in the front room. "That's Liam and this is Miranda." She kissed the baby on her head.

"Lovely," Mac murmured.

"Sit," Ben said, and they all took a seat around the table. "What is it you want?"

Cain glanced at Mac and then Dane.

Mac cleared her throat. This was her area more than theirs. "Ben, first let me extend my condolences on losing your team leader."

He didn't say a word but just nodded. When Darinda let out a snort, Ben sent her a look that said *keep your mouth shut*. At least, that was how Mac interpreted it.

"We have reason to believe Owens was smuggling drugs and...other things into Oahu," Mac began. "We can prove that he did a drug exchange the other night, and we can prove how he brought the drugs into Oahu. We know from our investigation that your team members all knew about this."

"I didn't know a thing. I—"

Mac cut him off. "We have Owens notebook, Ben." That stopped him cold. "We have dates and quantities. We have dollar amounts and initials. *Your* initials. At least at the beginning. You need to tell us about that."

Ben stayed silent. Darinda looked worried. The baby started to cry. Darinda took the baby down the hallway off the kitchen, trying to shush her the whole way.

Mac said, "I know this is hard, Ben. These people are your friends, your family —"

"They aren't my fucking family," he growled. Then he rubbed his face with both hands. "You have the book?"

She nodded.

He rubbed his face again. "Shit." He let out a long breath. "Yeah, Owens was smuggling shit. Drugs and guns. There was other shit, too. I… I got four kids. I'm drowning in mortgage payments and car payments and just trying to put food on the table. Owens said it was easy money. I…I just needed a break. So, I helped him a few times."

Darinda came down the hall again and through the kitchen. She walked up behind her husband and put her arms around him. He straightened and squared his shoulders, seeming to take strength from her embrace.

"I took the money, but after making one mortgage payment I just couldn't bring myself to use any of it. Then I told Owens I wanted out. I didn't want to do it anymore. I just wanted to do my job. I loved being MSRT. It's the best job in the world. At least, it was until Owens.

"He told me I could get out, but I had to stay part of the team and keep my mouth shut or something bad would happen to me. Bannister had just quit. Owens said I couldn't go too, or it would look like something was wrong."

Darinda went to the kitchen and got Ben a glass of water. She set it down on the table next to him. She didn't offer the rest of them anything, and Mac didn't blame her one bit. Hard to be hospitable to people who could take your husband away.

Ben looked at Dane for the first time. "I had no idea about what they were going to do to you. I swear it. I would never have gone along with it. I'm sorry, man."

Dane nodded.

"After what happened to you, when they were taking you away by medivac, Owens came up to me and said that's what would happen to me if I said anything. He said he'd make sure I died."

Dane ran a hand through his hair. "I get it. You've got a family. What choice did you have? He would've killed you. I know that. I'll make sure others know it, too."

Ben raised his eyebrows. "Others?"

"Ben, we need to know what you know about some other people. Craig Owens brought something onto Oahu this last time, something we need to find." Mac was trying to be gentle. Ben looked like he'd been through the wringer. The last thing he needed was to be yelled at. He'd clam up. "Do you know where we can find the stuff from the last shipment?" she asked in a calm voice.

Ben stayed silent. He looked at all three of them and reached for his wife's hand. "Am I going to go to jail?"

Mac hesitated. "To be honest, I don't know. It's hard to say. If you help us, it will go a long way toward showing remorse."

Dane leaned forward. "I'll go to bat for you, Ben. I promise. I'll tell them that Owens tried to kill me and I have no doubt he would have killed you, too. You were operating under duress."

Mac wouldn't have gone that far, and she couldn't guarantee anyone would buy it, but she loved that Dane offered to help Ben. Instead of being bitter about Ben's part in what happened to him, Dane chose to be the bigger man, a man she admired greatly because of it. She wanted to reach out and squeeze his hand. Instead, she folded her hands on the table.

Ben glanced up at Darinda. She nodded and he let out a long sigh. "I can tell you where the guns are. I think he already passed the drugs on. He was only ever the middleman on that. He got a percentage off the top for making sure they arrived safely. The weapons were something different. He made a lot of money off those."

Cain cleared his throat. "We need you to tell everything you know to a Special Agent Rutledge. Will you do that?"

"Yes." Ben took a sip of water, and Darinda put her arm around her husband.

Cain excused himself to make the call. Thirty minutes later, they met Sinclair in the driveway. "How the hell did you get him to flip? I took a run at him a couple of times, but he wasn't budging."

Mac crossed her arms over her chest. She felt the burden of turning Ben Hestman in. He'd made mistakes, but she wasn't sure he deserved jail time. "He's tired. I think if you'd tried again, he might have caved. But to answer your question, we found some evidence and when confronted with it, he decided to help himself."

Dane came up beside her and handed Sinclair the file with copies of the pictures and the pages from the little black book. "You'll need these."

Sinclair studied the items Dane had placed in his hands. "What are these?"

"Proof," Dane said. "Craig Owens was smuggling drugs and guns into Oahu. Ben can tell you where he thinks the weapons are and provide the details you'll need to arrest the rest of the team. But I want you to give him every consideration you can. Owens would have killed him if he didn't go along, just like he tried to do to me. Ben Hestman didn't have a choice. I want that noted. He shouldn't go down for something he did under duress."

Sinclair nodded slowly. "I can't make any promises, but I will do my best. Owens wrecked a lot of lives. We'll try to limit the damage to anyone else. Hopefully, when we find the rest of the team, they will cooperate as well, and we can figure out the whole network."

Dane shook his head. "I wouldn't hold your breath on cooperating. They've got nothing to gain now."

"You're probably right," Sinclair agreed. He turned to Mac. "You must be relieved, Mac. This takes the pressure off. Once these guys are in custody, you'll be safe."

She sent him a quick smile. "It still hasn't sunk in yet, and I don't have an apartment to go back to but, yeah, it's good."

A car pulled up to the curb and a short, stocky man got out. "That's my NCIS partner, Ron Daily," Sinclair said by way of introduction. Everyone shook hands.

Sinclair tapped the file against his leg. "Okay then. Let me get in there and get started with Ben. Thanks for trusting me with this. I appreciate it. I've already spoken to my boss, and he is coordinating with some of the top officials at CGIS. We'll take it from here."

Dismissed. Mac would normally argue about it, but what did it matter? She was too close to things, so they weren't going to let her work it anyway. Cross would find someone to represent CGIS during the interviews, and Sinclair would get all the information he needed. At least, she hoped he would.

"Where do we go from here?" she asked as they piled into the SUV.

"The hangar," Cain said. "We still have to find the motherboards and figure out who TigerKing is."

"Is it alright if I come along?" She looked at Cain, who gave her a quick nod.

"We need all the help we can get. Besides, Grady, Cameron, and the others from Owens's team aren't in custody yet. We need eyes on you."

With that settled, she leaned back in her seat and closed her eyes. Her body was sore and her mind was heavy, and she was barely able to hold her head upright. After the drive-by shooting last night, she couldn't sleep. She just kept replaying it in her mind. What if Dane hadn't grabbed her in time? Or worse, what if he'd been shot? That had caused more than a little anxiety.

They'd only known each other for a couple of days, but she couldn't believe how much she liked him. Damn, he'd gotten under her skin. Dane was a good man. A strong man that she could draw strength from when she needed it. He was supportive and kind. He had a great sense of humor, and he was hot as hell. He even liked cats. She was sure she'd heard him talking to Beans. That had been the icing on the cake.

Too bad they couldn't date. Not only had she done that in the past and it blew up in her face, but now she no longer had a team. With everything that had happened, she would be under scrutiny for a long time to come. Her boss had been a crook, and her partner had been undercover with another agency, and she had been unaware. Yeah, there was no coming back from the office gossip around that stuff. She'd end up bringing Dane down with her. A clean start was the only way. CGIS had offices all over, didn't they?

But first things first. They had to find the motherboards. If they could figure out who the mastermind was, then they could find the stolen merchandise.

That thought niggled again. A tickle in the back of her brain. Something she knew… but remained just out of reach.

CHAPTER NINETEEN

Dane sat down at his desk and winced. A sharp tearing sensation rippled through his obliques, making him hiss quietly. He checked the time and saw it was too early for his next dose of Advil. *Dammit.* He was also slightly pissed off that Mac had sat down next to Cass, which was stupid. What the hell? Were they in grade school? It was ridiculous, yet he was grumpy about it. He couldn't even blame it on needing sleep. He'd slept more last night than he had in the last few months.

He sent a text to his neighbor, Mrs. Palakiko, asking about Beans. He never thought of himself as a cat guy, but once Beans had shown up on his doorstep and refused to leave, well, he was a goner. He never realized how much company a cat could be, or how soothing it was to sit with Beans on his lap purring. He needed that now. The purr. It relaxed him.

He got up, went back to the kitchen, and poured himself a coffee. Jace had just made a fresh pot and the aroma was nearly nirvana. Cain walked out of his office. Dane raised his cup and his eyebrows, but Cain shook his head no.

Tac wandered over and poured a cup. "I need this today."

"I hear that," Dane agreed.

"I just got off the phone with Bertrand," Cain addressed the occupants of the room, which got everyone's attention quickly. "He's happy that we figured out what Craig Owens was up to, and he's thrilled it's a joint Navy/Coast Guard ring because then no one is going to want to bash the other in the press and in Washington. But…he's less happy that we haven't found the motherboards."

Dane and Tac both returned to their desks and sat. Bertrand not being happy was understandable, and par for the course. Dane was pissed about that too.

Cain went to the front of the room by the whiteboard so he could address all of them. "By the way," Cain added, "Sinclair pulled off the raid and found some of the missing weapons with help from one of the other Coast Guard Special Ops teams. That pleased Bertrand, taking some of the pressure off us."

"Thank fuck," Dane muttered.

Cain shot him a side-eye glance, then continued. "They arrested Cameron, Grady, and Anderson. They were hiding out with the weapons. They also arrested Probert over on Kauai."

"Why didn't we do the raid?" Jace asked.

"Because it's a waste of time. We knew the motherboards wouldn't be there," Dane said and blew on his coffee. "Did they say why they shot at us? It seems like such a stupid move."

"Yeah, it was," Cain agreed "But they were desperate. Apparently, they figured without the file, there was no real evidence against them. They ditched the bike and got rid of everything else and were in the process of getting rid of the weapons when the raid happened. According to Sinclair, Cameron thought without evidence they might be kicked out of the Coast Guard but at least they wouldn't go to jail."

Cass piped up. "So, are we thinking that Cross is the head of the snake? That he organized stealing the weapons and getting them to Oahu to sell them?"

That was the million-dollar question.

Mac leaned back in her chair. "Well, he did go to Princeton so TigerKing could fit."

"Yeah, but so did a pile of other people around here," Jace said.

Dane had no idea who he was talking about, but it was a fair point. "Well, he also was the one with the connection to the container ship company. Cross's office set up the training runs. That can't be a coincidence."

Mac turned and looked back at Dane. "But he would argue that while he had the connection, Owens had been the one who worked it out with the captains of the ships, or that one of the shipping executives and the captains had turned a blind eye. It doesn't necessarily link him directly. If we're going to accuse the Deputy Director of CGIS of selling American weaponry on the black market, then we better be damn sure we have solid proof."

Koa stood and walked back to the kitchen. "She's right." A splash of coffee splattered the counter. He wiped it with a paper towel as he said, "We got nothing."

"So, let's get something," Cain said. "It's just gone twelve-hundred. Go home and get some sleep. Two together in shifts starting at sixteen-hundred. We're gonna follow Cross until we catch him with his hand in the cookie jar, or something else breaks."

"Why sixteen-hundred hours?" Cass demanded. "Why not start following him now?"

Dane sighed. "I can answer that. Because Cross is a political animal. They just found the weapons, and unless I miss my guess, Sinclair used mostly Navy guys to do it. Cross didn't know Sinclair was undercover. He's gonna be spitting mad. There will be lots of phone calls and name-calling and back and forth all afternoon. You gotta figure it will be at least sixteen-hundred before it gets sorted."

Cain nodded. "Uh-huh, that's what I figure. Then if he really is involved, he's gonna want to check on his plans for the motherboards."

"Why do we think they're still on the island?" Mac asked. "I mean, think about it. Why wouldn't he have sold them right away and gotten them out of here pronto?"

"It's a good point," Tac agreed.

Dane took another sip of his coffee. They weren't wrong. Were they too late to find the motherboards? His gut said no. "Mac, you said he wanted the flow of information to go through him and only him, correct?"

She nodded.

"Well, what if there was a delay? What if he took the risk of riling everyone up to look for these things because he knew it would take a while to get them off Oahu?"

Mac frowned. "I'm not following you."

"He knew the Navy would be looking for the motherboards, so he couldn't move them quickly. What better way to control things than tell his people to look for them but keep him abreast of any tiny detail? He would know if someone was getting close and, better yet, all those people looking would scare informants and the like away. CGIS out there banging around as well as the Navy, there's no way that wouldn't cause a stir and he'd be in a position to control it."

"He even said in his briefing to make as little noise as possible about this," Mac added. "How can you send out an office full of agents and not make noise? That had to drive the Navy crazy because now everyone is talking about the weapons. They're gonna get all kinds of false leads on one side of things, and people are going to disappear on the other. It's brilliant when you think of it."

Koa put his coffee cup in the sink. "Except now the other weapons have been found. So, what does that mean?"

Everyone stayed silent.

"It means we're running out of time," Dane said finally. "We have to find those motherboards soon, or they will be gone forever. Ben Hestman flipping sped up the timing on finding the weapons. Let's hope Cross still isn't quite ready to move the motherboards."

"You know, you all are presuming that what you saw on the beach wasn't the sale. That it was a delivery," Mac pointed out. "It could have been the sale of the motherboards, and they could be long gone. Think about it. Owens had already collected the motherboards from the ship. Who would he be giving them to other than the buyer?"

"Fair point," Cain agreed.

"My gut says no." Dane just didn't buy it. "I think he was delivering the motherboards to his boss."

"Explain," Cass demanded.

Dane mulled it over for a minute before speaking. He wanted to get everything straight in his head before spewing his theory. "I think Owens didn't know who he was working for. Sinclair said the guy in San Diego didn't know who the players were. He was kept in the dark for a reason. What if Owens was the same? He knew Casper was working for the same guy, but who's to say he knew more than that? He knew Casper, and Casper knew the big boss. Casper kills Owens on the boss's orders and then the boss kills him. Wraps everything up in a neat little bow. Hell, Owens's team implodes all on their own, and I'm guessing they didn't know anything beyond Casper either. Cross, or whoever the boss is, is home free.

"Now he has the motherboards and needs to sell them.

Whatever the holdup was, it's got to be close to being over. Cross is going to sell those motherboards in the next day or two, and then he really is home free."

I agree," Cain said. "With all these agents pounding around and asking questions, it would be damn hard to get the motherboards off the island. My gut says they're still here. I have no idea if Cross has them, but whoever it is will probably want to move them quickly now. We just have to figure out how they're going to do it."

"You mean like a private jet or boat? There are how many of those on this island?" Cass demanded.

"Yeah, but maybe only a half dozen people who could be buyers," Cain said. "Finn Walsh has been working on a list. There aren't that many names. He said he'll send it this afternoon. So I repeat—go home, get some rest, and be back here at sixteen-hundred. And, Mac, congratulations on being free."

Mac stood. "Thanks. It's kind of nice to know no one wants to kill me. Now, I just need a place to live, all new stuff, and possibly a new job, but hey, it's all good."

Jace guffawed. "That's the spirit."

Mac rolled her eyes but smiled. "Thanks."

Dane put his mug in the sink and then walked over to her. "Do you need a lift to the hotel?"

"Er, Cass is going to drive me." She glanced up at his face but wouldn't look him in the eye.

He wasn't sure what had happened but he was now *persona non grata*. "I see. Okay, then. Don't forget to grab your cell phone. I think Cain has the box that we stored them in." Cass had gone to get her backpack. As she walked up, Dane said, "Hey, Cass, if you're going to the hotel, would you mind grabbing my go bag? I left it in the room."

"Sure, no problem."

"Thanks." He gave Mac a terse nod and then headed out

the door. He didn't have time for whatever game she wanted to play. If it was only supposed to be a one-night stand, then he was good with that. Not really, but he'd make himself good with it. Life was too damn short, as he'd learned recently. He was done playing games. He was going home to spend time with his cat.

"Dane," Mac called. "On second thought, since you have a bag there, would you mind dropping me? Cass has someplace she needs to be."

He glanced at Cass, but her face was blank. "Sure."

Ten minutes later, they were on the highway headed back to the hotel. "So, um, you said 'a new job' back there. You worried they're gonna fire you?" Dane kept his eyes on the road. He wasn't sure he wanted to see Mac's expression.

"It's a possibility."

"But you don't think so." He braced himself. This was what he was afraid of. She would leave, not because she had to but because she wanted to. How could she have become so important to him in such a short span of time?

"I think life at the CGIS office will be difficult for me. I didn't know my boss was crooked, or that my partner was undercover from another law enforcement agency. Neither one looks good for me. The question on everybody's mind will be is she crooked, too? How could she not know Sinclair was with NCIS? Maybe she did know and just didn't tell anyone. So either I'm stupid, or I betrayed their trust. I just can't see an upside."

"I thought you liked it here. The people at your office will get over it. Don't let them drive you out."

"I did like it here. Right up until all this started. It was a fresh start, one I desperately needed. I made a huge mistake in Minneapolis, and I thought being here was wiping the slate clean, but it turns out I made the same mistake." She shook her head. "I'll tell you about it later maybe."

Whatever it was, she wasn't keen to talk about it. He was going to have to live with that, but he couldn't live with the thought that she might leave town. He'd just started to get to know her. Leaving wasn't the answer, at least not as far as he was concerned. He wanted more, but it wasn't up to him.

They were pulling up at the hotel. Dane parked the SUV and walked with her inside. They got to the room, and she opened the door to the foyer. He followed her in and then went to the room he'd slept in while she went into her room. Grabbing his bag, he glanced around the room to make sure there was nothing else he'd forgotten.

She was waiting in the foyer, leaning against her doorjamb, arms crossed over her chest.

"You gonna be okay?" he asked. "It's been a hell of a day for you."

She nodded. "I feel about a million years old."

"I hear that."

"Your back. I'm so sorry. You hurt yourself saving me. I feel guilty about it."

He shook his head. "Please don't. It was my job to protect you. I did my job. If I can't make my back function, then I can't do the job. It's that simple." And that scary. He was in pain. All bruised up. At least, he hoped it was just bruised.

Dane shifted his go-bag from one hand to the other. "Well, I'll leave you unless you need something else."

She stared at him as if she was making some sort of decision.

He cocked an eyebrow.

"You know what I need?" she said as she straightened.

He tipped his head.

"You. I need you to take me to bed. I just need to lose myself in you. Like we did before. I need to bury myself in your arms where I know I'll be safe for a while. I'm not asking for any kind of relationship. I just need a distraction. A chance to come down from all the adrenaline of the last few days. In short, Dane Landry, I want to use you for your body and then I want you to go. Can you deal with that?"

Dane stood there, mouth hanging open. No one had ever propositioned him so bluntly before. Did he want what she wanted? No. He wanted more. He wanted to hold her, but not just this once. He wanted her in his bed for the foreseeable future. Her expression was neutral as if his answer didn't matter, but her hazel eyes told him it did. She needed him, needed comfort, and he was not going to deny her that. Not now. Not ever.

He gave her a wicked grin. "I'd be an idiot to refuse an offer like that." He dropped his duffel bag and opened his arms.

She smiled and stepped into his embrace.

His fingers wound through her hair as his lips crashed into hers with an intensity that spoke of his need for her. His tongue sought out every intimate space in her mouth, battling in a heated dance of pleasure. He ran his hands down over her back and gripped her ass, holding her against his body, letting her feel the evidence of his desire. He wanted her like he'd never wanted another woman. Seeing her under the debris of the explosion and then hearing the gunshots of the drive-by had all been too much. The thought of someone hurting her was terrifying to him. He needed her to be safe.

Mac answered his advances by slipping her hands under his shirt and setting fire to his skin with her touch. He gasped at the sensation and scooped her up in one quick movement. Then he swore.

"Your back!" she said. "Put me down."

"I'm planning on it," he grinned as he walked her over to the bed and then set her down.

He dropped his shirt on the floor and then brought her in for another kiss that left them both breathless. He was determined to help her forget. To make her feel safe and secure. To make her relax and trust him. To offer her the safe harbor she needed whether it was for one day, or if he had his way, much longer. She was his. She just didn't know it yet, but he was determined to show her in every way possible.

Mac reached for his belt. He let out a deep growl as she started to undress him, pulling his jeans down over his hips. He helped her and kicked them off. He pulled her T-shirt off over her head and then swiftly undid her bra. He stripped it off her arms and then dropped the scrap of fabric on the floor. Then he helped her with her jeans until she stood there only in a black lace thong.

His hungry gaze raked over every inch of her beautiful body. He wanted to touch her everywhere. He nudged her to her back on the bed. His heart raced as he lowered his weight slowly down onto her. He captured her left nipple with his mouth. Her back arched as he swirled his tongue around it. The lacy fabric of her thong against his stomach flipped a switch on his desire. His cock strained against his underwear as his lust for her grew.

He brushed his lips against her neck as he whispered, "Fuck, I want you."

"I want you, too. Now. Inside me."

He cupped her face with both hands and claimed another passionate kiss. Her hands ran down his abs until they found their way to the waistband of his underwear. His breath caught in his throat as she teased him through the fabric of his black boxer briefs.

The scent of her need drove him to distraction, and he wanted nothing more than to feel that moisture on his tongue. He started at her nipples and dropped a series of kisses down her stomach until he reached her thong. The sight of it made him even harder, and as his fingers touched the lace, he heard her whimper his name. It was so sexy he almost lost control.

He peeled off the thong and hovered above her, blowing gently on her skin. She called his name again. He lifted her hips as he settled his mouth on her and flicked his tongue over her clit. He wanted her to know who was making her feel so incredible he wanted his name imprinted in her brain. If they were through, he wanted this, him, to stick in her mind just like she would be stuck in his.

He teased and tortured her with his mouth until she was straining for him, begging for more. He added his fingers and moved them in and out of her slick heat, faster and faster, until she breathlessly panted his name. He almost lost it himself when she shuddered beneath him.

When she reached for him, he crawled up on the bed next to her. She kissed him hard on the mouth as she jerked him free from the confines of his underwear, pushing them down off his legs. Then she brought him on top of her and wrapped her legs around the back of his thighs. "I need you, Dane. Now."

She arched into him. He wanted to wait, go slower, but it was too much. He entered her a little bit at a time, but when she lifted her legs higher, he buried himself to the hilt. She felt so good. So tight. He moved slowly at first, but she pushed against him, increasing the tempo.

He bit down on her neck and matched her hips. He thrust inside her again and again until she arched off the bed and moaned his name as she climaxed. With a few more thrusts, he was there with her. She said his name one more time before he collapsed back onto the sheets pulling her with him.

He lay there with her, catching his breath. Mac was an amazing woman. He wanted to be with her, to start a relationship, to romance her and learn everything about her, but he knew it wasn't up to him. She had to want to stay in Hawai'i, and this interlude was just going to make it harder for him if she decided to go.

Mac got off the bed and went to the bathroom. She came back in a minute and offered him a bottle of water. He sat up and took a drink. "What will you do tonight while we follow Cross around?"

She shrugged. "Not sure. I guess I have some decisions to make."

"There's no rush."

She took the water bottle from him and took a swig before handing it back. "There kind of is."

He frowned. "What do you mean?"

"I don't have a place to live. I can't stay at hotels forever. So I need to decide what I want before I can get settled again."

"You can stay at my place." He saw her hesitate, so he added, "Or Cass's. I'm sure she'd put you up for a bit."

She shook her head. "I'm not much good at couch surfing. I like my own space."

"Fair enough." He glanced at the clock. "I need to get moving. I have to go check on Beans and grab a shower. I can swing by later maybe. Bring you some dinner or something."

She stared at her hands as she twined her fingers in and out. "No, Dane. I... This was the last time we can be together. That mistake I mentioned...I had an affair with someone I worked with, and it didn't end so well for me. I won't go through that again."

What was she talking about? His stomach knotted. "What's that got to do with this?"

"Everything. Yeah, we don't work as closely as what

happened before, but we still work together. I won't go down that road again."

"I hate to tell you this, but it's a bit late for that."

She bit her lip and lowered her head. "I know. I'm sorry. That's why this has to be the last time."

He was trying not to panic. Was she really calling it quits? "What happened at your old job?"

"I slept with another cop. We dated for a few months, but then the top brass found out. He'd been a cop a lot longer and was my superior officer. He told them I came on to him, I seduced him, and then I stalked him when he wanted to break up with me. It was all bullshit, but Command believed him, or more likely, they sided with him, because he came from a long line of cops. His family was practically legendary. I only had one uncle on the force, and even he didn't really stand up for me. Anyway, it was humiliating. I moved here to get away from it, and I ended up—"

"Sleeping with me." Dane wanted to kill the cop back in Minneapolis for hurting Mac. It was his protective nature. But she was comparing him to some asshole cop. That wasn't fair.

"I'm not going to screw you over. I'm not some asshole."

She grabbed her T-shirt and threw it on over her head. "I want to believe that, but he said the same thing and then did anyway. It's just better we end this here and now. I don't want to have to work with someone I used to date. It's weird."

"Are you staying on Oahu then?" he demanded. Was she going to be on Sand Island, but he couldn't see her? Jesus, was she going to date other guys and he'd have to watch? Maybe it was better if she left. Seeing her with someone else would be utter torture.

She shook her head as she bent down and gathered up his clothing from the floor. She put it on the bed next to him. "I don't know what I'm doing, but I do know either way, I don't want to mess up again. This was a one-off."

"But it was twice." He stood now and stared at her. She was throwing something good away because of some prick from her past. "You're blaming me for some other asshole's actions."

"You know what I mean. It just doesn't work. Having sex and working together. And I'm blaming myself, not you. I shouldn't have slept with you either time, but I was very clear with you both times what I wanted."

"Why doesn't it work? It's not like we work out of the same office."

Mac sighed. "Please get dressed."

Dane pulled on his clothes. "I don't see the problem."

"The problem is colleagues take sides when it doesn't work out, and it all gets complicated. I am so fucking tired of complicated. I loved my job at CGIS, but then this case and you happened, and it all just went downhill."

"So, let me get this straight, you regret sleeping with me and think I'm part of the reason your dream job went downhill."

"No. Well, yes, but it wasn't like you did it on purpose. It was my mistake. Like I said, I made the same mistake *twice*. I'm an idiot." She had her hands on her hips. "Do you know why I brought Cain to the meeting with Sinclair? I mean, why he was sitting at the table?"

What in the hell was she talking about now?

"Because I knew if something bad was going to come from that conversation, I needed a witness, and it couldn't be you. We slept together, which meant your opinion, your witnessing of the event, would be called into question. We can't work in the same place and expect it not to have repercussions. I just don't want that. I've worked too hard to create this career to lose it to another stupid mistake."

He was having a hard time keeping his breathing even. "So…not only am I a mistake, but I've cost you your dream job. I'm the asshole, is that it? Fine. Roger that. Point taken. Understood."

"Dane," she said. "Look, I didn't mean to hurt you. I just… It's complicated."

"No, it's simple. We're done. See you around Special Agent Rankin." He breezed past her, grabbed his duffel, and slammed the door on his way out.

She wanted uncomplicated; she got it. His sole purpose now would be to find the motherboards and get back into shape, more time at the gym, more time with a physical therapist, and no more time thinking about her. Now, if he could just figure out how to do that last part, life would be good again.

CHAPTER TWENTY

Mac collapsed on the foot of the bed in the hotel room. What the hell had she just done? She had been blunt and mean on purpose because she didn't have the strength to resist Dane any other way. When Cass had gotten a call and backed out of giving her a lift, Mac knew she'd end up in bed with Dane again. She didn't have the will to fight her desire for him, but more, she wanted the comfort that his arms offered her. The warmth, the feeling of safety. She knew the moment she sat in the truck she'd invite him back to her bed as soon as they got to the hotel.

But they couldn't stay together for all the reasons she'd said. And not because she was falling for him, either. It was stupid and weird and probably because they'd been through so much together, but she couldn't help it. The thing was, she felt like she was already in quicksand. She needed a strong base, a foundation to build her life on. The one she'd started here had already been blown to smithereens. Starting something with Dane was out of the question, no matter how much she cared for him.

She really did need a fresh start. The more time she spent around Dane, the more she'd fall for him, and then she wouldn't want to leave. She'd be caught in that horrible vortex of caring for him and being with him but hating her job and everything else. She had been the subject of the water cooler gossip once before, and the hateful things people she respected had said about her still stung. More than that. It was devastating.

She didn't want to go through that again. Casper and Sinclair had made that inevitable. They'd destroyed her credibility. Who would respect her now? But she could leave. Start over once again. Find another CGIS office. It would be better, but she wouldn't do that if she were with Dane. She'd stay.

She ran her hands over her face. She had never considered herself a runner, but here she was again, one foot already out the door for a second time. And this time, she could honestly tell herself it wasn't her fault. She didn't start this clusterfuck, but she could head for the hills before it got out of control.

She hung her head. Staying just wasn't an option. There was a whole world out there. She could go anywhere really. Work in any sort of law enforcement department. Hell, she didn't even have to worry about moving at this point. She had nothing to move. It would be the easiest relocation ever.

Except, of course, she'd be leaving behind her heart. Dane Landry had gotten under her skin, and no matter how hard she wanted to deny it or say it wasn't true, she knew deep down that she was going to mourn the loss of him for a long time.

And Hawai'i. She loved the islands. Other people said they got island fever, that suddenly they couldn't get away, they felt claustrophobic for something new, but not her. Not so far. It was beautiful here, and the people were amazing. The energy of the islands spoke to her. She would miss that.

Mac glanced at the clock and did the calculations. Her parents would be home from work. They would want to hear all about what happened. They would want to see her. She could hop a flight home and spend a couple of weeks recuperating in her childhood room.

But she made no move to pick up her phone. Instead, she laid back on the bed and closed her eyes.

How had her life become such a mess? Too many traumatic events happening in too short a timeframe? She needed a chance to process things. A moment to breathe.

Dalton Sinclair. She could call him and ask him about working for NCIS in San Diego. She thought he'd put a good word in for her. They'd made a good team for the short amount of time they'd worked together. He was a good investigator, and now that she knew the truth, she'd trust him wholeheartedly, which would make for a nice change. And San Diego was warm and sunny. It was drier than Hawai'i and the water was colder, but she'd adjust. Maybe that was the smart play.

She yawned. She would think about it more after she napped. But the hint of that niggling thought popped to the surface once again, and she opened her eyes, mentally stretching for whatever it was that was taunting her. Did she have it? No. It was gone again. She sighed. It would come to her at some point. She just hoped it was in time. She had a sense of a looming deadline, and it made her stomach knot. They were all running out of time.

Her ringing phone jarred her from a deep sleep. She'd been having a weird, jumbled-up dream. Confused, she stared into the darkness and tried to place where she was. It all came back in a rush. The explosion. The Kahala. The second attempt on her life. She was at the hotel because she no longer had an apartment.

Her cell stopped ringing. They'd put the batteries back in their phones earlier since there didn't seem to be a worry about being tracked anymore. She'd liked it better when no one could reach her.

She started to move but froze when every part of her body protested in agony. She was bruised from head to toe, and stiff from falling asleep in an awkward position. She rolled slowly to her side to grab her cell off the nightstand. The screen lit up, and she didn't recognize the number from the missed call.

Tossing the phone aside she rose slowly, her body working like it was one hundred years old, not in her early thirties. Moving with slow, deliberate steps, she made her way to the bathroom. Her mind was on fire, too, thoughts swirling around in her head of the last few days. Cross, Casper, and Owens. It was all so much to take in, to sort through.

And her heart ached as much as her body. *Dane*. She would love to be curled up with him right now, but instead, she'd pushed him away because she was too weak to behave like an adult. It was stupid, but she felt like adulting was beyond her at the moment.

She flicked on the light in the bathroom, flipped on the shower, and started peeling off her clothes. The hot water would help fix her up, and maybe some Advil. She smiled wryly. She was becoming just like Dane's team. Another misfit and broken toy.

The pounding spray was heavenly, and she stayed in the shower much longer than was necessary. Finally, she got out and toweled herself off. After brushing out her hair, she went through to the bedroom and turned on the lights. She rooted through the pile of clothes Cass had bought for her and pulled out faded jeans, a white tank top, and an off-the-shoulder black sweater. She also dug out a filmy cream-color bra and thong set. Cass sure knew her way around clothes.

She pulled on her underwear, did a few stretches to try and loosen up her muscles, and then pulled on her clothes. Her stomach growled. She glanced at the clock. It was 10:35 p.m. No wonder she was hungry. She'd slept for hours. Grabbing her cell, she saw that she'd missed another five calls from the same number. It wasn't one of the guys because she'd programmed their numbers into her phone. It wasn't work either, or it would come up as such. She gave a mental shrug as she slid her feet into a pair of black mules, grabbed her cell and her purse, and headed to the door. She opened the inner door and then opened the door to the hallway and let out a small scream.

"Sorry I didn't mean to startle you." Neil Ainsley stood there, staring at her.

"Mr. Ainsley." She clutched a hand to her chest. "You scared the hell out of me."

"Sorry. I did try to call. And it's Neil."

She blinked. "That was you? I didn't recognize the number. Is there something you wanted?"

He smiled at her. "I wanted to check on you. Make sure you're okay. John is concerned about you."

Alarming tingles rippled across Mac's back. Something was off. "I'm fine. Thanks for checking."

"Have you eaten dinner? I would be happy to take you out for a meal." Ainsley raked her body with his eyes. "You look like you're dressed to go out."

He, on the other hand, looked like he hadn't slept in weeks. His hair was standing up in tufts and he was wearing the same clothes as he'd had on yesterday. He usually looked harried and harassed, but this was next level. And started alarm bells clanging in Mac's head.

"You know, that's very kind of you, but I'm okay, thanks. I'm sure you could use a night off anyway. Thanks for coming to check on me, though. I'll be sure to thank Deputy Director Cross as well."

Ainsley didn't budge, just stared at her with a strange look in his eye. "I'm afraid I must insist. John won't be happy if you're not looked after. Let me buy you dinner."

Her stomach rolled as the smile on her face froze into a grimace. Could she get back into the foyer and close the door before he blocked it? She glanced down. Not a chance. His foot was already lodged there. He was prepared for her to do that. *Shit.* Her instincts told her she was in serious trouble. "Mr. Ainsley—"

"Neil."

"Neil. I really need to go. I'm meeting someone. If you wouldn't mind moving."

His face hardened. "There's no need to lie. I know Cass is otherwise engaged for the evening, and you don't have friends here."

"What the hell? Are you spying on me?" She tried for indignant, but the note of fear in her voice gave her away.

Ainsley moved swiftly and, suddenly, she was staring at a nine-millimeter semi-automatic. "I don't have time for games. I did try to do this the easy way. Now we'll do it the hard way."

He seized her arm and dragged her into the hallway. Then he put an arm around her waist and pushed the gun into her ribs. "Place your purse so it hides my gun."

She hesitated, but he pushed the barrel hard into her side. "Fine." She adjusted her purse.

"Now we're going to walk right out of here and get into

the SUV. If you make a fuss or draw any attention to us, I will pull this trigger. Are we clear?"

His eyes said he wasn't joking. He'd pull the trigger. Her throat had gone dry. She nodded.

"Good. Here we go. And McKenna, I truly am sorry it had to end this way."

CHAPTER TWENTY-ONE

Dane sat in the rented SUV and stared through the window of the upscale restaurant where Cross was having dinner. As usual, the streets in downtown Oahu were crowded. He grunted into his comms. "I don't think Cross is our guy."

Koa grunted beside him. "I agree. He's got too much to lose."

Jace arrived at the table, smiling at Cross and his dinner companions, the base commander, and the head of Naval Base Pearl Harbor. Through the earbud, Dane could hear Jace acting as the waiter. "Here are your drinks, gentlemen. Have you had a chance to look at the menu?" After a pause, "No problem, take your time." Jace sailed away from the table again. His voice was low when he said, "I agree with Dane. Cross has spent the last twenty minutes trying to find anyone but himself to blame for this mess. He's trying to share it with the Navy and asked what they're all gonna do about it. Underneath his suave exterior, he's sweatin' it. Big time."

"If it's not Cross, then who is it?" Tac asked from his place at the bar.

"Let's review what we know," Cain directed.

Cass shifted on the bench at the bus stop down the street from the restaurant. "One, Cross has the connections to bring the drugs and weapons in. Two, he went to Princeton, and the title TigerKing works for him. Three..." She paused. "Is there a three?"

"He knew Casper and he knew Owens, but then again so did a lot of people," Tac said. "Princeton also graduates a lot of people every year."

"His office," Dane said.

"What?" Koa grunted.

Dane adjusted his position to relieve the spasm in his back. "Cain, you said the connection to the container ships to do the drills was through Cross's office. Did you mean Cross directly or his office?"

Cain was parked in another SUV down the block. "Huh. I ran it through Wainwright, who said it came from Cross's office. One of his assistants called me to let me know we could practice that day."

"Maybe call—"

"On it," Cain replied. There was silence so Cain must have taken out his earbud.

"So, if it's not Cross, then who are we left with? It's got to be someone on base. Someone with access." Dane stared across the street, tapping his fingers on the steering wheel in thought. "Someone who could have contact with Casper and Owens and have it not seem out of place."

His mind wandered. What was Mac doing right now? Sleeping? Did it matter? She'd made herself crystal clear. He needed to let it go.

"Ainsley." Cain's voice came back online. "Neil Ainsley set up the training on the container ships."

"Shit. He never even entered my mind," Jace said.

Dane's adrenaline kicked up in a rush. "That's the whole point. He's good at being in the background, keeps a low profile so no one notices him." They were following the wrong person.

Cain added, "Wainwright said that no way could Cross arrange something like using the container ships. He's not organized enough. Ainsley is the real power behind the power. He takes care of everything."

"How'd you get him to open up to you like that?" Cass asked. "He's a by-the-book kind of guy. Not like him to step outside the formality of the ranks."

"He's had a few drinks, and I told him the Admiral has us on special assignment. His help could be instrumental to our success. No one wants a pissed-off Admiral to know their name."

"Nice to be able to call out the big guns," Koa said.

Dane shifted in the driver's seat. "We're following the wrong guy then. We need to find Ainsley. He's gonna be the one selling the motherboards if he hasn't done so already."

"How are we gonna find him?" Tac asked.

"Good question," Jace said. "I can ask Cross to call him and see where he is."

Cain said, "But then we'd have to bring Cross into this. I think it's better if he stays on the outside of it at the moment."

"Agreed." Dane didn't want any more bigwigs involved in this than absolutely necessary. It always meant trouble.

"We could call Manu and ask him to triangulate Ainsley's cell," Tac suggested.

"That's an idea," Cass agreed. "Do you think the kid is home?"

"Dunno. I'll call him." Cain clicked off the earbud again.

Dane stared through the restaurant window at Cross.

"Do you think he knows anything about all this? He made that whole speech about everything going through him. He tasked the entire CGIS staff to search for the Navy's missing weapons. It's a hell of a way to control the board when you're playing a dangerous game."

Koa rubbed his stomach. "Yes, but did he decide to do that on his own, or did Ainsley suggest it to him and manipulate him into doing it? Ainsley is the organizer, so it strikes me as something he would do."

Cain's voice came through the comms again. "I'm waiting for Manu to get back to me. I asked Finn Walsh about Cross," he said. "According to office scuttlebutt, Cross had an affair with a married co-worker who happened to be the daughter of a senator. It caused a huge mess, and Cross was sent out here as punishment. He's desperate to get back to the mainland and get his career back on track. Finding the missing weapons was his ticket out of here."

"That makes sense," Cass said. "Ainsley suggests it, and Cross jumps at the chance. Wonder what will happen now?"

"Manu," Cain said, and then silence resonated through Dane's earbud. Then, "Got it. Yeah. Will do. Everyone back in your cars. Jace, ride with Tac and Cass. Ainsley is currently heading away from the Kahala. Mac's cell pings with his."

Breath whooshed out of Dane's lungs like someone had just sucker-punched him in the gut. He couldn't suck in any oxygen. He couldn't connect two thoughts, as if his brain was short circuiting. Mac was with Ainsley. Was she safe? Did she know he was behind it all, or was it just some innocent thing? Dane trusted his instincts and nothing felt innocent with Ainsley.

"Dane, call her," Koa demanded.

Dane pulled out his cell and hit the call button as he took off down the street. Cain was behind him, and the others were in a van at the end of the convoy. The call went to voicemail. He tried again, but still no answer. He told the others.

"That's not good," Jace said.

"No, it's not." Cain agreed.

Dane couldn't think like that. He had to believe she was okay. That she was safe. That Ainsley was just checking on her. Because if it was something different, if he had her hostage, Dane would kill him. He wouldn't hesitate. Not one second. If he hurt a hair on Mac's head, Dane would make sure Ainsley paid dearly.

He weaved in and out of traffic. "Do we know exactly where they are? What's Ainsley driving?"

"Manu is keeping me updated. Ainsley is heading to the other side of the island. Traffic's light. We should be able to catch up to him in about ten minutes if we're lucky," Cain said. "I'll call Sinclair and ask him about Ainsley's car."

Dane stepped on the accelerator harder. Ten minutes would be excruciating if she was being held captive. He didn't want anything else to happen to her. She'd been through enough. Icy fingers touched his heart at the thought of Ainsley holding Mac hostage. It was incomprehensible that this was happening. He tossed his cell to Koa. "Try her again."

Koa hit the button on the phone and listened but then shook his head. "No answer."

Cain came back online. "Sinclair says Ainsley drives a Tesla, but he's not in it now."

"How does he know that?" Dane demanded.

"Because he's staring at it in the parking lot at CGIS headquarters."

Fuck! Dane ground his teeth. What the hell was he driving? How were they going to find them?

"Where are they?" he demanded.

"Manu says they're…shit." Cain went silent.

"What? What is it?"

"They're at the East Island Marina. It looks like they might be headed out on the water."

Dane couldn't believe it. How the hell were they going to find them now? They needed one of the RHIBs, which was back in the other direction. "We need to reach out and see if anyone is out here on the water. Any Coast Guard vessel will do."

"Roger that," Jace said. "I'll make calls."

Panic nibbled at the edges of his brain. This just couldn't be happening. If Ainsley got her out on the water away from shore, they had no way to find them. "What boat is he taking out? Does Ainsley own a boat?"

"Checking," Cass called. "No boat that I can see."

What boat was he using? If he went to the marina, then he had to know there was a boat available to use. *Hang in there, Mac. We're coming.* He just prayed they wouldn't be too late.

CHAPTER TWENTY-TWO

"Don't try anything. I've already warned you that I will not hesitate to shoot." Ainsley had her by the arm again and had his gun poked into her side. They'd arrived at a marina, and he was escorting her down a pier.

"Where are we going?" Her stomach rolled at the thought of going out on the water with him. She didn't have to be a rocket scientist to know she wouldn't make it back.

"Where do you think?" he snarled.

They approached the end of the pier and then turned right. There, on the left, was a Hatteras sport fishing boat. Something she only knew because the vessel was Casper's boat, the *Lucky Lady*. When she'd first joined the team, he'd taken her out on a tour around Oahu. "You have the keys to Casper's boat?"

"Shut up and get on board. If you try anything, I will shoot you." Ainsley was nervous, judging by how he was repeating himself.

She scampered over the edge of the pier and onto the boat. Ainsley had made her drive over here. He'd taken the time to put a suppressor on the end of his gun as she drove.

He was going to kill her. There was no question. But did she fight him now and hope he was a lousy shot, or did she wait until they were out at sea in the hope that someone would come for her?

Where was Dane? Did he even know she was in trouble? After the way she'd treated him, she doubted he'd even care. No. That wasn't true. He'd care, but would he check on her? She'd been pretty firm in her dismissal of him. He'd come if he knew she was in trouble, but how was he to know?

Ainsley climbed onto the boat and then gestured with the gun for her to climb the ladder to the fly deck. She did as she was told. Once up there, he started the boat and waved the gun her direction. "Now, go down and undo the ropes. If you run, I'll shoot you."

Making her way back down the ladder, she reviewed her options. She could dive over the side and hide under the dock. If Ainsley didn't get her with the first couple of shots, she stood a chance of surviving until help came. Maybe.

She stepped onto the dock again and released the stern rope, glancing up at the fly deck as she did. Ainsley was staring down at her, gun pointing directly at her. It came down to how good of a shot he was.

"I won the state shooting contest four years running. I'm a crack shot." Her indecision must have shown on her face. It was as if he'd read her mind.

Her stomach plummeted to her shoes. Sweat broke out across her back. She said nothing but headed to the bow of the boat. He could be lying, but could she take that chance? He could be telling the truth as easily as he could be lying. Which meant the chances of her surviving were slim. The possibility she was going to get out of this at all was close to nil. But the longer she was alive, the more opportunity she had for someone to come to her rescue. She just had to hold onto hope.

After she threw the bow line onto the boat, Ainsley waved the gun at her, gesturing for her to climb back onboard. She jumped from the pier to the deck and wobbled a moment. As soon as she was steady, she climbed the ladder. He nodded to the seat with a scowl, and she plopped down. Her hands were shaking slightly as they pulled away from the dock.

"You killed Casper."

He glanced over at her as they headed out of the marina. A ghost of a smile lit his face. "Trying to get me to confess?"

Trying to distract him so she could make a play for the gun resting on the controls next to him was more like it, but she'd take anything at this point.

"So did you do it?" she pressed.

He shot her a glance, then tilted his head. "Why not? Sure. Yeah, I killed Casper. Tying up loose ends. He was becoming a pain in the ass," Ainsley yelled over the wind. They were picking up speed as they left the marina and entered open water. "He kept trying to get more money. He'd been satisfied with dribs and drabs all the way along, but then suddenly he wanted a bigger piece of the pie."

"Because he killed Owens," she yelled back.

Ainsley nodded. "He did, and he didn't even do that right."

"Who was with him?"

"What do you mean?" Ainsley demanded.

"Someone else had to be there. Casper didn't scuba dive and couldn't have tied Owens to the anchor on deck and then thrown him overboard. The body wasn't secured well enough."

He scowled at her. "Fucking smart bitch. You're too smart for your own good." He adjusted the controls a bit and goosed the throttle. The bow lifted higher. "He took one of the heavies that worked for his bookie. Once the guy got

Owens attached to the chain, he came back up. Owens helped the guy off with his tanks while he sat on the side of the boat and then shot him. The body fell overboard and floated away. If only he'd done that with Owens, we wouldn't be in this mess. But he had to get fucking creative. Thought finding the floating muscle that was known to the police for being involved in illegal gambling would make it look like Owens was killed because of that. Of course it didn't happen. Idiot." He shook his head.

She eyed the gun. It was on his right, a bit too far from her to make a move. If she shoved him, she might have a chance to get it, but it was a crapshoot. Last resort. Not that she had any other ideas at the moment.

She kept up her diversionary tactic. "So Casper wanted more money because he killed Owens. Thought he deserved more."

"Asshole had to pay for the muscle he killed. The bookie just tacked it onto his debt. Casper needed real cash." He looked at her. "And I wasn't willing to give it up." Ainsley's smile took an evil turn. "We're coming up to your final destination. I won't mess up in case you're wondering. I know what the fuck I'm doing. We're not by any shipping lanes. There's nothing out here but ocean for miles and miles."

Her heart slammed into her ribcage. There had to be something she could do. Something to stop this from happening. She looked over the ocean for lights. Anything.

"You looking for your boyfriend, Landry?"

How the hell did Ainsley know about Dane? It wasn't like he was the only one who'd stayed at the hotel with her. The team had been coming and going for days.

"What? You didn't think we knew about that? We've been following you for a while. He's not coming to rescue you. Right now, he's following Cross. The poor bastard thinks

Cross is behind all this." Ainsley snorted. "Cross doesn't have the balls for it or the brains. You're on your own."

Fear spiked through her as the hope in her heart flickered out. Maybe this was it. She was going to die on a boat in the middle of the ocean. She should've called her folks, and she shouldn't have pushed Dane away. The last memory he would have of her was her being a bitch.

That stung. She couldn't have that. No giving up. There had to be a way. She just had to find it before her time ran out.

CHAPTER TWENTY-THREE

"Any word on a boat?" Dane tried to be patient, but Mac's life was in danger so all bets were off.

"There's nothing close by. Hold one," Jace said. He was gone for thirty seconds. Then, "Okay. Spoke to Sinclair. Explained the situation and asked him to keep it under his hat. He wasn't keen, but he agreed. He's on his way. He's on a RHIB. He'll be here in twenty. Best I could do."

Twenty minutes was way too long. They could be anywhere by that point. Mac could be dead. Dane pulled into the marina, found a spot in a dark corner, and parked.

"I'll check it out but I'm sure they're already on the water," Koa said as he climbed out of the SUV.

Cain had pulled in beside them. He got out and came over to the driver's side window. Dane opened it.

"Look," Cain said, "I know exactly how you're feeling right now, and I'm gonna tell you what someone once told me. Have your moment, feel it, and then put it back in the box, or you won't be any help to Mac."

"I don't know what you are talking about," Dane deflected.

"Fuck that noise. We all know you've got something going with Mac. She's in danger, and now you can't function. Can't think straight. I'm giving you until Koa gets back here to feel what you need to and then you pack that shit away and do your job. That's what's gonna bring her home safe. You got me?"

Dane didn't know what to say. He just nodded, and Cain walked away from the vehicle. In the side mirror, Dane watched him go and then took a deep breath. He was right. Being all over the place wasn't going to help Mac any.

A spike of adrenaline rushed sickeningly through him. Just the thought of her out there with Ainsley was terrifying. If anything happened to her, he knew it would be the end of him. He just couldn't take another hit. He needed Mac to be okay like he needed to take his next breath. If they didn't find her safe and sound, he'd—

Stop right there, Landry. Pull your shit together.

Maybe she was right. Maybe them being together was a bad idea if this was any indication. He couldn't function if he was constantly worried that she was in danger. And with her job, she'd be in danger a lot. Mac leaving Hawai'i might be the best thing for both of their careers.

He sucked in a deep breath and hissed it out. First, he had to get her back. Nothing was going to stop that from happening. Cain was right. He needed to focus. Go cold. He took one last breath and got out of the SUV as Koa approached. Ainsley was his, alive or dead, made no difference to him.

"Nothing," Koa said. "Not even anyone around to ask. There are some cameras, but by the time we get anyone down here to access them…" His voice trailed off.

"It will just confirm what we know," Cain said as he rejoined the group. "Ainsley has Mac and they took a boat. The question is what boat?"

"I can answer that," Jace said out the window as he, Cass, and Tac parked beside them. "My money is on Ainsley taking Casper's boat. This is the marina where he typically docked."

"What berth?" Dane asked.

"Fifty-Two."

"Koa, check it just to make sure," instructed Dane.

Koa took off at a jog.

Dane pulled out his cell but then thought the better of it. "Anyone got a sat phone?"

Cain went to his vehicle and came back with one. Dane took it and dialed. "This is Chief Petty Officer Dane Landry. I need the location of a boat named *Lucky Lady*." He provided as many details as he had to the dispatcher. "I need that location ASAP." He gave the dispatcher the sat phone number and hung up.

"What are you thinking?" Cain asked.

"The *Wally* is out there somewhere along with a few other boats. There's a chance someone will see it ping on their radar. I'm thinking we ask Sinclair to ask his friends at Pearl to see if they can come up with something, too."

Cain jabbed a number into his cell. "Finn, yeah, I know it's the middle of the night there. Find me a satellite over Oahu. Specifically, the ocean off the east side of the island. I need to find a small fishing boat. And you might want to wake up the Admiral. A CGIS agent is being held hostage by Neil Ainsley—" Cain's jaw ticked, clearly annoyed by an interruption. "Yes, that Ainsley, Deputy Director Cross's assistant. We believe he is behind the motherboard theft." Cain hung up. "Someone will find them, and then we'll be on our way."

"Waiting is the worst," Cass said, "but we might as well suit up while we wait." She went around to the back of the SUV and opened the hatch. "Come get your gear."

The next few minutes were spent quietly dressing in tactical gear and adding a lot more weapons. They were going fully loaded and red hot.

"This is what Casper's boat looks like." Jace pulled the picture up on a laptop they had in the back of the SUV.

The fishing boat was a thirty-footer, designed with an elevated fly bridge to make spotting large sport fish easier. For several minutes they tossed around boarding strategies, trying to figure out if there was a way to get on board without anyone seeing them, but unless they had a whole lot more time and scuba gear the possibility was zilch.

"We're just going to have to go right at him and hope he's distracted." Cain shot Dane a look. "Mac is smart, she'll understand what's going on and help if she can."

"Agreed," Dane said.

There wasn't another option. He was just gonna make damn sure he was front and center on the RHIB so he could be the first one on Casper's boat.

He looked at Cass. "Bring the sniper rifle."

She looked at him, eyebrows raised. "That's a hard shot. At sea on the waves at any amount of distance?" She shook her head. "I could hit Mac."

Fucking adrenaline. He needed it to stop pulsing through him. His gut was a knotted, tarry ball of tension. "I know, but we may not have much in the way of options." Dane wasn't fooling himself. Cain had been right. He needed to look at this as if Mac was a total stranger, and not the woman he wanted in his bed for the rest of his life. Her odds were not looking good right now. Anything they could do to up those chances had to be done.

"I agree with Dane. Take the rifle," Cain ordered. "You're the best shot with it, Cass. We may need it out there."

Cass's lips went into a hard line. "Okay." She pulled out

the case that held her sniper rifle and set it on the ground beside her.

The sound of a boat engine reached their ears. As a cohesive unit, they sped to the end of the dock. Sinclair pulled up on the RHIB.

"Thank God," Dane said as they all jumped on board.

"Any idea where we're headed?" Sinclair asked. He was wearing full tactical gear and had a machine gun hanging around his shoulders.

Dane studied him. "You've done this before and not just with NCIS."

Sinclair nodded. "Former Marine Force RECON."

"Well, shit. That might've been nice to know."

He shrugged. "Again. Undercover. And it didn't come up since we met."

"Glad to have you with us."

The sat phone buzzed. Cain answered. He yelled out a heading to the Petty Officer driving the boat.

The petty officer steered the boat into open water, then shoved the throttle into a wide open position. The bow lifted and Dane braced himself on the rigid orange hull. The night was calm, the sea was flat, and the RHIB practically flew across the water. The great big ops clock in Dane's head was ticking faster. It was all down to timing now.

CHAPTER TWENTY-FOUR

"But why do you want me dead?" she asked Ainsley as he started to slow the boat. "I don't have anything on you. I had the file, which implicated Owens' whole team and Casper, but nothing on you." The full moon shone brightly in a cloudless night sky. She looked around but still no sign of help on the horizon.

Ainsley decreased their speed even further while checking the radar. She was running out of time. As he pulled the throttle back, the gun started to slide so he moved it to the left side of the console. A spark flared in her brain. Maybe there was hope.

"You are another loose end," he said finally.

"But why," she demanded. "I don't know anything. How can I be…" She stopped when the realization hit her. "You have a partner, and they are worried about me. They think I know something."

He stared at the navigation screen and then slowed the boat to a crawl.

She glanced at the gun. Could she get it? She moved slightly to gauge Ainsley's reaction.

He immediately put his hand on the gun and glared at her.

So much for that idea. She was going to have to think of something very quickly because they were stopping.

He turned off the motor. The boat started to drift. The waves were small, the ocean calm. Under normal circumstances, Mac was sure she'd be nauseous by now, but the power of adrenaline was amazing. She was too worried about dying to feel like puking.

"Now"—he turned to her—"no one is going to find you out here. You can yell and scream all you want, so go for it if it makes you feel better."

She stared at him. There was no way she was going to give him the satisfaction of breaking down. He was a truly evil asshole, and she wouldn't let him win if she didn't have to. "Who is your partner? Who is the TigerKing?"

"Maybe it's me. I like animals. Maybe I'm the TigerKing."

She shook her head. "No, it's not your style. You're not savvy enough to think to use a drone for transporting..." The missing piece fell into place. She couldn't believe it. How could she have missed it? The niggling thought floated to the surface, and this time it finally gelled. A snippet of conversation that her subconscious had logged but her conscious did not. "Holy shit!" she breathed. "Answer me one more question. What was the delay?"

Ainsley frowned. "What are you talking about?"

"The delay. The motherboards are still here. Your partner must be selling them since you're out here dealing with me. I assume you want to get rid of them as soon as possible, and since most of the other weapons have been found, now is your moment to get rid of them. So who is the buyer and what was the delay?"

"That's two questions, but I'll answer one. There was

never a delay. It was always part of the plan. I orchestrated this whole thing, and now those motherboards are about to fly off to their new owners, and in the next twenty-four hours I'm about to become crazy rich. No more running around after Cross for me. That asshole is on his own." A smile grew on Ainsley's face. "Now you've put it together. He was stupid and made one small error. No one seemed to notice, but I told him you would eventually put it together. And just in time because now you have all the answers you wanted, right before you die." He stood, grabbed the gun, and pointed it at her. "On your feet."

She didn't move.

"Now," he growled.

She slid off the seat but had to grab onto it when her knees buckled.

"Move!"

Letting go of the seat, she took a tentative step. Her knees held, and she slowly made her way over to the ladder. He gestured for her to climb down. She moved at a glacial pace. Her hands and legs were trembling with anticipation. Ainsley would have to tuck his gun somewhere to descend the ladder. Was this her moment to jump for it? She could go underwater and hope for the best. It was better than dying on deck and being thrown in.

Her foot hit the deck and she moved to the left side of the ladder. Looking up, she held her breath. What he did with the gun determined her fate. He stared at her for a moment, not moving. Could he read her mind? "I'm coming down. If you try anything I will make your death painful. Do you understand me?"

She nodded once.

He had the gun in his right hand. He turned and started down, only holding on with his left.

She debated grabbing his ankle and jerking him from the

ladder as he descended. He'd land flat on his back, allowing her to grab the gun if he dropped it. If he didn't let it go then she'd have to fight him for it. But she'd lose if they got into a wrestling match for it. He outweighed her by at least fifty pounds, and she'd be toast if he wound up on top. He'd kill her with his bare hands. No, she was going to have to take her chances in the water.

She leaped to her left and pushed off the side of the boat, diving into the water. Shots rang out around her. One grazed her arm. She pulled herself deeper and deeper into the inky blackness. Eventually, she would have to surface to breathe, but maybe she could confuse him. She swam under the boat, with her lungs burning for air and fighting the primal urge to open her mouth to breathe. *Hold it together* she admonished herself as she reached the far side of the boat and neared the surface. Although she desperately wanted to gulp air, she controlled the urge and broke through the water line as quietly as she could.

Sucking in oxygen at an alarming rate, she went back under and tried to put as much distance between her and the boat as possible. She waited until her lungs were screaming for oxygen before she surfaced again. She pulled in more air. Turning slightly, she glanced back at the boat. Ainsley was leaning over the far side. She went under again.

When she surfaced this time, she was about thirty feet away from the boat. Ainsley was looking for her. His face was mottled with anger. He slammed the side of the boat with his hand but then straightened and smiled. The smile turned into laughter, and soon he was doubled over.

A minute later, he was calm again.

"I know you're out there, Mac, and I know I at least grazed your arm. That's okay. I drove us out here on purpose. You're in a current that runs away from the islands. You will never make it back to shore. No one is going to find you. The current will carry you out into the middle of the Pacific like the rest of the garbage. It's going to be a long, slow terrifying death for you, Mac. Enjoy!" He turned, went up to the fly bridge, and fired up the engines.

There was another sound. A buzzing. Mac turned and searched the horizon. There. It was a boat coming straight at them. Did she raise her arms and wave for help? If she did, Ainsley could still shoot her.

Ainsley turned and saw the boat coming. He gunned the engines and took off.

The boat continued coming. Mac raised her arms in the air and started waving them frantically.

The boat, an RHIB, had a spotlight that was dancing over the waves. It hit her square in the face. She waved frantically and the boat swerved in her direction. She was going to be saved. She couldn't believe it. Suddenly, a new sound hit her ear. She turned. Ainsley had turned and was coming back. He was aiming directly at her. *Shit*! She couldn't outswim the boat.

Her life depended on who reached her first.

CHAPTER TWENTY-FIVE

"Shoot him!" Dane demanded.

"You can't," Sinclair yelled. "He doesn't have Mac on the boat. If you shoot him, he'll claim he was just coming out here to help Mac and you shot an unarmed man."

"But she can testify that he kidnapped her."

Sinclair said, "Only if she survives." He turned to Cass. "Do not shoot Ainsley unless you see a gun in his hand. We need to get Mac before he does."

They were getting closer, but it was going to be tight. Dane's heart was in his throat. This could not go wrong. They were this close to saving Mac.

Dane watched helplessly as they both zoomed toward the target. Mac tried to swim toward them, but Ainsley adjusted. "He's not going to shoot her. He's going to hit her!"

Cain stared at Dane and then back at Ainsley. "Fuck. You're right. And without her to testify against him, he gets off. He'll tell them he was trying to help her and accidentally hit her with the boat. It's dark and very hard to see out here."

He turned to Cass. "Wait until the last possible moment and then take him out."

"No. Sinclair is right. Scuttle the boat," Dane demanded.

"What?" Cass looked at him as if he were crazy.

Dane moved on deck to brace himself and raised his weapon. "If we all shoot at the hull below the water line it will slow him down. We'll figure the rest out later."

Cain nodded, and the entire team lined up on the RHIB and took aim.

"Mac, please keep your head down," Dane murmured before they opened fire, peppering the hull of Casper's boat. Chunks of fiberglass flew, and the boat started to slow. They were coming up fast on Mac. Ainsley had ducked at first but now realized what they were doing. He gunned the engines, but with the water pouring in, the boat was seriously slowing down.

Dane stopped shooting and picked up the bullhorn. "It's over, Ainsley," he hollered. They started slowing down. Mac was just off their port side. The driver brought the RHIB down to a crawl so they could reach out and grab Mac.

Dane handed the bullhorn off to Cain. He leaned over and reached for Mac.

"Thank God!" she said as she reached for his hands. Bullets sprayed the water, and she disappeared. Dane fell back. Dropping his weapon, he dove in the water while his teammates fired on Ainsley. Ainsley took more rounds than could be counted full-on in the chest. He fell into the water.

Where the hell was Mac? Dane looked around, but the water was dark. He couldn't see anything. He surfaced. "Mac!" He yelled again. "Mac!" Nothing. He dove under again, searching frantically. Where the hell was she?

Then he saw her. She was floating about four feet under the surface. He dove, wrapped an arm over her chest and gripped under her armpit, then kicked like hell toward the moonlight shining above. Jace and Cass helped get her into the boat. Cass immediately started working on Mac as Jace and Sinclair helped Dane into the boat.

"C'mon, Mac. Breathe," Cass begged and then went back to mouth-to-mouth. She was doing chest compressions when Mac suddenly started choking. They rolled her over, and she spewed water.

"Mac, open your eyes," Dane demanded.

Mac's eyelids fluttered, and then she looked up at him.

He'd never been so happy to see those hazel eyes in all his life. "Are you okay? Where did he get you?"

She stared at him. "Ainsley," she mumbled.

"He's dead. We've called for backup."

"My arm," she said. "Grazed it."

He glanced at her arm long enough to confirm it was just a graze and then even though he didn't see any blood, he searched the rest of her for any other injuries. He needed to know for sure she was okay. *Nothing.* His pulse settled back to a normal rhythm when he noticed blood on the floor of the RHIB. Where was it coming from? Not her arm. It was on the wrong side.

"Mac, honey, I'm gonna have to roll you over."

She grunted as he moved her. "Shit. Get me some more bandages. The bastard got her in the back. I think it's just a graze, but it went right across her shoulder blades."

Cass handed him bandages, and they patched her up as best they could. They were just finishing when reinforcements arrived. The driver brought the RHIB alongside the *Wally*. "How the hell did they get here so fast?" Cass asked.

Cain smiled. "Finn Walsh. He called Bertrand, and the Admiral called out the *Wally.*" He squeezed Dane's shoulder. "They're gonna take her on board. They've got a medical bay. They'll see to her and make sure she's okay."

Dane leaned against the hard rubber, covering his face with his hands.

Mac reached up and took his hand in hers. "Thank you for coming to get me."

He locked gazes with her. "I'm only sorry we weren't here sooner."

She smiled weakly, but gratitude and something more glittered in her eyes. "You were here in time. That's all that matters."

He squeezed her hand. There was a lot he wanted to say, to tell her, but this wasn't the time.

The crew from the *Wally* strapped her to a stretcher and lifted her on board. Dane and the entire team followed her onto the *Wally*. She was being carried to the medical bay when she stopped them. "Wait. Dane," she called.

He walked over to the side of the stretcher. "Honey, you have to let them take care of you."

"I know, but I need to tell you something. Ainsley has a partner."

Dane stared at her for a moment before he called out, "Cain! You're gonna want to hear this. Everyone will." They all walked over and surrounded Mac.

She held onto Dane's hand as she spoke. "Ainsley had a partner. The person who arranged the drone thing and the payment by bitcoin. Ainsley didn't have the skillset for that. The TigerKing."

"Who is it?" Dane asked.

"Manu."

"No fucking way," Tac said. "He's just a kid!"

Jace froze and then swore. "Yeah, but he's a smart one. He went to Princeton, too. Was the head of the chess society or something."

Mac nodded. "He had a failed tech startup, something to do with AI software. He'd gotten lots of backing but couldn't provide what he'd promised. He came back to Hawai'i to lick his wounds."

"He's been using the system to reroute the weapons," Sinclair said.

She nodded. "He'd have the skill for it." She swallowed. "Ainsley said the deal is going down soon. He said the motherboards were leaving tonight and he was going to be rich in the next twenty-four hours."

Dane wracked his brain for anything they were missing. "Leaving how? And why twenty-four hours to wait?"

"Flying," Mac supplied. "Ainsley said they were flying out of here tonight. That there never was a delay. Everything was part of a plan."

"Sir, we need to get her to the med bay," said one of the seamen carrying Mac. "She's losing a lot of blood."

"Right." He looked down at her. "Rest up. Call us if you think of anything else." He desperately wanted to kiss her. Right here, right now, in front of his team and the crew of the *Wally.* But no one needed the distraction. This was work. She was right. The line between personal and professional would be too blurred if they worked together and dated. He gave her hand a squeeze and let them take her away.

He watched their retreat until he couldn't see her, feeling like his heart was being ripped out and stomped on. Blowing out a breath, he turned toward Cain. "What the hell do we do now?"

Cain shook his head. "I have no idea. We need to get back to Oahu and find Manu. I can't believe that kid is behind all this."

"Yeah. Shocking doesn't quite cover it. Do we have any way to track him?"

Sinclair snorted. "That kid is brilliant. There's no way he'd let himself be tracked."

Jace nodded. "He used a drone and bitcoin for taking delivery. Remember?"

They got back on the RHIB and headed back to the

marina. Dane checked his gear and tightened the straps as they sped across the water. Mac's words swirled around in his head. The delay wasn't a delay; it was all planned. Scheduled.

They arrived back at the marina and disembarked. Sinclair was still on the RHIB. Dane nudged Cain and tilted his head toward Sinclair. "Technically, it's the Navy's missing shit."

Cain gave Sinclair the once-over. "Hey, Dalton, you want to join us?"

A smile lit the man's face. "Thought you'd never ask." He hopped off the RHIB and followed them to the parking lot. They stood next to their vehicles.

"Where do we go from here?" Sinclair asked.

"Good fucking question." Cain shook his head. "Ideas, anyone?"

Dane leaned against the SUV. "I've been thinking. If I were Manu and had to meet someone to give them the motherboards, what would I do?"

"Probably won't take his own car," Jace offered.

"Agreed," Dane grunted.

"Ride-share service has got to be out. It's not like you're gonna depend on an Uber driver to take you somewhere and then wait for you," Koa said. Then frowned. "But then he's young. Maybe he would use Uber."

Cain put a foot up on the bumper. "He's a smart kid. He'd have to plan for a quick getaway on the off chance he'd need it. I'm sure he doesn't think he will, but I don't think he'd be so arrogant that he wouldn't at least give himself the option of a quick getaway."

"So, no on Uber or Lyft." Dane cocked his head. "He's tech savvy so he's not going to rent anything either because it can all be tracked. He wouldn't borrow from a friend because that's more witnesses."

"Steal one?" Tac asked. "Seems stupid, but it's a

possibility."

Dane nodded. "There's that. But you know, I'm willing to bet he took one of the CGIS cars from the motor pool. It's Sunday. No one is there. He can take the car and clean the log, so it looks like it never left."

Koa smiled. "But the car has a GPS locator built in."

"Who do we call to get the information?" Cain asked.

Sinclair pulled out his cell. "I'll call the guy in charge of the equipment sign-out." He put the phone to his ear and walked away.

Dane tried to relax, but it was hard. Mac wasn't in danger, but she was hurt, and he couldn't be there. He needed to focus on getting the guys that hurt her. He'd deal with how he felt about her later, after everything died down, assuming this went well. If they screwed this up, he might be looking for a new job, too.

Sinclair came back. "Can I borrow the laptop?"

Jace brought it out of the trunk and opened it on the hood of Dane's SUV. Sinclair still held the phone to his ear. He logged into his email and then clicked on a link. It brought up a map. "Thanks, Dave. Yeah, I appreciate it." He tucked the phone back in his pocket.

Sinclair looked at the dots on the screen. "So, there are only three cars in use at the moment. One is downtown Oahu, one is at a restaurant on the north shore, and the last one is at Kalaeloa Airport."

"Bingo," Dane said. "That's got to be Manu."

"You think the buyer is at Kalaeloa?" Cass asked. "We use it to launch search and rescue missions, the flight school uses it, and the National Guard does, too, on occasion. Also, small planes, you know general aviation stuff. The private jets usually fly into Inouye. What kind of a buyer would use Kalaeloa?"

"The kind that comes for unofficial official visits to the Coast Guard," Dane supplied.

"Shit, you mean Senator Weston?" Jace squeaked.

Dane nodded.

Cain pulled his phone out of his pocket and checked something. "The senator is wheels up in forty minutes. Explain your theory on the way. We need to get there before Manu leaves."

Dane, Koa, and Sinclair got into Dane's rented SUV. Cass and Cain were in Cain's vehicle, and Jace and Tac were in Jace's rental. Dane took the lead as they tore out of the parking lot and raced toward Kalaeloa.

Dane handed his cell to Koa. "Get both cars in on a conference call so we can talk. It's easier than using the earbuds while we drive."

Two minutes later, they were all on a video call. "Tell us your theory," Cain said.

"Mac told me that the whole thing was on a schedule. The deal was planned to go down a few days after the arrival of the motherboards. Why? Why would they want to wait? Because they couldn't change the schedule. If it was all planned, then this was done well in advance. They knew the schedule because it's not the buyer's schedule; it's the seller's. They could plan around it.

"Senator Weston is heading out to Singapore tonight. His plane won't be searched. He'll be cleared to go no matter what. He can take the motherboards to Singapore and sell them to China."

"Jesus, you're accusing a sitting US senator of selling highly classified equipment to China?" Jace said.

"Yeah, I guess I am. Or, at least, to someone. It fits. Weston arrived, and all hell broke loose. He's flying out right when the motherboards are leaving, according to what Ainsley told Mac. Can you think of a better way to get them out than on a private jet of a sitting US senator? Besides, think about it. He's not selling them to be used against us. We all know these are going to go to Russia. China has its own shit. And Jace said that the senator is up for re-election. I imagine he needs some serious cash to do it."

Jace added, "The other party is setting up a big hitter to run against him. It's going to be an expensive race. Selling the motherboards gives him money, and this trip gives him publicity and credibility."

Dane changed lanes. "And don't forget, Manu is at the same airport. I'm thinking that's not a coincidence."

"*If* he's there," Cain cautioned. "We don't know for sure yet."

"It's a strong likelihood," Sinclair said. "I checked with my guy again. The other two cars are signed out. The one at Kalaeloa is not. It's supposed to be back at the lot."

"What are we gonna do when we get there?" Tac asked. "Assuming this is all true. I mean, we can round up Manu, but unless we catch him red-handed, we've got nothing on him. Ainsley is dead. There's no one to testify to anything."

The truth of Tac's words hit Dane dead center in his chest. They had nothing on Manu, one of the main players who wanted to hurt Mac, and there was nothing they could prove.

"We're just gonna have to find the motherboards and hope they're covered in his prints," Cass said. "Or we could leave him in a room with Dane for a few minutes, and I'm willing to bet he'd confess. You didn't hear that, Sinclair."

"I didn't hear a thing," he agreed.

"There will be no alone time," Cain said. "Unless absolutely necessary," he added with a smirk.

The team chuckled. Dane knew Cain was joking. And he wouldn't do it anyway, but Manu didn't know that. And as smart and tech-savvy as the kid was, Dane was willing to bet he'd never been faced with an angry MRST operative before. There were all kinds of things he could do to Manu without ever laying a finger on him. Although, one good punch would make him feel so much better.

CHAPTER TWENTY-SIX

Dane rolled the SUV to a stop outside the squat building that housed the waiting area for passengers and pilots. "What do you think?" he asked. They still had an open phone line to the other SUVs.

"I don't think they'd be in the Fixed Base Operator lounge. I think we need to go out on the tarmac and find what hangar they're in," Tac said. "The exchange will take place there. That's the most logical thing to do."

Koa grunted, "Agreed. I'll go find out what hangar Weston's jet is in. Sinclair, check the cars again and make sure Manu isn't on the move."

"Roger that." He brought it up on his phone this time. "Still here. The airport isn't that big. I'm sure we can find them quickly."

"True, but we need some kind of plan. We can't just roll up and hope for the best." Dane was already running ideas. "I'm thinking we come from two directions and have people at the hangar's back door, just in case."

Koa climbed back into the SUV. "Hangar five."

Cain and Cass led the way, followed by Dane's SUV. "I

like Dane's plan," Cain said. "Let's do it. Jace, you and Tac cover the back of the hangar. Dane, follow my lead and block the front of the hangar with the SUVs."

Dane rolled to a stop behind Cain and watched in his rearview as Jace and Tac got out and made their way toward hangar five. They disappeared behind hangar four. "We don't have an earbud for you, Sinclair. Just follow my lead. It'll be fine. I'll let you know if anything is happening unless you want to stay in the SUV. Nothing wrong with that. You're at a disadvantage."

Sinclair snorted. "Yeah, I'll be with you. I'm not really a sit in the car kind of guy."

Jace's voice came over the earbud. "In position."

Dane said, "They're in position."

"On me." Cain's SUV took off and Dane slammed his foot on the gas pedal. He followed Cain to the hangar. "Now!" yelled Cain as they screamed to a halt and jumped out of the SUV in front of the structure. It was empty.

"What the fuck?" Dane said. He looked around. Then he looked outside. Two hangars over, there was an unmarked CGIS car. "Shit. Two hangars down!" He pointed. They all got back in the SUVs and shot down the tarmac.

A jet came out of the hangar and turned away from them. It was heading for the runway. They roared up to the hangar and screamed to a stop. Dane hopped out and ran around the SUV to catch Manu just as he was getting into the car.

"Where are the motherboards?" he yelled.

Manu stared at him before a slow smile lit his face. Then he cleared his features and said, "Dane! What are you guys doing here?"

"We know everything, you little shit. The motherboards. Are they on the plane?"

Manu stared at him, looking perplexed. "I have no idea what you're talking about."

Dane wanted to hit him so badly his hand itched. "Drop the fucking act. It's over."

"I still have no idea."

Dane turned away. The jet was rolling toward the runway. Cain was on his phone, trying to get the jet stopped. "The tower has issued a hold order, but they're still going."

"Shit." Dane stood there, rage and helplessness roaring through him. "What are we gonna do?"

"We can try and get ahead of them on the runway," Tac said.

"Too late." Cain pointed at the jet that had already turned onto the runway.

Dane whirled around and went nose-to-nose with Manu. The kid reared back but was trapped against the car.

"What's wrong? What's going on?" he demanded, still doing his innocent act.

Dane leaned in. "You know what, kid? You think you're safe because you've killed everyone that had any evidence against you. You think you're gonna get away with this, but what you haven't accounted for is National Security. See, we have enough circumstantial evidence to say we suspect you are a threat, a fucking domestic terrorist. Know what that means? No trial. No jail. Just some deep dark hole somewhere until the CIA decides what to do with you. They can keep you there for years. National security threat. No lawyer in the world can get you out of that one.

Manu's eyes narrowed just before the sound of the jet engines increased to a roar.

"I'm not lying to you, kid. Are the motherboards on that airplane? Yes or no. Your future depends on it."

Dane didn't blink. He didn't flinch. He stared into Manu's soul and sent his message. This little shit was not getting away with selling out his country on top of killing a lot of people.

Fear crept into Manu's features. His eyes started darting around. Sweat broke out on his upper lip. The roar of the jet engines hit a new level of brutal.

Manu gave the smallest of nods.

"They're on the plane," Dane yelled as he moved away from Manu. He needed distance, or he'd hurt the kid.

Cain yelled, "Bertrand says stop the plane."

The jet was picking up speed as it taxied away. Sinclair was closest to the SUV. He hopped into the driver's seat while Dane dove into the passenger side and Koa jumped in the back. They took off across the access road and through the grass before swinging onto the runway.

Sinclair gunned it until they were next to the plane. He hit the horn, trying to get the pilot's attention. But nothing.

Cain's voice came through the earbud. "You're running out of runway. Stop that goddamn plane from taking off."

Dane brought up his gun. "We have to stop the plane. Koa, take out the tires. I'll hit the engine."

Koa snorted as he pulled out his weapon. "We're so screwed after this. Firing on a US Senator is going to make us cellmates with the kid."

They put down the windows and opened fire. The tires deflated and then the rubber started to peel off, hurtling through the air like steel-belted missiles. The airplane weaved on the runway, but they kept going. Dane laid down another spray of bullets and the engine caught fire.

Sinclair hit the brakes as the plane veered in their direction. But then the jet swung back toward the middle of the runway. It was slowing down, and Sinclair kept well back. One engine was engulfed in flames. Then there was an explosion and bits of metal went everywhere. The airplane crashed onto the right-side wing and came to an abrupt halt.

Sinclair pulled up about thirty feet away, and they all got out. Dane ran to the door just as it opened. Weston came out first. Then a couple of people in suits. Next were the pilots. "That it?"

The pilot nodded.

"Weston," Dane called over the cacophony of the approaching emergency vehicles. "Where are the motherboards?"

He looked blankly at Dane. "I have no idea what you're talking about."

Sonofabitch. It was all over. Weston was going to get away with it if they didn't find those motherboards. "No fucking way." Dane hauled ass into the burning airplane.

"Dane, brother. What the fuck?" Koa yelled.

Dane went to the back of the plane and looked in every bin and under every seat. The smoke was getting thick, and he couldn't hold back a cough.

Nothing. Where the hell could they be? There was no way Weston would've put them in the cargo hold. He looked around again. Only the emergency lights were on, and with the smoke, it was getting harder and harder to see. There was nowhere else to look.

"Dane, get your ass out of there now. That's an order," Cain instructed through his earbud.

He stayed silent. Come on. *Think.* Then it hit him. He went back to the bathroom and ripped open the cupboards. There was the case. Beside the toilet. He ripped a curtain off the side of a window and used it to pick up the box. But as he tried to move, he stumbled and fell. Pain pierced his back like an ice pick, burning hot and weirdly cold. He coughed hard as he struggled to breathe. He rolled to his hands and knees, feeling like every muscle in his back was being ripped apart. Keeping his head as low as possible, he sucked in a huge breath before he stood and limped down the aisle. He made it to the open door before he took another breath.

"Here," he thrust the curtain-wrapped box toward Jace.

"Got it," Jace said. He moved away from the airplane.

Koa and Cain reached up and helped Dane out. Supporting him under his arms, they ran with him all the way behind the fire trucks. When he stopped, he started coughing again. An EMT brought him over to an ambulance and stuck an oxygen mask over his face.

"Jesus, Dane," Cain said. "That was risky and stupid. Don't ever pull that shit again."

Dane just coughed and pulled in oxygen.

"But the admiral is pleased you got the motherboards. He's not so happy about the exploding airplane."

Dane met Cain's gaze, and the two of them broke into laughter until Dane started coughing again.

Once he stopped coughing, he pinned a stare on his team leader. "Where's the Senator?"

Cain gestured behind them. "He's sitting in the back of an ambulance. I have Cass and Tac watching him. If he moves, they'll arrest him. The EMTs have already been told not to transport him anywhere. The admiral is trying to find someone to take him."

Sinclair came over and stood beside them. "People are coming from Pearl for the motherboards and the senator."

Dane stared at him. "Shit. Will they do the right thing, or is this gonna get swept under the rug?"

"If I had to guess?" Sinclair shrugged. "The latter."

Dane's stomach dropped. All that work. Everyone whose lives had been torn apart, or ended by this… All for fucking nothing. Bile rose savagely in his throat.

Cain's voice came through the earbud. "Jace, you still have the motherboards?"

"Roger that."

"Sinclair, who do you trust to lift some prints?"

He smiled. "I know just the person. I'll give her a call. Get your people on the road. We'll get this done and then the guys from Pearl can have them."

"Jace, take Tac with you and head to Sand Island. Go to the CGIS building. A person named—" Cain looked at Sinclair, who responded with, "Miranda Hill."

"Miranda Hill will meet you at the doors. Go with her and keep the motherboards in sight the whole time."

"Roger that," Jace acknowledged.

"Cass stay focused on the Senator." Cain grinned. "Shoot him if he moves."

"That would be my distinct pleasure," she replied.

The EMT gave Dane the once-over. "He needs to go to the hospital for observation."

Cain glanced at Dane. "I don't think he's going to argue with you."

"What do you mean?" Dane demanded. He didn't want to be evaluated. He was fine. He started to take off the oxygen mask.

Cain grabbed his arm. "You want to go to the hospital where Mac happens to be, don't you? Here's your ride. No waiting around."

Dane blinked as he tried to understand what Cain was saying, and then his heart soared. He was going to Mac.

"Um, yeah. Hospital. Sure. Yeah. I might need some respiratory therapy after all. Let's go get checked out."

Koa snorted and shook his head. Sinclair grinned, and Cain just nodded at him. They put him on the stretcher and closed the back doors of the ambulance. His team was awesome, but even better, he'd managed to do his job with minimal interference from his back. But best of all, he was going to see Mac. Now he just had to convince her not to leave Hawai'i.

CHAPTER TWENTY-SEVEN

Mac winced when she moved. The bandage was protecting her back, but it wasn't the most comfortable thing in the world. Fortunately, both gunshots she was dealing with now were just grazes. The nurses had cleaned them and bandaged her up. The doctor had told her she could go home tomorrow. She snorted. In the hospital two times in less than forty-eight hours. Had to be some kind of record. Then of course, there was the question of home. Hers had been blown to bits. Where, exactly, was she supposed to go tomorrow?

She shifted on the bed, trying to get comfortable. Maybe it was time to see her folks. She'd called them earlier just after the nurses had finished with her. Her mom was thrilled to hear from her and prattled on about them coming to visit Oahu and Mac soon. She didn't have the heart or the stamina to break her mother's heart and tell her the truth. Instead, she'd signed off by saying how much she was looking forward to her parents' visit. She'd have to tell them the truth, but she could put it off for another day, couldn't she?

She closed her eyes. Her headache had started pounding

again, and it was painful. The meds they'd given her when she'd first arrived had been pretty intense but left her feeling woozy, and her wounds were starting to hurt again. Maybe she should ask the nurse if all this was normal.

She opened her eyes. "Oh, shit. You scared the life out of me. I didn't hear you come in."

John Bishop Cross stood beside her bed. He offered her a smile. "Sorry. I just thought I'd better check on my favorite CGIS agent. You've been through quite a lot these last few days."

"Um, yeah." She tried to pull herself up higher on the pillows, but it hurt to move. She looked around for the call button. She wanted the nurse, but it was on the far side of the table next to her bed. She couldn't reach it.

"Could you—"

"So how are you feeling?"

"A bit sore, but I'll live. Got a drumline rehearsal going on in my head, though."

He nodded.

Something was off. She could feel it, but her brain was foggy. The headache and the pain, not to mention the meds and the whole events of the last twenty-four hours, had left her feeling fuzzy. What was it? What was wrong with this situation?

"Well, I'm sure once you get some rest you'll be back on your feet in no time." He moved so he was leaning a hip on her bed. His hand was close to hers.

"Um, I appreciate the visit, but I think I'd like to sleep."

"I'm sure," he said but made no move to leave. "What did Ainsley say to you out there? I had no idea about any of it. Hard to believe, I know, but he completely pulled the wool over my eyes."

She wanted Cross gone. He was creeping her out. "Um, well, he said a lot of things. I can't remember much at the moment. You know, it was traumatic, and I'm just not sure…" She didn't know what to say. The whole conversation was triggering alarm bells in her gut.

She glanced around him at the door to see it was closed. He'd closed it on his way in. *What the hell?* "What do you want, Cross?" Her stomach knotted. The back of her hospital gown was damp with sweat.

"Want? Like I said, I came to check on you. And apologize, of course. I can't believe Ainsley was involved in this mess. Running drugs and stealing from the Navy. It's unbelievable."

Suddenly, it hit her. His shirt was wrinkled, and his eyes darted all over the place, never focusing on any one thing. The typically charming, charismatic deputy director was … frazzled. Not a look she'd ever seen on him before. More than that, his brow was taut and his mouth gaped open a bit. She recognized panic, even through the fog shrouding her brain.

"Yes, it is but, you know, we rarely ever know someone, right?" She was babbling. She needed to calm down. "I'm sure Ainsley had his reasons."

"Um, I guess. He didn't tell you anything about it, did he?"

She shook her head and immediately regretted it. A steely ball of pain rattled around her brain. She was seeing stars as she replied, "He didn't say much."

"Really? I heard that you said he confessed everything to you."

She blinked. "Er, no. Not really."

"Which is it? No? Or not really?" He moved, shifting his weight so he was evenly balanced.

He was going to attack her. No. That was stupid. Must be the meds. Why would he want to attack her? "Because you were in on it." The words came out of her mouth without thinking. Damn meds were making her do stupid things.

His entire body stilled. Then he grabbed her arm and squeezed. "What did he say? What did Ainsley say to you?"

"Nothing. He said you weren't involved. You couldn't be. You didn't have the organizational skills necessary for this kind of operation."

His eyes narrowed. "I don't believe you. What did he really say?" When she just stared back at him, he shook her. "What did he say?"

He leaned over her and got right in her face. His lips had thinned into an angry seam, and the skin around his eyes was pinched and pale. Fear glinted in his stare, and she knew he was going to hurt her. Maybe kill her.

She struggled to free her arm. "He didn't say anything, but you *were* involved. You knew what was going on. You're a traitor and a murderer!" She clenched her teeth and fought to get her arm back. When he reached for her other arm, she smashed his jaw as hard as she could.

He stumbled backward, wrenching her arm in the process. A roar filled the room. She yanked to free herself from his grasp, and he actually let go. But that was because Dane had pulled him away from her. Dane slammed him against the wall and pinned him with a forearm across Cross's chest.

"What the hell are you doing?" Cross roared.

Dane smashed his fist into Cross's jaw, and the man wobbled on his feet and then slid down the wall. Dane stepped back. "I'm done with these assholes." He turned around. "Are you okay?"

Mac ignored the pain searing her shoulders and stared at him. "Um, yeah. I can't believe you're here. I… Thanks for saving me. Again."

He smiled. "I think you had it under control." He turned his head and started coughing.

"Are you okay?"

"Long story," he rasped and then coughed some more. He moved around her bed and went to the rolling table where there was water. There were traces of soot under his nostrils. He took a sip but then covered his mouth with his arm as he continued to cough. He was still in his tactical gear and had his handgun strapped to the front of his leg.

"What happened to you?" Mac asked. What was wrong with Dane? Why was he coughing so much? "Are you okay? Maybe I should call the nurse." She turned as Cross was lifting his gun. She grabbed Dane's gun and fired.

Her aim was true, and the bullet struck Cross center mass and he went down, dropping his gun beside him.

"Holy shit." Dane stared at Cross and then at Mac. "Thanks for saving my life."

She smiled up at him as the door burst open and the world rushed in.

CHAPTER TWENTY-EIGHT

"French fry?" Dane offered.

"Sure." Mac grabbed a fry from his plate and bit into it. She turned to admire their surroundings. "You have a great backyard. The view is awesome." This was the first free moment she'd had since everything had gone to shit, and she'd decided she and Dane needed to talk. Nerves fluttered in her belly as she'd approached his front door, and the soft beat of butterflies had since morphed into raucous, beating crows' wings.

"Thanks. I was lucky to find this place." He popped a fry into his mouth.

"How did you find it?" she asked.

He smiled. "Believe it or not, through my mother."

"Your mother?" Out of all the things he could've said, that wasn't remotely what she was expecting.

He nodded. "A friend of hers retired out here and then decided it was too far away from family. She was homesick. So I asked if I could rent the place, and she agreed. She didn't want to sell it anyway because eventually, she wants to give it to her kids to use."

"That's cool. Do her kids want it? Will they kick you out soon?"

"Her kids live in Switzerland and Italy. They don't want it as far as I can tell, so I think I'm good for a while."

She grinned and took a sip of her beer. It was nice to be sitting here in the sun with Dane. It had been a long three weeks of meetings and discussions and debriefings as everyone tried to put together what happened.

"It's still hard to believe, you know?" she said as she leaned back in her chair.

"Yeah. Cross was a surprise. We'd eliminated him. Figured Manu for being the tech mastermind behind everything."

"And he was. Ainsley was just too loyal, I guess. He cut Cross in on the deal so that they could both make money." She grabbed another fry off his plate. "I think Ainsley wanted to be close to the limelight, and the only way that was going to happen for him was if he stuck with Cross. The higher Cross went, the better it was for Ainsley."

"And then he pulled Cross down with him." Dane took a swig of his beer. "The whole thing was freaking audacious. Casper found out Owens was smuggling drugs, and telling Ainsley about it was what gave Ainsley the idea. He approached some cousin of his, a guy named, Bob Thornton, because he mentioned at last years' Thanksgiving how easy it would be to steal the stuff. Apparently Thorton worked in the Naval depot at San Diego. When Sinclair was on to their set up, then Ainsley brought in Manu to reroute the stuff and then remove it from the system. It all worked beautifully until they went for the motherboards."

"What I don't understand is how Weston got involved."

"No one does, and he's not talking. They suspect that Ainsley or Cross or maybe both approached him, knowing he needed a lot of money for his re-election campaign."

"Scary though, isn't it? We're all at the mercy of the moral compass of those in government."

He snorted. "That's enough to keep me up at night." Dane pushed his fries toward Mac. "I don't know why you ordered a salad if you wanted fries."

"Because sometimes I don't know what I want until it's in front of my face." She gazed into his eyes.

"Why do I get the feeling that we're not talking about French fries anymore?"

Mac's lips turned down. "I owe you an apology."

"You saved my life, so I think we're even."

She pushed away her plate and leaned forward, folding her arms on the table. "No. I panicked after the last time we were together. I knew I was starting to care about you, and I guess I just couldn't take anything else going wrong. I was thinking it was better to cut ties before everything blew up in my face. It would hurt less."

"I get that. I might've had a similar thought or two."

She gave him a half smile. "But I have since realized that if I didn't have you in my life, I'd be missing out on something pretty special. There's always going to be a bit of a bumpy road ahead since we work in the same place, but I'm willing to give it a try if you are." There, she'd laid it all out for him. Her pulse ticked up wildly and her stomach rolled as she waited for his response. Would he take her up on her offer, or was it too late?

"When Ainsley held you hostage, I realized that every day I would be terrified watching you go to work. The fact that your job has moments when it's damn dangerous is a tough one to swallow. I want to always be there to protect you." He immediately held up his hands. "Not that you need my protection. You've shown again and again how tough and resilient you are. But that doesn't mean I don't want to keep you safe. It's just a lot."

"I see." So he was opting out. The fries she'd just gobbled soured in her stomach.

"But, not having you in my life would be much harder to take." He reached across the table and grabbed her hand, pulling her from her chair as he stood up and came around the table. "Mac, I would so much rather see your face every day than live without you. I know you decided to stay on Oahu, and I would love it if you'd give us a chance."

Fighting tears of relief, she wrapped her arms around his neck. "I think that can be arranged. How would you like a roommate for a few weeks until I find a new place?"

He paused. "Well, I'll have to ask my other roommate. He's quite fussy."

She grinned. "I already spoke with Beans. He says it's fine as long as I feed him treats."

"Then I guess we're good." With that, he leaned down and sealed his lips, and his fate, to hers with a searing kiss.

The End

Keep reading for a sneak peek at *Diverted*, Book 1 in the Coast Guard RECON Series

SNEAK PEEK: DIVERTED

COAST GUARD RECON BOOK 1

Nick Taggert was injured on his last assignment for the Coast Guard. Now, too hurt to go back to his former position and not wounded enough to be benched, he's assigned as the new Coast Guard team leader in…Panama. They're there as part of a drug interdiction unit, but really, they're Team RECON. Recon as in reconstructed. Each of the four men is like him; a Humpty Dumpty. Except they were trying to put themselves back together so they could do what they loved best, kicking ass and taking names.

Dr. Carolina Alvarez had moved on from research and was working for Doctors Without Borders. A chance meeting with her old boss set her on a dangerous mission to deliver much-needed medicine to South America. Her failure would mean the sure extinction of a tribe clinging to their ancient ways.

Nick should have realized from the instant Carolina walked back into his life things would not go according to plan. But harbored resentment still clouded his vision. Now they were on the trail of the missing vaccine, and the assignment just turned deadly

DIVERTED: PROLOGUE

February 9th, 2021

Alejandro Garcia glanced at his watch and seethed. He abhorred tardiness, and the man was late. Stirring his coffee, he watched people stroll by the cafe window. He, unlike most of the world, hated Paris, especially in January. The cold invaded his bones, and gray skies hung heavy overhead. Even the Eiffel Tower looked dirty and dingy in the falling mist.

Garcia sighed. He found the French to be tedious. They thought too highly of themselves, and their lack of work ethic astounded him. The constant rioting about trivial things illustrated a society too pampered to be taken seriously. He had no idea why the French government tolerated such behavior.

He rechecked his timepiece and took a sip from his cup. However, they did serve excellent coffee, and for that, he was willing to forgive quite a bit.

A black car pulled up to the curb. The driver came around and opened the door. A tall distinguished-looking gentleman emerged. "Finally," Garcia mumbled as his ten o'clock appointment entered the café twenty minutes late.

Edward Langston approached the table, hand outstretched. "Sorry, I'm late. Ran into a traffic snarl. Protesters wouldn't let the car past."

Garcia stood and shook hands. "Of course. Please." He gestured toward the opposite chair. "May I get you something? Coffee perhaps?" It galled him to play host to this American, but it was a small price to pay for the benefits this man could provide to Garcia's country.

"I'm fine. Can't stay long." The men sat. "Look." Langston leaned forward. "Our agreement… I must say I have some misgivings."

Garcia ground his teeth. Langston couldn't back out now. Not when Garcia was so close to sealing his country's future on the world stage. "You don't want to run a live test of your experiment?"

"Of course, we want to run the test," Langston said. "Don't be stupid. I want to make sure you understand the risk you're taking. None of this can come out. Ever."

Garcia nodded. "Agreed. It would be bad for all of us and, yes, we understand the risk. Your mosquitoes will save millions of lives and change the world. We want to provide you with the opportunity to prove their efficacy. Many of our population are affected by mosquito-borne diseases; it is perfectly logical for you to test your theory in our country. As to the other part, that will remain a secret, I can assure you."

Langston hesitated before giving a curt nod. "We have a deal."

"When will the testing begin?"

Langston frowned. "Our people should be in place at the end of March, maybe slightly later. By the summer, we should know if it's working or not."

Garcia nodded again. "Good. The sooner, the better. No delays."

"Obviously," Langston snarled. "I'll be in touch when we're ready to go."

"Everything will be ready to proceed." Garcia forced a smile.

"Make sure it is. This is very important. To both sides."

Garcia's jaw ached. The American's attitude was insufferable. "It will be smooth on my end, I can assure you."

Langston studied him for a minute. "You're sure your boss is on board with this?"

"You need not worry, Mr. Langston. As I said, things will flow smoothly on my end." Garcia curled his hand around the coffee cup and squeezed. He would prefer if the cup were Langston's neck, but that was not in the cards. At least not yet. He reminded himself there must be sacrifice to achieve success. His day would come.

"Fine." Langston stood up, and Garcia rose with him. "I'll be in touch," Langston stated, then turned and exited the cafe. He got into his car and drove off.

Garcia returned to his seat and signaled the waiter, who brought another piping-hot coffee.

Americans. Another group Garcia hated. Not so different from the French. Always thinking they knew better and possessed the upper hand. Not this time. This time, Garcia had the advantage, and things were just as they should be.

DIVERTED: CHAPTER 1

"Bring him over here, Muhammed!" Dr Carolina Alvarez pointed to the now empty table along the wall of the tent in the makeshift hospital. Two local men half carried half dragged the unconscious man between them over to Carolina and put him face down in front of her. The sound of sporadic gunfire erupted, but everyone in the tent ignored it.

"We found him washed up on the beach," stated Muhammed, the taller of the two. "We didn't want to just leave him there. It would not be right."

Carolina gave him a brief smile as Gabe, a nurse, came over and helped her move the injured soldier onto the table. The man was dressed in military fatigues so helping him could be risky for Muhammed and his son, but they were good people. They put politics and religion aside to help someone in need. Carolina had seen that a lot in Yemen. What the world was told about the Yemenese, and the truth of the matter wasn't even close. Of course, she'd found that was the way of it in most of the countries she'd worked in. Doctors Without Borders only went to places in need, and most of those countries had political problems.

"Thanks for rescuing him, Muhammed. Do you know where he got shot?" Muhammed and his son Ahmed both shook their heads. The son was the spitting image of the father. It was like seeing double.

"He's not shot." Ahmed turned and mumbled something to his father in Arabic and then said, "Stabbed. In the back." It was hard to hear him over the din of voices in the tent.

Carolina helped Gabe turned the man onto his side. "Take his vitals," she said as she leaned over to see the injured man's back.

Muhammed cleared his throat. "We go now."

Carolina nodded. "*Shukran*, Muhammed," she said, trying to thank him in his own language but he was gone. Probably good he wasn't there to hear her butcher it.

There was a lot of blood soaking into the man's shirt. She peeled it back to reveal a long, deep gash that went right across the man's back from his right shoulder to his left hip. "Jesus. He was hacked, not stabbed." She peered closer at the wound. It was ugly and it was going to take a lot of work to fix. She cursed silently. A slash like this needed a plastic surgeon in a real hospital not a general surgeon in a makeshift hospital tent. She'd do what she could, but it wasn't going to be pretty. "Colin, I'm going to need your help!" Carolina didn't even look up as she yelled for the other doctor. "Gabe, how are his vitals?"

"They suck," he stated. "His pulse is weak and his pressure is low. His breathing is shallow."

"Hang a unit of blood and then grab the portable x-ray. I need to see if his ribs are broken."

Gabe quickly hooked the man up to the IV and then skirted the table and moved to the other end of the room.

"Colin?" Carolina called again as she noticed a birthmark on the man's right shoulder. It looked sort of like a four-leaf clover. Another flurry of gunfire sounded, drowning out

Colin's answer. Just then the flap of the tent was pushed open wider, and a new group of injured were brought in.

"You're on your own," Colin called. "I'll take the new ones."

"Shit," Carolina mumbled. "Let's hope your birthmark is a sign you're lucky." *You're going to need it.*

Gabe came back with the portable x-ray and set it up. He quickly took pictures of the man's torso. After a brief pause, he consulted the tablet on the machine's stand. "Look like four broken ribs."

"That's not good. Okay, let's get his wound cleaned and stitch it up. But first we need to see if any of his organs were damaged either by the hacking or from the broken ribs." She leaned closer. "It looks like it missed his spine completely. This guy is lucky as hell. Half an inch more, and his spine would have been severed."

She heard a grunt and straightened, looking down at her patient's face. The lines on the exposed side of his face were etched into his skin and his eyes were open. They were a very distinctive shade of blue. Like the sky on a cold day in winter. "Hey, can you tell me your name?"

He remained silent, staring at her.

"Do you know where you are?"

He watched her but said nothing.

"Okay, well then, whoever you are. We're going to take care of you. I'm going to give you something for the pain, and then I'm going to stitch you up. You were very lucky."

He raised an eyebrow. "Lucky. Sure." He closed his eyes again.

READ THESE OTHER EXCITING TITLES BY LORI MATTHEWS

Callahan Security

Break and Enter

Smash And Grab

Hit And Run

Evade and Capture

Catch and Release

Cease and Desist

Coast Guard Recon

Diverted

Incinerated

Conflicted

Subverted

Terminated

Brotherhood Protectors World

Justified Misfortune

Justified Burden

Justified Vengeance

Free with Newsletter Sign Up

Falling For The Witness

Risk Assessment

Visit Https://www.lorimatthewsbooks.com for details on how to purchase these novels or sign up for my newsletter.

ABOUT LORI MATTHEWS

I grew up in a house filled with books and readers. Some of my fondest memories are of reading in the same room with my mother and sisters, arguing about whose turn it was to make tea. No one wanted to put their book down!

I was introduced to romance because of my mom's habit of leaving books all over the house. One day I picked one up. I still remember the cover. It was a Harlequin by Janet Daily. Little did I know at the time that it would set the stage for my future. I went on to discover mystery novels. Agatha Christie was my favorite. And then suspense with Wilber Smith and Ian Fleming.

I loved the thought of combining my favorite genres, and during high school, I attempted to write my first romantic suspense novel. I wrote the first four chapters and then exams happened and that was the end of that. I desperately hope that book died a quiet death somewhere in a computer recycling facility.

A few years later, (okay, quite a few) after two degrees, a husband and two kids, I attended a workshop in Tuscany that lit that spark for writing again. I have been pounding the keyboard ever since here in New Jersey, where I live with my children—who are thrilled with my writing as it means they get to eat more pizza—and my very supportive husband.

Please visit my webpage at https://lorimatthewsbooks.com to keep up on my news.

Made in the USA
Coppell, TX
22 July 2023

19492983R00184